Dear Reader:

We are especially proud to be bringing you this book, which is an iPublish.com original publication.

What that means is this book was discovered and endorsed for publication by other readers like you.

The author submitted the manuscript to iPublish.com, where it received ratings and reviews from other writers and readers. Their overwhelming enthusiasm for the submission brought it to the attention of the iPublish.com editors. We agreed this is a book that deserves to be enjoyed by many readers.

And one of them is you! We hope you agree it's a real find.

Sincerely,
The iPublish Editors

P.S. If you're interested in submitting your own work for publication consideration, visit us at www.ipublish.com to find out how!

"I had my novel, but how to get it published? Like many writers, I was caught in a frustrating catch-22. Only a few publishing houses will look at manuscripts that aren't coming from an agent. And how do you get an agent? Well, you have to publish first. Aaarrrgh!

"Then I learned about iPublish from an Internet ad. I saw it as a win-win situation. Here is a place where you're encouraged to write and improve. I went for it. And I'm glad I did!"

The son of an inventor, JERRY J. DAVIS is an ex–professional photographer and a journalist who was kicked out of journalism class. He currently works as a computer technologist in the Dallas area, where he's known for having too vivid an imagination. He has a beautiful wife and two lovely daughters, three pesky cats, and a rambunctious dog.

TRAVELS

TRAVELS

JERRY J. DAVIS

iPUBLISH
at Time Warner Books

For information address iPublish.com, 135 West
50th Street, NY 10020.

 An AOL Time Warner Company

ISBN 0-7595-5024-7

First edition: October 2001

Visit our Web site at www.iPublish.com

1. Anarchists

THE PHONE HAD BEEN RINGING FOR QUITE A WHILE.

Dodd noticed the ringing. Then he noticed it more. It was like he was coming back from somewhere down a long hallway to find a phone ringing at the very end. Then it took him a moment to realize that he should answer it, since—after all—it *was* his phone.

He tore his eyes away from the large 3-D screen and looked around his living room. His girlfriend was there along with some other friends, all of them staring at the screen. The phone rang on. No one was noticing but him.

I should answer it, he thought.

Dodd struggled to his feet and walked across the living room to the adjacent kitchen. He groaned; the time display on the telephone's screen read seven past midnight. What was he doing still awake? It was a work night. This was probably Toby's wife calling to get him to come home.

He picked up the handset and touched the button to accept video. Instead of Toby's wife, a bearded face with unkempt hair appeared. "Dodd!" the face said.

"Danny?" Dodd said back to it. He was alarmed—like dark clouds at sea, the appearance of Danny Marauder usually foretold trouble.

"Sorry I woke you up. You know I wouldn't be bothering you if it wasn't important."

"I . . . you didn't wake me."

"Me and a couple of friends are kinda caught out in the open, if you know what I mean. We need a place to crash."

Dodd fidgeted. *Anarchists in my apartment?* If it were just Marauder, it would be okay—but his *friends*? "Well, I . . . I have company over here, Danny."

"We'll stay in your garage if you want us to, man. I mean, we have to get under a roof. You understand?"

"You mean the . . ." Dodd cut himself off. He didn't want to know.

"I really need this favor, Dodd," Danny told him. "If you do this for me, we'll be all even. Hell—I'll be owing you."

Dodd hesitated.

"Come on, man." Danny was pleading.

"You just want to stay in my garage?"

"That's all I'm asking."

"Okay. Okay, I can do that. But"—he gave Danny a warning look—"don't bring any . . . you know. Just don't." Dodd could imagine a half dozen anarchists getting drunk and shooting up his garage with high-powered energy weapons. What a nightmare!

"I love you, man," Danny was saying. "We'll be around in a little while, very quiet. No problems."

Dodd nodded, said good-bye, and hung up. He immediately wanted to call Danny back and cancel the whole thing, but of course he had no idea where Danny had been calling from.

The time display now read 12:10 A.M. He had to get up for work at 5:30. I've got to get these people out of here, he thought, and walked back into the living room. "Okay, it's time to call it a night. It's way past my bedtime."

No one looked away from the television. No one made a move. His girlfriend, Sheila, was only a meter away, and she hadn't heard a word he'd said. She stared at the screen with glazed eyes, breathing slowly through her slack mouth. Colors from the giant screen reflected from her white face.

He reached over and shook her shoulder. "Are you asleep?" he asked.

"Huh?" She blinked, then turned and looked at him. "What?"

"I said, are you asleep?"

"Oh." She held out her empty wineglass. "Can I have a refill?"

"A refill?"

"Yes, please."

"Sheila, I . . ."

She was smiling sweetly at him. "Please?" she said.

Dodd took the glass and headed back toward the kitchen. This is getting out of hand, he thought. I'm just going to go to bed with them here.

In the kitchen, he opened the refrigerator and knelt, holding Sheila's glass under the tiny silicon spigot. A pale red liquid dribbled out, Vinny's Uncommon '41, *The best hydroponic wine money can buy."* Haunting, racing music drifted in from the television—the endless sound track of the Travels station. It seemed to spin around him in the air, the holographic sound bouncing through the kitchen. As he listened, he forgot what he was doing, his head beginning to sway back and forth to the gentle rhythm. He finished filling Sheila's glass, then got another for himself and began filling that as well. The Travels music was so relaxing. He felt light. He took the two glasses of wine back into the living room and eased himself down on the couch next to Sheila.

"Here," he said.

Sheila took the glass wordlessly and ducked as he put his free arm around her. Dodd sipped the wine, and the image of the rolling ball on the screen pulled at his eyes like a magnet. For a moment he resisted, looking over at his friend and coworker Bob Recent. He was cuddling with his wife, Denise, at the opposite end of the couch. Both held empty wineglasses in their slack hands, and Dodd felt guilty that he hadn't given them refills. His other friend, Toby Whitehouse, was beside the Recents in an overstuffed chair. He, too, was holding an empty glass.

Didn't I have something to tell them? Dodd asked himself.

He couldn't remember. The screen reclaimed his attention.

The surreal, multicolored sphere had made its way down to a virgin beach; early-morning sunlight streamed through large, mist-shrouded waves as they crashed ashore, and gulls whirled and soared in the lazy glowing sky . . . The music surged and ebbed with the scenery, never stopping and never repeating itself. Dodd raised his wineglass to his mouth but nothing came out; it was already gone. He let his hand drop, forgetting the glass, watching as the sphere bounced higher up on the beach, rebounding off rocks and driftwood, hitting patches of sand and sending up clouds of slow-mo drifting particles.

Suddenly he couldn't see the screen. His eyes struggled to focus on a dark silhouette centimeters from his face. "Hey," a voice said.

"Danny?"

"Yeah, you noticed. Been ringing for a while, man. Had to finally let myself in."

Dodd glanced over at the time display. It was close to 2:00 A.M. "Jesus!" he exclaimed.

"You're frying your brain watching that stuff."

Dodd nodded. That was true. He stood and turned around to say something to Sheila, but she was still staring at the screen. Bob and Denise were oblivious, and so was Toby. They just stared at the screen. It seemed unreal.

"Hello," he said to his guests. "Hello?"

"Want me to get their attention?" Danny asked.

"No." *God no!* "Let's go out to the garage."

They went out the front door, then around to the side of the small apartment complex. There was a row of garage doors with brightly lit numbers above them. Dodd led Danny over to one of them and unlocked the door with his voice. It opened with an electric whine, revealing an empty space with a few boxes in one corner.

"No car?" Danny asked.

"Haven't had one for years."

"Damn. I was going to ask if I could borrow it."

Dodd laughed, short and sharp.

Two men and a woman Dodd had never met emerged from the bushes and hurried into the garage. Danny Marauder gave Dodd a hug, and said, "Good night, and thank you." He followed his companions in and closed the garage door with the inside button, leaving Dodd alone outside. He looked up involuntarily and searched the sky for police drones, but without a pair of spotters he would never be able to see one—at least not at night.

He reentered his apartment and stood looking at his friends. For a moment he considered just going to bed and leaving them to themselves, but then he remembered that Bob and Toby had to work just like he did. Maybe all he had to do was remind them of the fact. Dodd leaned over his stack of video components and hit the main power button. "Hey," he said in a loud voice, "it's after two in the morning!"

His friends' expressions would have been funny had Dodd been in a better mood. They looked like they were in shock. Sheila looked angry.

"Come on, guys," Dodd pleaded, "let's ambulate. The theater's closed."

"I didn't realize it was so late," Bob Recent said. He yawned, and the yawn spread to his wife.

Toby was the first one to stand up. He looked sheepish. "I had no intention of staying this late," he said. He was a naturalized Jamaican-American from when his country had become an American state, and his accent was still very prominent. "I am going to catch hell from my wife."

Dodd shrugged. "I tried to get you guys outta here two hours ago."

"You did?" Bob said.

"Yeah, you were all on another planet." Dodd looked over at Sheila. She glared back at him. Uh-oh, he thought.

Toby, Bob, and Denise said their good-byes and exited gracefully, leaving Sheila behind in the apartment. As soon as Dodd shut the door, Sheila said, "Are you throwing me out, too?"

"You can stay if you want to go to sleep." Dodd pushed a button on the computer panel beside the door, starting the routine that would shut off the lights and silently take phone messages. There was a solid, loud *clunk* as the front door locked itself.

"I want to watch Travels a little longer," Sheila said.

"It's two in the morning."

Sheila's expression softened. Now she was pouting. "Can't I watch it for just a little bit?"

"Sheila, look! Even if I go to sleep right now, I'll only get three and a half hours in before I have to get up and go to work!"

"Please?"

"I don't function well with only three and a half hours sleep! Can't you understand that?"

"Oh, come on—please?" She made a big pout.

Dodd tromped angrily over to the video components and turned them back on. He adjusted the volume, and said, "Please don't turn this up." He walked out of the room and down the hall to his bedroom, closing the door behind him and falling into bed.

Within minutes she had turned the volume up.

Dodd was angry for a while, but then he relaxed as the music worked on him. It was nice, really. It was also haunting, seeming to spin through time from eternity, passing through him and on ... it was sparkling, pure. It brought images to mind of the rolling Travels sphere, flashing its colors as it bounced along a misty beach, bouncing on and on, never slowing, never stopping, taking him into his dreams, becoming his dreams, displacing his dreams.

2. Mutant

THE SETTING SUN WAS FAT, RED—A GLOBE OF HELL DESCENDING TO THE ocean.

And he was staring at it.

His eyes began to char and burn in his head.

Saul exhaled sharply and forced himself to look away. The setting sun was real despite the effects of the drug. It was real, and he shouldn't be staring at it. He held his left hand against his closed eyes and felt a distant sensation of pain. Colors swam under his eyelids, brightly glowing shapes and patterns, shifting and melting and forming new ones. His right hand held his drink; he took a sip and blindly set it down where he could find it again without having to open his eyes. Over the railing came the distant booming hiss of ocean waves crashing ashore—the sound was altered by the Mataphin drug, giving him the distinct impression of someone whispering to him through a cardboard tube.

Saul took several long, deep breaths, easing his muscles, relaxing and clearing his mind. The patterns became less random, the colors more subdued. In the center of his mind's eye he visualized a sphere, the Travels sphere, and imagined it rolling along. As he relaxed the image solidified, became three-dimensional. With the aid of the Mataphin he was entering a lucid-dream state while remaining fully conscious. It was a powerful and dangerous drug, and he'd been abusing it lately, but he *needed* it.

I'm almost there, Saul thought.

He watched the ball rolling through iridescent red-and-black landscapes; through oddly symmetrical forests where the leaves shone like neon; through glassy, shimmering shores where all the rocks had perfectly flat tops covered in tiny, glowing beads of moisture. Perfect images, and flawless movements as graceful as running water. I'm there, he thought. I'm there. Saul moved his hand in slow motion toward the small cerebral recorder in his pocket, the input plugged right into the base of his skull—straight into his visual cortex. His finger touched the record button.

There was a sudden scream, a sound as loud as an air-raid siren. Saul's body jerked, and his eyes opened wide. He felt as if someone had hit him over the head with a chair. "Mirro!" he yelled. "Mirrrrooo!" No one answered him, and the baby kept crying.

Trying to ignore the shrieks, Saul took a few deep breaths and closed his eyes, watching the visions. He tried to bring back the clarity, the flow and balance, but every time the mournful scream reached a crescendo his visions shattered like glass plates. He was never going to get any work done with the baby crying. Saul sat up, calling out his wife's name again. There was still no answer, so he stood up and walked through the hanging beads into the house, cringing at the shrieks, trying to keep his balance under the effects of the drug.

"Oh, sweetheart," he muttered emptily. "Oh, honey, what's wrong?" He stroked his daughter's flaccid skin, trying to calm her. She was fourteen years old, weighed over four hundred pounds, and had a brain the size of a small lizard thanks to her mother's continued use of Lottalove, the pheromone perfume Mirro had worn when she and Saul were first married.

His daughter settled down and grinned at him, gurgling as he gently stroked her stomach. Her enormous round face wrinkled grotesquely with the grin, drool running down her cheek and mingling with tears. Her eyes and mouth were tiny, her hair fine and golden. Her arms and legs were very short. From the smell of her, she needed her diaper changed.

"Oh God," Saul muttered, standing over her and trying to prepare himself for the task. Changing the diaper of a four-hundred-pound perpetual baby was, for him, a half hour job. As he was preparing the bedside hoist he heard the front door open, and, hoping it was his wife, called out, "Is that you?"

"Silly question," her voice came back. "Anyone would answer that 'yes.'"

Saul frowned. "The baby was crying. Where were you?"

"Seeing Vicky. Are you getting any work done?" She appeared in the doorway of their daughter's room, scantily clad and looking as if she'd been asleep. There was something different about her this evening; it took Saul a few minutes to figure out what it was. The tips of her golden hair had been dyed powder blue. "Oh," she said, sniffing the air, "time for a change-change."

"I was about to do it."

"Oh, it takes you forever. Go on, get back to work."

Saul turned and walked out of the room, brushing past her in the doorway. "Could you stay and keep her quiet, please?" he said as he walked down the hallway. "At least until I come down?"

"Sorry, honey," she said.

"Yeah," he muttered, thinking: If you weren't so fucking sorry maybe we could stick this freak child of yours into a Home. Or better yet into one of those euthanasia centers. We could live like royalty on the money we spend keeping that thing alive.

Saul stopped in mid-stride, standing in the long west-wing hall, horrified at his own thoughts. Is that me? he wondered. Is that really me? My God, it must be the drug. It *must* be. The Mataphin amplifies . . . it must be amplifying my resentment. I don't wish death for her. Poor baby, it's not her fault she's like that.

Saul made his way back to the oceanfront porch, taking deep breaths to clear his mind of the ugliness and depression. He settled himself into the couch and sipped his drink, closing his eyes, seeing the red of the sunset through his eyelids. It looked like fire. Raging red fire, sprays of molten rock, and through it rolled the sphere, the Travels sphere, and with it came relaxation and peace. The fire faded, other images came to mind, beautiful images luxurious and deep, the ball rolling and rebounding, and Saul followed along behind it, watching closely, controlling its direction, and forgetting about his mutant daughter and bisexual wife and his lost chance to have a true family. The sphere led the way. Soon he arrived where he wanted to be, and he slid his hand up to the small recorder in his pocket, and once again pushed RECORD.

3. Testicles

DODD WAS GROGGY AND ILL-TEMPERED WHEN HE LEFT HIS APARTMENT FOR work the next morning. When the house computer woke him at 5:30 A.M., the television in the front room was still going, the twenty-four-hour Travels channel continuing its coverage of the rolling ball with no interruptions or commercial breaks. Sheila was asleep, so there was no argument from her when he turned off the TV, but by the time he had showered, shaved, dressed, and eaten breakfast, she was awake again, and the Travels channel was back on the screen.

The anarchists in his garage were already gone, but he found a note of thanks spray-painted on one of the walls.

BEWARE THE ANTICHRIST AI!

it read, luminous red words outlined in black. They had dug through his boxes of junk and taken a few cooking utensils. This made Dodd mad, not because he had cherished the old stained utensils—far from it, they were *junk*—but it was the way they had just taken it; they hadn't even thought about asking. And the spray paint! He was going to have to paint the whole wall to cover it, and he'd have to do it soon, too—the apartment management was rarely understanding about this sort of thing. Dodd was sure that somewhere in his lease agreement was the clause, "Letting anarchists sleep in your garage unit is terms for eviction."

Dodd joined the other pedestrians on the sidewalk, walking the six blocks down the street toward the subway terminal.

BEWARE THE ANTICHRIST AI!

What the hell was that supposed to mean? Either Danny Marauder had finally gone over the edge, or it was something the anarchists were into. There was no way of telling—the anarchists seemed to be into everything. Like Dodd, many of them were veterans. That's where he'd met Danny—they had served together in the South American War. Carrying guns powerful enough to blow up a truck with a single round, never firing a shot, wading through cities of dead people who couldn't decay. It was graveyard duty. Dodd had been able to maintain his grasp on reality; he returned home to lead a normal life. But the others, the ones that ended up anarchists, they had lost their grip.

His train hissed to a halt, and Dodd boarded, packing himself in with a hundred other bodies, standing because all the seats were taken. The ride was uneventful. He endured it as usual by escaping into a trancelike state until an amplified voice announced his stop. "Cherokee. Cherokee Station." Dodd made his way to the door and waited. Beyond the yellowed windows of the subway car, the brick walls of the station blurred past and slowed, graffiti everywhere, layer upon layer.

BEWARE THE ANTICHRIST AI!

The doors opened, and Dodd stepped out, walking involuntarily up to the painted letters, looking closely, as if he would find meaning in the texture of the painted brick. Danny must have been here, he thought. Shaking his head, he turned and trudged up the escalator. The main gate of Honda Aerospace was seven blocks away.

At Honda he presented his union card to a machine and was cleared through by a smirking, smoking, gruff-looking old lady in a guard's uniform. Beyond the gates, all across the sprawling plant, people and machines rushed to and fro in the early sunlight, impossibly busy. Dodd made his way to the forklift station, checked in, bought a cup of freshly brewed coffee from the garage's machine, and slowly, carefully climbed aboard his semiautonomic rig. The forklift came to life as he keyed in his employee number; on a screen behind the controls his morning assignment appeared. Dodd instructed the forklift to go—it knew the way— then settled back in the comfortable black seat to enjoy his coffee and try to wake up.

When Dodd saw Bob Recent, Bob was just getting through the front gate; he was thirty-five minutes late. Dodd brought his rig to a stop and waved, but either Bob didn't see or he was ignoring Dodd; Bob walked past without acknowledging. Is he mad at me? Dodd wondered. Why, because I kicked him out of my apartment at two in the morning? No. He's probably mad because I didn't kick him out sooner.

Dodd made his way over to the shipping warehouse and gently dropped off his sixth load of inertia-null units. He watched for a moment as two spidery robots began sorting them out, preparing them for inventory. Dodd disliked these two little robots—he'd known the workers they replaced.

On his way back to production/inspection for another load he saw Bob Recent again, this time standing with one of the big bosses near the administration office. Dodd sipped the last of his lukewarm coffee and watched them, wanting to see if Bob was being chewed out for being late. It would be a first. Bob was habitually late, but never seemed to get caught. It would serve him right if they fired his ass, Dodd thought. But then again, he really didn't want that to happen. A fully autonomic forklift, not a human driver, would replace Bob. Dodd didn't need any more "smart" forklifts running around reminding him that his job was more of a union-management compromise than something vital and necessary to the company.

It didn't look like Bob was being fired. He and the big boss were shaking hands. They passed out of sight behind the edge of

14   a building, leaving Dodd with an unpleasant feeling in his bowels. *Bob Recent? No. No way.*

A few hours later Dodd saw a little white cart racing toward him across the smooth concrete plain, the driver waving for him to stop. Dodd felt a headache coming on. It was Bob Recent.

Dodd pulled to a stop as the cart came alongside him. Bob's smile was large, his eyes glassy. There was the flush of blood in his cheeks. "Hey, guess what happened."

"You're management now."

"Right! I'm section foreman. I'm this section's foreman."

"You're my boss."

"Yeah! Isn't it great? Me, section foreman!" He laughed like a kid.

"Well, I'm happy for you, Bob," Dodd lied.

"Oh, boy, so am I! Wow. I can't wait to tell Denise about this, she'll be thrilled!"

"I'm sure she will." Dodd felt obligated to hold out his hand. "Congratulations."

Bob shook. "Thank you."

"How did you manage this, anyway?"

"Well, it's funny, it all started when I put in my resignation—"

"Resignation?"

"Oh, yeah. Well," Bob fidgeted, becoming self-conscious. "Well, you see, Denise quit her job—"

"Denise quit her job?"

"Yes."

"I thought she loved that job!"

"Well, she did, but it didn't leave her with a whole lot of free time. Denise wanted to stay home and watch Travels during the day."

"Travels?"

"Yeah, and well, I thought that, hell . . . if she did that, I didn't see why I shouldn't. So I discussed it with her, and we decided that I should quit and go on compensation—"

"Compensation? Bob, what kind of compensation?"

"Progeny compensation," Bob said defensively.

"I was afraid of that. Bob, I thought you wanted kids. You told me that's why you and Denise got married, why you stuck around here doing a robot's job."

"Well—"

"*You* told me that. Those were your words."

"I know. My God, you make me feel like I'm a traitor or something."

"I just don't want you to do something you'll regret. I mean, it used to mean something to you, something to work for, a goal. How much progeny tax do you have saved up, Bob? Last time we talked about it, you had over five hundred thousand. You're almost there! You're going to throw that all away on something else?"

"I'm not throwing it away on anything," Bob said, angry now. "Sometimes people's priorities change, sometimes people acquire new goals instead of hanging on to old, outdated ones. Denise has decided she doesn't want a baby, Dodd. And that's her right—it's *her* body. So if she doesn't want a baby, what difference does it make if I get a vasectomy? I can't start a family without my wife, can I?"

"This was Denise's decision, then?"

"No, it was both of ours!"

"Okay. I think it's a mistake, but hey, it's your life."

"That's right, it's *my* life."

"Right."

"And I don't think it's a mistake."

"Okay. Sure."

"I mean it."

"Hey, you're right, it's none of my business."

They stared at each other for a tense moment, then Bob said, "I'm going to let this drop. It doesn't matter why I was going to quit or what I was going to do, because I didn't. What *does* matter is that I'm your new foreman, and you'd better keep that in mind from now on."

"Whatever you say."

"Get back to work." Bob said it as if he were trying the words on for size.

Dodd stared at him in silent outrage. Bob, unable to look him in the eyes, turned and climbed into his little white cart. It lurched into motion, speeding off across the long, flat concrete, leaving Dodd cursing under his breath.

4. Come Knockin'

TOBY WHITEHOUSE LIVED IN AN OLD TAN HOUSE THAT HAD SOMEHOW evaded the great, sweeping renovations which had overtaken whole neighborhoods after the South American War. The front yard was kept neatly mowed, and the old house always seemed to have a fresh coat of paint. Even the picket fence out front was painted white, keeping it cheery. The wood of the picket fence was probably older than Dodd; it sagged in places where rot had set in, but the five dozen coats of paint held it together. On either side of the front door were gaudy stained-glass windows that ran from ground level to the top of the doorframe. Dodd rang the doorbell and tried to peer through the glass, but he couldn't see a thing— nothing but a multicolored blur. The glass itself depicted gruesome pictures of Jesus Christ hanging from the cross, blood gushing from His hands and feet.

The South American War had affected its veterans in different ways. Some had turned to anarchy, some had turned to drugs. Toby Whitehouse had turned to JTV, Jesus Television. It was a mild and somewhat positive preoccupation, and Dodd had no problem with it. Whatever made Toby and his family happy was okay with him. He rang the doorbell again and listened for footsteps.

There was the sound of wood sliding roughly against wood, and Dodd looked up to see Savina, Toby's seventeen-year-old daughter, poking her head and shoulders through her bedroom window. "Dodd," she said in a loud whisper. "I've got to talk to you."

Just then the front door opened, and Toby was smiling and greeting him. "Dodd! Dodd, come in." His accent was heavier than usual today, which told Dodd he was excited about something. Dodd smiled up at Savina before walking inside the house with her father.

"Today has been an incredible day," Dodd said.

Toby closed the door behind him. "That it has." He was grinning. "Come on in. Sit down."

"Thank you." Dodd followed him into the den and leaned against a wall, feeling too pent-up to sit down. "I'm troubled, Toby."

Toby paused in front of him, looking at him as if he had no right to be troubled. "And what is it that's bothering you on this incredible day?"

"Did you know that Bob was going to quit his job?"

"No, that I didn't."

"He went in and gave them his resignation, and they talked him out of it. They gave him a promotion—now he's my boss."

"You don't seem very happy about it."

"I'm not. We got into a fight."

"Oh, that's bad. Especially now that he's your boss."

Dodd gave him a brief summary of the argument, to which Toby made grave faces but little comment. Something else was on his mind. Savina made an appearance downstairs and Dodd smiled at her; she made mysterious hand signals behind her dad's back, then put her finger to her lips, telling Dodd to be quiet about something. He winked at her, ruffling her thin braids as she came close. She laughed, dodging away.

"So," Toby said, "have you heard the big news?"

"What big news?"

"About the Savior! The Second Coming."

"No, I think I've missed that one."

Toby's eyes were gleaming like the eyes of a used-robotics salesman. "You haven't heard, then?"

"What? No, I haven't."

"It's something *fantastic*," Toby said, exhilarated. "They announced it today on JTV. The Pope of the United Church was given a revelation. He's coming back!"

"Back where? To the Americas?"

"No, to Jerusalem!"

"The Pope's going to Jerusalem?" Dodd didn't understand. What was the big deal?

"No, not the *Pope*. The *Savior*!"

"The savior?" Dodd still didn't understand. "Which savior?"

Toby looked very disappointed in him. "You know, *the* Savior. The Son! Jesus Christ."

Dodd thought that he was still missing something. "Jesus Christ?" he said, hoping for some vital clue.

"Yes. *Jesus Christ*. The *Savior*."

"Jesus Christ is going back to Jerusalem." The sentence was meaningless to him. He waited for Toby to correct him.

"*Yes*. Is it not a spectacular revelation?"

"Jesus Christ is going back to Jerusalem. This is what you're trying to tell me?"

"Yes! That's it!"

"I don't get it," Dodd told Toby.

Toby took him by the shoulders and gently shook him back and forth. "Are you in shock? I'm telling you in the simplest words I know."

Dodd stared deep into his friend's eyes. In the background he could hear Savina laughing. Suddenly it dawned on him that Toby meant the actual words that he had said, "Jesus Christ is going back to Jerusalem." His mind tried to reject it again, but there was no other explanation. "Wait a minute," he said to Toby, "you're telling me the Pope came on JTV and made this announcement?"

"Yes!" Toby was grinning. "In eighteen days."

"What were his exact words?"

"This is what he said: 'Our Lord and Savior is returning to Earth in eighteen days. He's coming to Jerusalem.'"

"The Pope made this announcement?"

"Yes!"

"In all *seriousness*?"

"Yes!" Toby was grinning like a maniac, his white teeth shining in high contrast to his dark skin.

Dodd's skin had gone pale. The United Church was a very serious organization. They were not into making shocking, sensationalist statements. "Do you have this statement recorded?"

"No need, they've been repeating the Pope's announcement every five minutes." Toby led Dodd into the next room, where his video system was on with the sound turned way down. Toby turned the volume up and they watched the tail end of a PTL Cola commercial: thin and genetically perfect Believers guzzling from bright cans with obvious sexual delight. The music was very up, very bouncy. Then a JTV announcer was grinning, and just as Toby claimed, they were replaying the Pope's announcement. It was very calm and dignified, a news conference held in what had once been the Catholic Vatican. The Pope was old and dressed in white with gold trimmings, and he was surrounded by rich reds and purples. In the background were other old men in tall hats, smiling peacefully. "The Savior is returning to Earth. He will be in Jerusalem in eighteen days. Let us pray..." There was a long session of chanting, most of it in Latin, and then a lot of praising of God. The clip ended, leaving Dodd breathless.

"We're going to church tonight," Toby told him, catching him off guard. "It would give me great pleasure if you would attend with us."

No convenient excuse came to mind—indeed, Dodd's mind was blank. "I don't know, Toby."

"You don't know!" Toby was very displeased.

"I have to think this over."

"What is there to *think* about? You come to church with us, you pray to God, maybe your soul will be saved."

Wheels turned in Dodd's mind, thoughts that would only

offend his old friend. "Sorry, Toby, I'm in shock. Pray for me if you want, but I don't think I want church tonight."

"You pray for yourself," Toby said angrily.

"Please, Toby. Not tonight."

Toby searched his eyes. His expression softened, and he nodded. "If it is not right for you, it is not right. I will pray for you."

"Thank you. I think I'll be going now."

"Okay." Toby shrugged. He followed Dodd to the door and opened it for him, his daughter Savina trailing behind and giving Dodd meaningful looks. He said good-bye and left, walking in a hurry.

The United Church owned JTV, he thought. JTV is having a ratings slump. The church is losing money. So they have the Pope come on and announce something exciting to boost ratings.

Dodd thought the situation through very carefully. It seemed to make sense, though the letdown at the end of the eighteen days was going to be a big risk for the church. He couldn't understand why the church would take that big a chance, unless they were about to sell the network. That's it, he thought—boost the ratings, sell the network, say the Pope's vision was a little off, maybe he meant eighteen years instead of days. People would be a little disillusioned, but they would have to forgive their pope. Meanwhile, the church has made money and at the same time dumped a major obligation.

That's got to be it, he thought. It *had* to be the explanation, or at least close—because Dodd was positive the church couldn't be serious. The Savior returning? The Second Coming in *eighteen days?*

He paused a block away from his apartment complex, gazing across the skyline at the late-afternoon sunlight. All the buildings glinted, little sparkles reflecting off ten million windows. He bit his lower lip at a frightening thought that he could not dismiss: What if the Savior *was* coming back? Dodd lowered his head, looking at the sidewalk, eyeing the motion of a beetle that happened to be crawling a few centimeters from his feet.

During his childhood, back before the collapse of '26 and the wars that followed, Dodd had been forced to memorize the Bible by a wire-haired old man with bad breath who screamed at him and several other children every Sunday for six years. Jesus Christ was coming back, the man had insisted. He was coming back in fire and glory, yes, yes indeed, He was due to return, but at *the end of the world*.

The End of the World.

Of course this was from the old Bible, the King James Version, which according to the United Church was "grossly distorted and altered to serve the purposes of man." They made the same claims about every other edition predating their own "new translation," which came about after the collapse, after the United Church had swallowed up Christian Life, the Southern Baptists, the Mormons, and others . . . even the Catholics.

The End of the World. It certainly seemed to Dodd that the world was on the brink of chaos, that reality was growing feeble and order was disappearing. What was true one day was wrong the next. The idea of something being permanent was forgotten. There were always *New Advances*. And in his head the images of the war, the terrible silence, the endless marching through craters littered with dead women and children, all with their arms around each other, around their poor dead animals, dogs and chickens, blackened, bloating, eyes white and featureless like hard-boiled eggs. No rot, no stink. Perfectly sterile.

Dodd found himself wanting to believe Jesus Christ was coming back to save him. He wanted desperately to believe. He couldn't, though. He just couldn't find it in himself. He couldn't trust JTV, because it was big business, and this was a big event, and all he could see was the money they were going to make because of all the people who wanted so desperately to believe.

And yet, Dodd couldn't believe the United Church would risk the anger of a world of betrayed believers.

The beetle at his feet crawled down a crack, disappearing from sight. Dodd put his hands into his pockets and continued on his way, walking down the block to his apartment complex, a small, cheap dwelling compared to the massive corporate-housing complexes looming to the north, south, and west. He passed the row of garages, guiltily thought about the graffiti painted inside his own, and walked up to his front door. "Open please," he told it. Recognizing his voice, it obeyed.

The television was silent. Dodd was amazed. He wondered where Sheila had gone, and walking down to the bedroom he was tickled to find her taking a nap in his bed. He stood over her in the dim light that filtered through the electric shades, studying her prone, nude figure sprawled across the unmade sheets. Her bright red hair spilled across her shoulders and back, messy and unwashed. Seeing her like this made Dodd feel better, and he bent over and gave her a gentle kiss on the small of her back. Her shoulder blades twitched, and after a moment she raised her head, turning and looking over her shoulder. Seeing him, she smiled and rolled over on her back, splaying her legs. She took a hold of his arm and pulled him insistently down.

5. Expecting

SAVINA WATCHED DODD WALKING AWAY FROM THE HOUSE, HER SMOOTH face set into a frustrated expression. She needed to talk to him, and her father had scared him away. Her father also forbade her to leave the house because they were going to church that night, so she couldn't go chasing after him.

"What's wrong, child?" her father asked her.

"Nothing," she replied.

Behind both of them the television showed one of the JTV choirs that the Church was so proud of, a gathering of perfect-faced men and women singing with all the enthusiasm their hearts and lungs could muster. ". . . blood runs so red to my face," they sang, ". . . I am awash in shame . . . when the Savior arrived . . . I had not yet been saved . . ." Savina wanted to gag.

Her father spontaneously hugged her, kissing her hair. Religious things always made him so emotional. "I love you, child," he said.

"I love you too, Daddy." She hugged him back, and something flashed in her mind in the mutual squeeze. An idea. "Can I invite a friend along to church tonight?"

"What friend is this?" her father asked.

"A girl from one of my classes." Savina thought frantically. "Her name is Lamissa."

"She isn't going to church with her own family?"

"Her family are atheists—I'm trying to convert her."

"Ah, now!" He seemed very pleased.

Here's the trick, Savina thought. "They don't have a phone. I have to go over to her house to ask her to come."

"No phone, child? What kind of family has no phone?" His voice was suspicious.

"They're Luddites, Daddy. Back-to-the-trees people. But Lamissa's not like that—she believes in God, and she really needs guidance."

"Where does Lamissa live?"

"Not far, between here and Dodd's."

Her father seemed to deliberate. "Okay, child. But you be back before we go to church—we are not going to wait around. If you make us late for church, you'll be paying for it later." He pronounced it "lay-tah," stretching the word out for emphasis.

"It won't take long, Daddy," she promised. She gave him a kiss, and smiled. "Bye!"

"Remember what I said."

"I will!" She was already on her way to the door.

"Bye-bye now," he said, "and good luck with Lamissa's parents."

"Thanks!" She opened the door, then dashed outside. In reality there *was* a Lamissa in one of her classes, but Savina hardly knew her. She certainly had no intention of inviting the girl to church. When she got back from Dodd's she would simply tell her father that Lamissa's parents wouldn't let their daughter go.

She trotted across the front walk and down to the sidewalk. Dodd was nowhere in sight—he had quite a lead on her—and she wanted to catch him before he got home and Sheila got her hands on him. With Sheila around he wouldn't talk to her.

Savina remembered the days when Dodd had been living with Leslie. She thought of the time as BS—Before Sheila—a happy time of warmth and excitement and freedom. Her parents used to let her stay with Dodd and Leslie, and they had taken her to the coast, to the mountains, out skiing; these were some of the happiest memories she had. Dodd and Leslie were so easy to talk to, she kept no secrets from them, and felt free to ask any questions she liked. They were open, honest. Savina had learned a lot about sex. It was no big deal. She and Dodd and Leslie had grown to be very close friends, and then Leslie was transferred to a new job, and she left. She just left. Dodd had said it was okay, that Leslie had to leave because of her career, and he had to stay because of his job, and that was life. He tried to hide it, but Savina could tell his heart was broken. Savina was fifteen at the time, and had an enormous crush on him. She would have done anything to make him feel better.

That's when Sheila came into the picture. Sheila was the woman in the apartment upstairs, the woman who'd been watching Dodd through the window and panting over him in the hall. She'd gotten to him when he was vulnerable and used sex to keep him. Savina thought she was a slut. Even her parents thought the woman was a slut, and had abruptly stopped allowing Savina to hang out at Dodd's place.

That hurt Savina, and made her dislike Sheila even more. Dodd was her *friend*, the only person she had left whom she could open up to, and the only person who could give her advice that was worth anything. The only one who supported her dreams. Savina needed him now more than ever.

She reached his apartment without seeing him. Dammit, she thought. Reaching out an index finger, she touched the burnished metal beside the blue-gray door and stood nervously waiting. After a minute she touched the button again.

No answer. Savina began to wonder if Dodd hadn't come straight home, if he'd stopped somewhere else. She touched the button again, standing on one foot, then the other. She was beginning to feel a little foolish, just standing there. Where else could he be? she wondered. He occasionally went to a bar about seven blocks away, but that wouldn't do her any good—they wouldn't let her in.

After ringing the bell again and waiting another minute, Savina walked with crossed arms around to Dodd's bedroom window and peered through the shades. At first she couldn't see anything—

there was only a small slit she could see through—but in the dimness beyond she could make out the bed, and figures on the bed . . . pale, moving . . . and Savina ducked and moved away from the window, heart hammering and face flushed. She felt guilty and frustrated. Sheila! She hated Sheila. The slut had firmly wedged herself in between her and Dodd, cutting Savina off completely. What could Dodd possibly see in her?

Savina strode away, face burning, arms crossed. Her hopes were crushed—she couldn't talk to Dodd and it was all Sheila's fault. She walked in the direction of the neighborhood subway station, heading reluctantly to her boyfriend's house. Her boyfriend by all rights should be the first to know, but Savina would have felt more secure if she'd talked to Dodd first.

At the entrance to the subway station Savina halted, watching the people emerge, staring at the old men, the women, the kids, the occasional raggedly dressed anarchist . . . She realized she had no idea of what to say to Greg. She was so angry she could slap his face, and at the same time she wanted to hug and kiss him until the fear was washed away. What am I going to *say*? she thought. How am I going to break the news? It was so hard to talk to him.

Abruptly she decided not to.

Her shoulders slumped, her head down, she turned and walked back to her parents' house.

6. Jesus Thing

SAUL KALMAN RETRIEVED AN URGENT MESSAGE ON HIS DESK TERMINAL—A new account had been set up for a Russian company: Jacovik Premium Imported Vodka. It was to be advertised subliminally on the Travels network, and it was part of Saul's job to supervise the design of the subliminal message.

"Shit," he muttered to himself as he stared at the screen. He was feeling more than a little dizzy. Saul didn't approve of advertising on Travels; the company didn't need it, subscriber fees paid for the channel. Ratings were phenomenally high for the network and still growing; Travels had a continuous 27 percent to 39 percent share of the total television audience. Telcron Systems, Inc., the company that produced Travels, was upsetting the balance of the entire video industry, dominating the other networks—and Telcron was yielding, at last, to advertisers clamoring to use the Travels medium, and to Telcron stockholders who wanted the advertising for the tripled income. Commercials were now present on Travels, but they did not interrupt the program—the program must remain endless, uninterrupted—so advertisers were paying multimillions to be part of the background, the commercials entirely subliminal. Also, there was a maximum limit of commercial accounts accepted by Telcron; advertisers fought and backstabbed each other to acquire accounts. Saul wondered uneasily about the hoops Jacovik Vodka had gone through to secure this new account.

"Shit," he said again. It was hard for him to concentrate on the problem; it was too early in the morning. He gave up, deciding to drop the whole matter in the lap of Vicky Zcavowitz, his assistant creative engineer. Pushing a button on his terminal, he sent the memo and information down to her and paused for a moment to add a few suggestions to help her along. Maybe, he thought, we could stick it on a billboard in the background. Hell, have the ball bounce *off* the billboard, slo-mo, in an erotic and suggestive way.

He shook his head. That was too obvious. Hell, he thought, let *her* think about it. With a decisive motion he slammed the SEND button and his notes joined the rest of the problem down in Vicky's terminal, waiting for her just as it had been waiting for him. He looked at the time readout on the screen. Hmmmm. She would be calling in about five minutes, madder than hell, and he was going to have to placate her, calm her down, show confidence in her, and promise a raise or something, then pray she did a good job or it would be his neck. But *dammit*, he thought, I don't have time for this! Saul had to be out in the field in an hour, and he should be taking his morning dose of Mataphin about now. If they wanted advertising, they should have a whole department to take care of it—not just him.

The terminal in front of him buzzed as a call came in. The point of origin was the main fifty-fourth-floor terminal, probably Lisa Schemandle. If it was Lisa, Saul knew what it would be about—something related to the Second Coming stunt that JTV was pulling. Saul reached over and picked up his Mataphin dispenser, deciding to take a double dose of the creativity enhancer immediately, to get it into his system before having to deal with this money-head bitch.

Her face blinked onto the screen, off-center. It was ruddy and lined, her eyebrows clenched, her expression dour. "Saul," she said.

"Good morning, Lisa."

"We've got to do something about this Jesus thing. We've got to *neutralize* it somehow."

"Why?" Saul said.

"Well, Saul, use your goddamn head! They're trying to get their ratings back! If they pull this off, the bottom will drop out—isn't that *obvious* to you? We've got to take steps to neutralize it!"

"You really think they have a chance?"

"Saul, you know who owns JTV, right? The United Church! The United Church leases satellite time from the Swiss National Trust, which has large holdings in the U.S. Food & Materials Corporation. The USFMC is owned by the United States government. The United Church has special rates on their satellite time because they own a large chunk of Swiss Trust, and the USFMC donates a hell of a lot of money to the United Church. Do you get the picture, Saul? Do I have to spell it out any more? We're dealing with a giant, a megacorp! We can't take any chances."

Saul didn't appreciate this demeaning tone of hers; he glared at her, frowning. "Telcron is owned by Mitsubishi."

"That's not the point!"

"Well then, what is the point? We're a megacorp, too. Why should we panic? I mean, it's not like we can stage a counter spectacular. We can't change the format, Travels is Travels. People—"

"Shut up for a second and listen to me. Saul, my own personal neck is on the cutting block here. I have no idea what to do either, but something must be done—*something*. You and I can come up with something if we *think*. Muck with the AHL intensity, increase the pace, anything! We've got to. Those bastards have pulled a fast one, Saul. This is *serious*. But they're dough-heads, fucking god-freaks—not professionals like us, not artists like you. Consult with your expert systems, your staff, and phone me after you get back from the field. Around six o'clock." She cut the connection, leaving Saul with sweating palms. He took another two Mataphin tabs without realizing he'd already had double his morning dosage, and shuffled out of his office, escaping down the elevator.

The fresh morning air did nothing to cheer him, and he felt rotten about what he had done to Vicky. He dreaded facing her. She's in the same goddamned position I'm in, he realized. I've put her there, out of panic, just like Lisa Schemandle panicked and put *her* job on *my* lap.

The Mataphin began taking strong hold as he found himself a seat on the crew truck. He settled back, made himself comfortable, and tried to relax and think. The crew would be down in a few moments, along with a fuming Vicky Zcavowitz, but for the moment, at least, he had peace.

So, he thought. What to do?

Well, the strength of Travels was its high Attention Holding Level; motion and music created by the human mind for the human mind, enhanced and reinforced to produce a strong mesmerizing effect. When Saul had first joined Telcron Systems, the AHL was merely an afterthought, a study done by one of the Mitsubishi executives long since gone——the study did nothing more than pin down what it was that made beta-test versions of Travels so pleasant to watch. Later the idea was seized upon, developed, artificially enhanced by teams of creative engineers of which Saul had been a key member. Now the AHL was more important than the program itself——the "art" that had been Travels was relegated to the background. The AHL *was* Travels, and if there were an answer to the present problem, it had to lie in the AHL.

That was the solution.

If the viewers are already in heaven, Saul thought, what would they need a savior for? The AHL needs to be intensified. But that means a hell of a lot of work. The entire production system would have to be regeared.

Shit, he thought. Why do it? Why panic and overreact? Why couldn't we just ride it out? JTV's stunt, after all, is risky——it could backfire altogether, eliminate the need for a Travels response. And the "response," the compensation for their stunt, could backfire as well. The Politico Network could end up with all the ratings.

Nevertheless Saul had to do it. It was now his job. As he sat there thinking about all his problems, which were made colorful and even larger by the influence of Mataphin, Vicky arrived to complicate everything and make Saul even more miserable.

7. Kisses and Fellatio

THE SCREEN ON DODD'S BEDROOM TELEPHONE READ: MESSAGES: 00 MAIL: 01
Someone had sent him mail. Probably junk mail, he thought as he retrieved it to the screen. The ancient art of "spam." As the message flashed up in little glowing letters, Dodd wondered if it was junk mail or if it was truly directed at him:

> TO: **Dodd Corley**
> DATE: **6/1/42**
> FROM: **friends**
> SUBJECT: **your soul**
>
> **THESE are the LAST DAYS.**
> **BEWARE the ANTICHRIST AI!**
>
> **Don't be fooled by the LIAR which mixes Truth with his LIES.**
> **<<< BELIEVE NOTHING! >>>**
> **Believe nothing and nothing will fool you.**
> **Trust only what you can reach out and touch!**
> **GUARD your SOUL!**
> **BELIEVE NOTHING! BEWARE THE ANTICHRIST AI!**

Digital graffiti junk mail. Dodd erased the message, wishing he had an artificial intelligence program of his own to shield him from such things.

These are the last days.

Oh goddammit, he told himself. Stop it. *These are the last days. Beware the Antichrist AI.* He'd been reading in his old King James Bible again, confirming what he remembered from his childhood studies: When Christ returned, he would return at the end of the world. He had found several references to it, a phrase that Christ had apparently been fond of: ". . . I am the Alpha and Omega, the beginning and the end, the first and the last."

Of course nothing like this appeared in the United Church version. They seemed to have mixed in a little Eastern religion, changing it around so that the return of the Savior is a time of joy and new beginnings. The part about Armageddon was reduced to a time of "struggle and change," and war was eliminated altogether. They didn't even use the term *Armageddon*.

Or did they? Dodd punched keys on his phone terminal, calling up a copy of the United Church Bible. "Search for references to Armageddon," he told it. The reply came on the screen, little words between two asterisks:

* Not Found *

"Search for any occurrence of the word *Armageddon*," he asked.

* Not Found *

Dodd shook his head in wonder. *Armageddon* was missing. He asked it for references to the Rapture, and it retrieved passages where people were *in rapture* at the voice of the Savior, but never were they *raptured*, the true believers taken away to heaven before Armageddon, spared the pain and agony of the *Trials and Tribulations*. People who were taken away during *the Rapture* simply disappeared off the face of the Earth. Or so Dodd had been taught as a child.

* Not Found *

Jesus is the beginning and the end, Dodd thought. If Jesus shows up, it will be *the end*. The finish.

Two weeks from now. *Beware the Antichrist AI!* The slogan kept popping into his head. *These are the last days.*

It was depressing to Dodd, because he couldn't help but feel that these *were* the last days. The world was going to hell. Robots and AIs were taking all the jobs. The poor and the disturbed were disappearing into euthanasia centers. Child taxation was making it harder and harder to have children, unless one happened to qualify for the "special circumstance clause"—which Dodd didn't. People were selling their progeny rights. Things changed so fast that one was apt to wander around in confusion from one week to the next, forever trying to get used to their surroundings. Thirty years ago interstellar colonies were still an impractical dream, and now they were reality—normal, everyday people, Dodd's neighbors, were packing up and leaving. Going to the new frontier, billions upon billions of kilometers away. It was incredible. Dodd couldn't see how such upheaval could keep up, this constant change. It was like society was stretching reality to its limits, and like anything—it was a universal law—if you stretched something too far, by God it was going to break.

Maybe Jesus *is* coming, he thought.

The phone began ringing, startling him, and he exited the UC Bible. He touched the key to accept video and picked up the handset. He recognized the lurid, painted Oriental face of Mr. Chang, the apartment manager, as it appeared on the screen. "Is Sheila Dwaas there, Mr. Corley?" he asked in his pleasant, patient voice.

"Yes. Just a minute."

"Thank you."

Dodd touched the hold key and padded down the hall into the living room, stood in front of the television, and faced Sheila. "Hey," he said. "Telephone."

She stared at his legs, mouth slack and eyes half-open. She looked like she was either dead or dying.

"Hey," he said, waving his hand in front of her face. "Sheila. Sheila! *Sheila!*"

Sheila jumped, startled, covering her bare breasts with her arms. "What?" she said, irritation in her voice.

"The manager wants to talk to you."

"What manager?"

"The apartment manager."

"Is he here?" Sheila looked around the room.

Dodd sighed, shaking his head. He pointed toward the kitchen. "On the phone."

"Oh." Sheila snatched a robe that had been sitting in a heap on the floor. Dodd went back into the bedroom as she answered the call, but after a few minutes she appeared in the doorway. "Hi," she said.

Dodd was lying on his bed with the old King James. He threw it aside and said, "What?"

"The rent on my apartment is due."

Dodd nodded, accepting the inevitable. "I'll pick it up."

"You still want me to keep it?"

Dodd stared at her with a blank expression. Then his eyes lit up. "What, are you saying you want to move in with me?"

"I'm more or less moved in now."

"You said you wanted to keep your place."

She shrugged, the loose robe sliding down to expose one of her smooth shoulders. "It doesn't matter. I mean, you're the one paying for it."

True, Dodd thought. It would save money to get rid of her apartment . . . and if she were officially moved in, living with him, they would be that one step closer to a marriage contract, and—

With Sheila? he thought. Would he want to have a child with her? Would she *want* to have one?

She frowned at his odd expression. "What?" she said. "Look, it's okay, I don't have to move in. I mean—"

"You can move in," Dodd said. "I mean, why not? Why not make it official? Besides, we can use that money we're paying out for your apartment for something else."

"Really?" She smiled, walking gracefully from the door to the bed, sitting down next to him. "For what?"

"I don't know. We'll see."

"We will?"

"Yes." Dodd was smiling at her now, fingering the side of her thigh. He drew spirals inward, then outward. "I've got some money saved up, too. We can do something special with it."

"A trip?"

Dodd pursed his lips, tilting his head to one side. "Maybe. A trip would be nice, but we can take a trip anytime. I was thinking of something *really* special."

"Like what?"

The spirals Dodd had been drawing on her thigh now turned to figure eights, working their way, coaxing, up across her pelvis and inside her robe. He was leaning against her, his head almost touching hers; she was motionless, waiting. "How would you feel if," he started, then hesitated. He was staring into her eyes, and she stared back, unblinking.

"What?" she said.

"How would you feel if I suggested that we both stop taking our birth control pills?"

She continued staring at him for a long moment, unmoving, then at last she looked down and leaned her head against his. "You . . . you want a baby?"

"You know I do."

"I didn't know you were that serious about me."

"How do you feel about it?" Dodd listened very carefully for her answer.

"I've thought about it," she said after a long pause. Her voice was distant, without inflection; it sounded almost dead. It rang hollow. Dodd felt as though he hadn't heard it; he wanted her to say it again, louder, so he could guess what she was thinking.

She leaned forward, and there was a warm, wet feeling at his neck—she had started kissing him, bringing her hands up to caress his chest. Her fingers trembled, but he had no idea why— was it out of emotion, or nervousness? Was she saying yes with kisses, or avoiding an answer? She tongued his ear, growing more passionate, then pulled back, eyes closed, her nose touching his.

He kissed her hesitantly, but as soon as their lips touched she was fervid, pushing him backward and landing on top of him, her tongue twirling and probing in time with her entire body, squirming, grasping, rubbing.

She worked her way down his neck, kissing and licking, then down his exposed chest, his nipples, down across his stomach, and then her strong, short fingers were ripping at the cohesive tabs of his pants. He stared at the ceiling, trying to think, trying to interpret . . . lips and tongue touched his penis, and it was all ripped away, his mind was gone. He closed his eyes and let go. Travels music drifted down the hall, reeling, racing. Sheila made slurping sounds. Dodd began grasping desperately at the bed.

It was like the process of thought reduced to a laser tracking a spiral on a disk, and during sex there is no spiral, the disk is blank, so the laser searches for something to track and quickly moves from one side to another without finding anything. When it reaches the end there is an explosion, and the power goes off.

Dodd felt the explosion. Orgasm is a time of nonexistence, like dying or meeting God, or falling asleep in a sailboat in a calm, sunlit ocean, nowhere to go, nothing to hit, wander where you will. You hear waves, you hear gulls, there is an occasional cool breeze over your warm skin. A pillow beneath your head. No worries.

Dodd once had a lover named Leslie whom he'd wanted to marry, who'd wanted children. She and Dodd saw things from the same point of view. She was like a female version of himself, and they were so natural together, so comfortable. He never told her he wanted to marry her, he never suggested they have a child— Dodd had no idea why, he just didn't. She accepted a once-in-a-lifetime job offer and went away, and now she was married to some superterranean who took her on cruises through the rings of Saturn and was wealthy beyond belief. Intelligence on her part, stupidity on Dodd's. She would have stayed if he had asked her to, but she would have been stuck with him and his normal little life. He knew all along she was destined for more than that, and so he'd let her go. It was the hardest thing he had ever done.

I'm normal because of her, he thought. She helped me to make sense of the war, of the hell we toured. That was your part in my life, the good deed you did for me. I'll always love you for that.

Salt breezes, seagulls. The sails made small rippling-cloth sounds. Leslie was smiling at him. "I love you as much as you love me," she told him. "I would have been just as happy in your ordinary little life. I would have loved to give birth to your children."

"I would have felt guilty."

"There's no reason to."

"You've already given me a life. I was suicide bound when you came to me. I was thinking of the euthanasia center."

"I know. The war was hard."

Images of the war drifted by like clouds. Nothing in his life had prepared him for the sight of a dead rain forest, the skeletons of immense trees and vines with all the leaves blackened, dead animals covering the ground like a carpet, birds and lizards and small frogs, snakes and pigs, billions of insects like the bottom of a bug zapper. In a clearing would stand the flimsiest little huts and shacks, made from old plywood and grass and branches; the bombs didn't even knock them down. Blackened people bloating with internal gases, but no decomposition. Killed by intense radiation that was gone four hours later, but all protein in the area was destroyed, there weren't even any bacteria left to break things down. No nutrients in the soil. The only life in the area was what Dodd and the other troops brought with them.

They dug holes and pushed bodies into them with Stiletto tanks fitted with bulldozer blades, covering the graves and paving them over for an airstrip, a copter pad, a basketball court. He carried an immense weapon that he fired occasionally at a tree trunk, just to watch the trunk explode and the tree fall over. There was nothing else to shoot at. All the death-dealing blows were delivered from orbit. A bomb here, a scattering of beams over there. Backward twentieth-century enemies with twenty-first-century weapons. Their families, their children. Little babies, shielded by their mothers, not a scratch on them but stiff and dead in their ragged little diapers. Some of the men in Dodd's unit showed nothing; others shot themselves. Dodd did a lot of crying and cursing, and was labeled a discipline problem. One of the officers criticized him constantly, and Dodd had swung at him with a shovel, but missed. The officer snatched the shovel away and swung it back—

Dodd sat up suddenly, startling Sheila. He was sweating. "How long have I been asleep?" he asked.

"About a half hour."

"What time is it?"

"Five-thirty," said the clock beside the bed.

"I've got to take a shower," he said, feeling dirty. Dodd rolled off the bed and onto his feet, heading for the bathroom. In the shower he punched the recall for his favorite temperature and let the water spray over him, running down his arms and legs, intimate cleansing water massaging his muscles and scalp. It rinsed the sweat away, helped him to relax. There were two things he hated dreaming about, and he'd had both in the same dream.

After exiting and drying himself, Dodd slipped on a fresh set of clothes, soft blue pants with a white stripe down the leg and a green-and-blue-splotched shirt, and walked down the hall to find Sheila on the couch in front of the television. That annoyed him, but he forced himself not to care, and standing in view of the screen found that Travels was, for some reason, particularly interesting this evening. He went into the kitchen, had the robot arms prepare some snack sandwiches, and joined Sheila with a plate and two glasses of wine. The sphere was there, as always—planetlike, rolling its way through a sensuous and surrealistically lit crest of a sand dune.

The thick, rich scenery flowed past in slow motion, the ball rolling on endlessly, the only thing on the screen one could really see. Everything else was taken in with peripheral vision. The winding, reeling music worked on Dodd, soothing him, carrying him along with the scenery, along with the rolling multicolored sphere.

Sometimes it did not seem like it was moving forward but merely spinning as the world moved beneath it. It was like a gear connected to a giant motor that spun the Earth around—then it would bounce through rocks, with the music rebounding on each collision, and suddenly the music swelled—tingling and spiraling—as the ball dropped straight over a bluff, twirling slowly in midair, the sky full of red-and-purple sunset clouds. Dodd felt breathless, close to vertigo; a chill ran up and down his spine as the music reached a climax and the sphere, for a tantalizing split second, eclipsed perfectly the swollen red sun. It hit the ground, touched down on surf-wet sand, and continued a fast-paced bouncing roll down the beach parallel to the shore. The viewpoint changed, swinging around behind the sphere, following it, and ahead in the distance Dodd saw a pier and the seafront buildings of a quaint little town. The pier caught his attention, tore it away from the ball. He recognized the place. He had grown up there.

"That's Avila Beach!" he exclaimed out loud.

"What?"

"That's Avila Beach," he said again. "I had no idea they were making this down there."

"Oh." Sheila's attention slipped away.

Dodd looked down at the plate of sandwiches, intent on taking a bite, but the plate was empty. So was his wineglass. He looked at a clock and found almost three hours had gone by since he'd sat down. He was disgusted, turned off. He could see spending twenty minutes in front of the sphere, or maybe even an hour. But three—? No! It was stealing time from him, taking it away without his knowledge or permission. "Dammit," he said angrily, and stood up.

Sheila didn't notice.

"Dammit," he said again, louder but with less anger.

She seemed to hear him, but the television had too strong a hold on her. There was a stupid expression on her face, and watching her Dodd realized she had never answered his question about having children. Kisses and fellatio had distracted him, but latio itself had been a "yes." Somehow he doubted it.

He looked from her to the pulsing scenery on the screen then back. "Dammit," he said again, trying to get her attention.

"What?" she said vaguely.

"Let's go see some real scenery."

"What?" Total incomprehension.

"They're supposed to be landing a new bank at around sunset, maybe we can catch a glimpse of it."

"What?"

Dodd took her by her thin pale arm and pulled her up off the couch. "Come on."

"Where are we going?"

"To see Travels on a larger screen."

"What? Really?" Her voice was still vague, stupid. He led her stumbling out of the room, out of the apartment, around to the stairs that led up to the sun deck on the roof. When they stepped onto the sun deck there was still enough light in the sky to see a hulking square bulk surrounded by large construction fliers. It was about two kilometers away, being lowered slowly into the skyline.

"Here's the bigger screen," Dodd said. "There's Travels."

"What?"

"That's a new bank building."

"Oh," she said, looking at it with blinking eyes. She appeared to be waking up. "It's so big," she said with a hint of wonder in her voice. "How can they hold it up there?"

"It's light," Dodd told her. "It's a metal made from hydrogen, they build the whole thing in space."

"Oh." She pulled close to him, hugging his left arm. The evening breeze was a little cool, and they were dressed for sun-light.

"Have you made a decision yet?" he asked.

"About what?"

"About the question I asked and you never answered."

Sheila became very quiet, her body going still. She didn't answer him.

"Well? What are you going to do, leave me hanging?"

"I need to think about it, Dodd."

"What's there to think about? Either you want to or you don't. If you want to, say you want to. If you don't, say you don't."

"You're not being fair."

"Fair?"

"You shouldn't ask this, I mean, like such an ultimatum. I have to think about it."

"Sheila, I have to know." *I have to know if I'm wasting my time with you.* Fortunately Dodd was able to shut his mouth before the whole statement came out.

"I can't have time to think it over?"

"If you have to think it over, then it's obvious you don't want to."

"Well, I don't, really."

"Oh, well, there. What's there to think about, you have the answer right on your tongue."

"I don't want to lose you."

"I didn't expect you to be an unwilling mother. That's not what I want, either."

"Well, Dodd, a baby is such a big responsibility, and it'll take years and years to save the money——"

"I have the money already. I've been saving since after the war."

The idea of him having all that money seemed to shock her. She looked upset, confused. They both stared off at the skyline in silence as the new skyscraper was slowly lowered among its neighbors. Spotlights lit glowing pointers of light that swung across the fading sunset, outlining the building. Dodd felt heartbroken, but at the same time he was a little relieved.

8. Fast Forward

BOB RECENT DID NOT WATCH JTV, NOR DID HE WATCH THE POLITICO NET-
work. He didn't watch any of the sickly, gasping, once-giant broadcast networks—they were all hanging on to life by a few bare threads, depending entirely upon pornography to keep themselves afloat. Neither Bob nor his wife Denise had any interest in the local music-television stations filling the obsolete broadcast frequencies known as VHF and UHF. They rarely if ever watched theater disks even though their system was capable of playing them. Bob and Denise had only one real video interest, and that interest absorbed them. The JTV announcement didn't have any effect on them at all. They were unaware of the news until the announcement was days old.

One of Denise's old friends called to talk to her about the Second Coming, excited to the point of hysterics, asking Denise where she and her husband would be on that fantastic day. "I don't know. Home probably," Denise had told her. When she and her friend had hung up she wordlessly resumed her place beside her husband in front of the television, baffled by the whole conversation. It occurred to her that she hadn't understood most of what her friend had said.

"What was all that about?" her husband asked, his voice a monotone.

"I don't know," she replied, watching as the Travels sphere tumbled hectically down a grassy knoll, ricocheting between the trunks of large oak trees. "I've forgotten."

"I overheard something about the Savior."

"Mm-hmm. Something like that." Denise let out a small sigh, trying to concentrate. What was it? Something about "the Savior" coming back in two weeks. Something like that. She wondered vaguely if it was something that should be important to her. It was hard to think.

The sphere had gone down a mountainside and was heading for a ravine. Denise sat forward stiffly, her pulse racing, as the sphere went right over the edge of the ravine with her following. The angle of the view widened, trees rushing past in the background, and rocky cliff face, and swooping birds, and the ball was spinning and wavering from side to side as it fell. Dark and solid, rocks rushed up and the sphere hit, rebounding across a large waterfall, soaring through the mists, and was soon bouncing along beside a river as it raced the water downhill. Denise reached out and numbly picked up her drink from the coffee table. It was warm, the ice long since melted, but it was still good. Orange juice and Jacovik Premium Imported vodka, her favorite morning drink. It was called a, called a . . .

A what?

Denise couldn't remember, though she knew it was named after some sort of tool. It wasn't important. She set the glass down, forgetting about it, watching as the sphere rolled down into the depths of a canyon littered with fallen logs; it bounced between them and over them, graceful, nimble, with endless momentum . . . pine and sage rushed past, flat mossy boulders and deep pools of blue water, an occasional bird flying along for a moment or two, then zipping off. Denise closed her eyes, feeling warm and cozy, but when she opened them again she found a sharp pain in her neck, and her right arm was tingling. She'd been sleeping in an odd position, and she was surprised to find herself on the couch and not in bed. Where was her husband? At work? Denise had no idea; she didn't know if this was one of his work days or not. She couldn't remember what day of the week it was. It didn't matter, though; all she knew or cared about at the

moment was that she was very hungry. The Travels sphere was
hurtling down a narrow path through a yellow field of wheat, but
Denise managed to tear herself away. She pulled her body upright
and found her legs weak and her head spinning.

In the kitchen she keyed instructions into the Master Chef
and stood wearily against a wall while the insectile chrome arm
pulled bread and sandwich makings out of the refrigerator. With
quick, deft movements it built a ham and cheese sandwich, then
pulled a half-empty bottle of Jacovik vodka out of the liquor cabi-
net and fixed her another drink. Denise wolfed down the
sandwich, followed by the vodka and orange juice, and while the
robot arm mixed a refill she walked stiffly to the bathroom.

She peered at her reflection in the bathroom mirror with a
dull sense of shock—how long had it been since she'd last showered? How long had she been wearing these clothes? Her hair
hung in oily strings, and crusted food matter clung to the skin
around her mouth. With numb fingers Denise undid her clothing,
letting it fall to the floor, and punched in a temperature setting for
the shower.

After showering and changing, she picked up her fresh drink
from the kitchen and sat down in front of the television, watching
with excitement as the Travels sphere bounced off an old chunk
of cement, rolled up a broken piece of wood, sailed through the
air, and ricocheted off the side of a colorful billboard.

Her husband, Bob, shook her. "Ready for some dinner, darling?"

Denise looked at him, wondering where he had been. "No, I
just ate."

"Are you sure you don't want something? I'm getting a sandwich."

"Well . . ." Come to think of it, she *was* hungry. "All right. Thank
you, honey."

Denise looked back at the television, watched the sphere roll
across white sand with green, green trees in the background. She
yawned and, looking down, was surprised to find a half-eaten

sandwich in her limp hand. Bob reclined beside her, head lolling, eyes closed. A raw rasping noise was coming from his throat. She shoved him, and his body jerked. "You're snoring!" she snapped, as he blinked and looked around in confusion.

"I'm sorry," he said, his voice small and boyish.

Looking back at the screen, Denise bit down on the remainder of her sandwich and tasted nothing. Then a warm, strong hand had a hold on her shoulder, shaking her, and she opened her bleary eyes and looked up at her husband. "Baby, wake up," he said.

"Hmmmm?"

"I think you wet yourself."

"Hmmmm?" But then she noticed the wet stickiness between her legs, and she groaned. "Not *again*," she muttered, getting stiffly to her feet. She realized she was starving.

"I'll get the automaid up here, darling. You go change."

"Thank you." Denise waddled into the bathroom and stripped off her clothes. In the bathroom she wiped her legs and crotch with a warm, damp washcloth, then put on a clean pair of disposable panties. Over that she slipped on a silky black see-through robe. Why anything else? she thought. I'm not planning on going anywhere today.

Back in the living room there was a six-wheeled multilimbed metal creature busily dry-cleaning the couch. Denise wandered past, making her way into the kitchen. Through the kitchen window shone morning sunlight. How long was the morning going to last? she wondered. Meanwhile the kitchen arm swung back and forth with jerky motions, stopping suddenly here and there, fixing her another sandwich.

Three in one morning? Denise thought, munching it down. I'm going to get fat. But something struck Denise as wrong, and she realized this was a *new* morning, not an old one. Funny, she didn't remember much of last night.

In the living room, Denise waited for the automaid to leave, then sat back down on the newly cleaned couch and uttered a long, pleasant, "Mmmmmmmm . . ." as she found the Travels sphere careening down a luxurious expanse of deserted, golden beach. A moment later Bob, for some reason, kissed her—or did she imagine it? When she looked up, he was nowhere in sight. Off to work? she wondered. But no, he couldn't have gone to work because after a few minutes he was back, sitting down beside her. And the sandwich she thought she had finished minutes ago was sitting untouched on the coffee table in front of her, along with a fresh glass of orange juice and Jacovik vodka. She picked up the sandwich and began eating, chewing slowly, eyes glazed over like glass marbles.

9. Rape, Rape

SAVINA CAUGHT UP WITH HER BOYFRIEND AT SCHOOL. SHE WALKED RIGHT UP to him in class—he was linked to his instructor through a headset and was oblivious to his surroundings. She stood behind where he sat, staring down at the back of his head and feeling hatred. His hair was so blond, so fine. Such a beautiful boy, things coming to him so easily. She just hated him.

Quiet so as not to disturb the other students, Savina grasped his headset by the cord and slowly pulled. It slid off his blond locks and dropped to the floor. Greg looked around for a moment, disoriented.

"I need to talk to you," she said, keeping her voice low.

"What?" He stared at her without recognition for a full three seconds. "Savina," he said. His voice sounded vague, his words soft and not completely formed.

She peered into his eyes and saw the pupils fully dilated, then let out a wordless exclamation. This was adding insult to injury. *"Let's go outside,"* she said in a harsh whisper.

Greg rubbed his eyes. "What?"

Savina reached across him and punched the keys to bookmark his lesson and log him out of class. Unplugging his headset, she wound the cord up and handed it to him. Greg was looking around at the other students, dazed and blinking. He took the headset and put it in his backpack, then reluctantly stood up. She grabbed his arm and led him out of the class.

Outside the sidewalk was black, made of carbon concrete

mixed with tiny bits of recycled glass to make it sparkle in the sunlight. They walked across its hot surface and off onto the grass of the park where students took their lunches. Beyond the grass, on the far side of the park, was the border to the Lesser Depopulated Zone.

Greg was blinking rapidly in the sunlight. Savina stepped in front of him, blocking his path. "You've been doing Sulin-C again, haven't you?" she demanded.

"Sulin-C's too harsh," Greg said. "I'm on Mataphin." He grinned. "Stole it from my mom last time she came by."

"Shit, Greg!"

"You want some?"

"That stuff's *bad* for you!"

"Yeah, right. Why would they sell it then?" He put his arms out and spun around. *"Woooo!"*

"How much did you take?"

"Woooo . . ." Greg kept spinning.

"Greg!"

"Four tabs," he said, trying to stop his gyrations. He was wobbling on his feet.

"Four?"

"Any less just makes me space out." He laughed. "I'm dreaming. I'm living in my dreams . . ." He laughed again, and collapsed awkwardly onto the grass. Then he looked around with a startled expression. "How did I get out here?"

Savina remained standing, looking down at him with her arms crossed. "What?"

"How did I get outside? I was in the classroom."

"We walked out here, Greg."

"We did?" He looked confused. "When?"

"Greg . . . Stop it."

"I'm serious. I don't remember coming out here."

"You need to stop taking that stuff. Memory lapses are a sign of brain damage."

"They are?"

"Yes."

"Well. Shit. Maybe you're right."

They were both silent a moment, then Savina said, "Look, Greg, I came out here to ask you something."

"You did?"

"Yes. Why did you lie to me?"

"Lie to you? About what?"

"You told me you were on birth control." Savina was glaring at him.

"Birth control?" Greg looked bewildered for a few seconds, then the color drained from his face. "Did I say that?"

"Yes."

Greg's eyebrows lowered, and his thin mouth warped into a frown. "I thought *you* were on birth control."

"You know perfectly well I wasn't! I'm *underage*."

"That doesn't mean anything. You could have gotten them."

"The point is that you told me *you* were on it, Greg. Otherwise, I *would* have gone out and gotten something."

"Are you saying that you're pregnant?"

Savina wanted to hit him. "What do you *think* I'm saying?"

"Oh, *fuck*." Greg stared off into the distance for a moment, then looked down at his hands. *"Fuck."*

"If they abort this child," she said to him in a low, even voice, "they'll *sterilize* me. You know that, right? It's the law."

Greg didn't say anything. He looked like he was desperately trying to sober himself. He got back onto his feet, and they started walking slowly across the field.

"Why didn't you tell me you weren't protected?" she demanded. "Why did you have to lie to me?"

"I don't know."

"It's so stupid! This could have been prevented so easily!" She glared at him. "It's going to affect me for the rest of my life, Greg. *Me!* Because you were too lazy to prevent it."

His eyes were watering up. "I'm sorry."

"You know what the really stupid thing is, Greg——if this had happened two months from now, I would have been legal. I would have reached legal age."

"I'm sorry."

"All I would have had to do was worry about raising the baby tax. I might have been able to convince the Church to sponsor the baby." She was silent for a moment. They were slowly walking through a grove of oaks near the border of the Lesser Zone; beat-feet music boomed from the ruins beyond, anarchists having a party. Savina felt her anger slipping away, and she grabbed hold, pulling it back. "Goddamn you!" she suddenly shouted at Greg. "How can you be so irresponsible!"

"I didn't *want* this to happen!" he yelled back. "I didn't *plan* to lie!"

They stopped in the grass, standing and staring at each other.

"I *want* to have a baby, Greg. I don't want to be sterilized."

"I'm sorry!"

"I know you're sorry." It was gone, her anger was gone. Now she was just frightened. "I'm willing to forgive you if you'll help me."

"Help you? Of course I'll help you." He looked so ashamed that it was pitiful. Tears streaked his smooth, angular cheeks.

Savina sighed, and leaned up against the trunk of a big oak tree. "I've come up with some ideas," she told him. "If I can get a fake Idex, I can emigrate and have the baby."

Greg's blue eyes moved to and fro without focusing, as if he were searching around inside of his head. "Emigrate?" he exclaimed. "To where?"

Savina pointed up. "One of the colonies."

Greg stared at her. "That costs a fortune, and they don't let pregnant women on shuttles."

"Yes, they do," she said, but was unsure.

Greg put his hands to his head, as if trying to hold it together. Thoughts seemed to be painful. "Shuttles aren't as well shielded as the colonies," he said. "Space radiation turns babies into mutants. Besides, the government makes you wait and have the baby here so you have to pay the baby tax."

That idea shot down, Savina tried the next. "You and I can go down and apply for genetic testing. If we make it, they'll let me have it under the special circumstance thing. You know, for the gifted."

Greg was now wincing and shielding his eyes. "No. You're not old enough, and even if you had an Idex . . . they'd find out. They'd get you for a fake Idex, and for being pregnant." He slapped his forehead a few times. "Oh, man. You're going to lose me in a minute."

"Stay with me, Greg."

"The sky is on fire. The fire is *green.*"

"Don't phase out! I *need* you."

"Okay," he said, looking down at his feet. His chin was set in a determined expression. "Okay. Okay, I'm . . . Yeah."

Savina was silent for a second. "What if we go to the Church and apply for sponsorship?"

"No . . . You're underage, and we're not married."

"I'll get a fake Idex, we get married, we apply."

"They'd find you were pregnant before the marriage . . . and kick us out."

"We can have the certificate date changed."

"Christ, Savina. We can also end up in jail. Then you'd lose the baby and be sterilized anyway."

"We could go to the anarchists."

"What?" That seemed to snap him out of it for a moment.

"We could," Savina said. "They'd take us in." She pointed at the direction of the beat-feet music.

Greg was shaking his head, his eyes rolling around. "No way."

"They take in people. How else do you think they got there?"

"It's bizarre that you'd even think of that. Savina . . . you can't have the baby. You're underage. I haven't got any money . . . Savina, there's just *no way.*"

"The anarchists have children. They don't pay taxes. They—"

"Those people live like animals and eat bugs!"

"It's not my first choice, but I'll do it if I have to. Greg, I need you to help me think of a way we can do it! You're intelligent, you're creative . . . *help* me."

Greg looked away. "I think you should just have the abortion and get it over with."

"Oh, thanks a lot."

"Savina, it's the least painful way out of this."

"For *you*, maybe—not for me! How would you like me to tell them you raped me? Then you'd be up for sterilization, too!"

He turned to stare at her, his eyes wide. "You'd do that?" His voice was small, astonished.

"How would you feel? Don't you want kids someday?"

"You'd *do* that?"

"I will if you don't help me."

"Oh, well then. Okay, I raped you. I'll just go turn myself in." He turned around, taking wobbling steps back toward the school.

"Greg, come back here."

"No, no, I've got to turn myself in for raping you. It's the only decent thing to do."

"Greg!" She trotted after him. "Greg, I wouldn't do that! I *wouldn't*."

"No, get away from me, I'm a rapist! I might do it again. Get away from me."

"Greg, *stop*."

"Get away from me!" he shouted at her. "Go away!"

"*Greg!*"

He reached out and gave her a shove, perhaps a bit harder than he'd intended. She fell backward and sat in shock, watching him walk away across the park. In the background the lively beat-feet music continued, *wumpata-wumpata-wumpata*, punctuated by whoops and howls and dangerous laughter. Savina leaned forward and hugged her knees, crying.

10. Sex Toys

VICKY AGREED WITH MIRRO, SAUL KALMAN'S WIFE, THAT IT WOULD BE tasteful to keep it discreet. Saul knew what was going on between the two of them but was doing his best to ignore it. They didn't hide it from him, didn't try to keep the affair secret—but they didn't flaunt it in front of his face. Saul was Vicky's superior at Travels, after all. There was no reason to aggravate their already turbulent relationship.

Vicky waited for Saul to leave the house before she went up and rang the doorbell. She stood on the porch, scratching at her ribs and shifting her weight from one leg to the other, half-expecting Saul to come wandering back for some forgotten item, but the door opened and Mirro ushered her inside.

"How long is he going to be gone?" Vicky asked, touching the door switch. It closed behind her.

"He's gone off to get some Mataphin," Mirro said. "He usually takes about three hours . . . I don't know why. I think he takes some as soon as he gets it and goes on a long walk."

"You sure he'll be gone that long?"

"Yes." Mirro kissed Vicky, a tender touching of lips, then backed away. "Go get ready while I feed my kid. I'll be in there in a few minutes."

Vicky stifled a shudder at the mention of the poor monster Mirro and Saul had created. She hid her feelings, kept her face from showing it as Mirro turned and hurried off into the main part of the house. The child gave Vicky nightmares. It looked like a

giant bloated baby with a tiny head and no obvious sign of gender.
Totally useless, no hope for improving, the child was a mutant in
every sense of the word. How Mirro could love it so was beyond
her.

Vicky found her way to the large master bedroom with its
sauna and love pool and began removing her clothes. Each article
she folded as she took it off, stacked it nice and orderly on Mirro's
dresser. Mirro's daughter made some horrendous squeal that rattled the walls, and Vicky thanked the Lord that her one child was
normal. It was a gift, she thought, that her son Greg was so healthy
and perfect. It tore her up that the courts had given him to her ex-
husband. Sleazy bastard, she thought automatically. She regretted
having a child with a man. It would have been wonderful if she
could have had Greg with Mirro, but then, of course, it wouldn't
have been Greg. It could have ended up like Mirro's daughter—
but no, that must have come from Saul's genes. It couldn't have
come from Mirro. No way! Vicky slipped out of her tight, see-
through black panties, removed the Soft-Scent pad, and eased
herself daintily into the warm, vibrating love pool.

Such a waste, she thought. All that progeny tax money! And for
what, a thing that should have been miscarried. Saul and Mirro
should be entitled to a refund. The government doesn't give
refunds, though. Vicky remembered how much money she and her
ex-husband had shelled out to have Greg. A half million dollars.
Now it was even more than that, unless, of course, you were one
of the so-called genetically gifted. Then they'd *pay* you to have
children.

Mirro appeared, carrying a black-leather case in which she
kept what she termed her "love tools." She set it down beside the
pool, opening it up like a hardware display. "What should we use?
I put all the water and shockproof ones on this side."

"I don't like the vibros in the pool—it's redundant."

"True. Here's this, it's kind of old-fashioned, but it holds
memories . . ." Mirro held up a strap-on latex penis with lifelike
throbbing action.

Vicky shrugged and half smiled. "Then one of us has to be the man."

"I'll do it," Mirro offered.

"How about the Pushme-Pullyou?"

"Again?"

"I like it." Vicky smiled, self-consciously seductive, widening her eyes, then letting half her face sink into the water as she drifted.

Mirro dropped the latex penis back into the case, picking out another item. "How about the Two-Headed Snake?"

Vicky put on a mock pout.

"It's the same thing," Mirro said. "It just moves more."

"But it's not you moving. I want it to be just us doing the moving."

Mirro turned on the Two-Headed Snake, held it squirming and throbbing against her torso. She smiled, rubbing the lower end across her pubes. "You sure?"

"I'm sure. The Snake is too . . . It's got too much life of its own."

"Okay, the Pushme-Pullyou it is." Mirro put the tools aside and began tugging at her blouse buttons.

As Mirro undressed, Vicky clutched at her own breasts, squeezing as she watched, tickling her nipples and sliding her left hand down between her legs . . . warming herself up, as she thought of it. Mirro was gorgeous, full-bodied, a classically beautiful woman. So motherly, so self-assured. Vicky was out-of-control head-over-heels in love with this person, far more attached than she would let herself admit. Proclamations of undying love-worship, she knew from experience, always led to disaster. That's what she felt toward Mirro whether she would admit it to herself or not: undying love-worship. To Vicky, Mirro was the mother-god of all womanhood, and Vicky wanted every bit of her, for now and ever.

Naked, descending step after slow step into the water, holding the knobbed, erect latex device like a scepter, she slipped into the water with half-closed eyes, and Vicky reached out to her, eager, her tongue already out of her mouth. Together they slipped under the surface, embracing.

• • •

Saul Kalman reached the drugstore after walking the entire distance—four kilometers—only to find, while at the counter with everybody waiting behind him, that he'd forgotten his Mataphin license. The pharmacist waiting on him was new; he'd never seen Saul before even though Saul had been buying at that drugstore off and on for over five years. "Look," Saul told him, "check your computer. I have a license. I'm an exec at Travels."

The pharmacist's eyes flared at that. "Travels, huh? Big deal. Working for the devil doesn't impress me."

Saul blinked. He took a slow step back from the counter. "Oh, Christ," he muttered, staring at the man. He couldn't believe his rotten luck.

The pharmacist's thin, sharply detailed face darkened even further. His eyebrows were thick and black, and they arched over sunken eyes like storm clouds. "Don't say the name of our Lord in vain. It is written: 'Cry not in anger to the Lord. Speak not in fury to He whose Love has put the spark in your parent's seed; it is He to Whom you owe all, Who holds the scales where your soul will be judged, will be weighed amongst—'"

"Are you going to sell me my fucking drugs or not?"

"You are required by law to have a drug license on your person before any restricted drug or remedy is dispensed."

"You mean I have to go all the way back home just to get my goddamn Mataphin license? It's just a goddamn *Mataphin* license; it's not like I'm buying narcotics!"

"I'm not dispensing any Mataphin without seeing a current Mataphin license," the young pharmacist said frostily. "Especially to a heathen of deceit such as yourself."

"You jerk," Saul said. "You Jesus-freak *moron*."

"Hey," a voice said from behind him; it was deep and

dangerous-sounding. Saul turned to find that the people behind him in line were all glaring at him. One particularly big man, with ape-shoulders and a titanic brass cross hanging from his neck on a chain, said to Saul: "You'd better shut your mouth, fool, before you *really* put your foot in it."

Saul turned back to the pharmacist. "I'm never bringing my business back here again," he said. The pharmacist smirked, but Saul had already turned his back and was walking to the door.

Across the street he found a phone booth and with an angry finger jabbed at the keys, dialing an autocab number. Stupid *stupid* lost people, he thought. They don't have a fucking clue. He reached the autocab company, registered his request in the queue, and hung up. The cab would meet him there at the booth. He stood beside it, feeling uneasy and impatient.

The customers who had been behind him at the pharmacy departed the store one by one, giving him dirty looks before continuing on their way. One, an older woman, saw him and came walking toward him. Saul fidgeted, feeling trapped, but he refused to run away from a wrinkled old bat with a bouffant hairdo.

"I heard what you said!" Her voice was dry and brittle, softened by a slight lisp. "You work for Travels!"

"What about it?"

"I love it!" she said, clenching her frail fists and shaking them for emphasis. "I love Travels!"

Saul let his shoulders relax, and let out a breath. "Oh, well . . ."

"But I *hate* it!" the woman said. "It robs you of time. It's a devil's tool."

"Lady, I don't think you—"

"A devil's tool! Last night my husband and I were out shopping, and we had an overwhelming urge to buy Russian vodka. We *hate* vodka! But we couldn't resist, and it was on sale, so we bought it, and later I said to my husband, 'I bet it's that Travels station. I bet they're using that subconscious advertising stuff'—and I was right! I *saw* it! On a billboard in the background during a really exciting part—"

"Pardon me," Saul said with relief, "this is my taxi."

"You've got to repent for this!" she said with genuine concern. "You can't keep it up—you can't get away with it! The Savior is coming!"

The cab pulled up, one of the big boxlike ones with a scratched and almost opaque sunroof, and Saul snatched the handle of the big sliding door and gave it a yank—but the door was auto, not manual. There was a big warning sign on the glass that read:

**HANDLE IS FOR EMERGENCY USE ONLY—
BUZZER WILL SOUND.**

It did sound, loud and angry. Saul let it go, flustered, waiting for it to close and reset itself. "No savior is coming!" he yelled at the old woman. "It's nothing more than a JTV media event!"

The old woman crossed herself. "Blasphemy!"

The door to the cab cycled open, and he jumped in, inserting his moneycard in the appropriate slot and stating his home address to the grid. The door shut him off from the shocked, accusing stare of the old woman, shut him off from the rest of the world. The vehicle rolled forward, video eyes alert and watching for traffic and pedestrians. Within a few minutes Saul was home.

He stepped quickly through the front door, his mouth drawn into a tight, unhappy line. No Mataphin, he thought. I still have to go get my Mataphin. Behind him the door slid shut and he stopped, rubbing his face with his hand. *Where's my Mataphin license anyway?* He stood there a long moment, trying to remember, feeling that he should know. It was strange that he couldn't remember.

I'm too shook up, he thought. I can't concentrate. Damn—I need my dose! As he stood there, something else occurred to him: Why was the house so quiet? Where was Mirro? He stood there, listening. There was no TV, no music . . . no baby crying. Nothing . . . yet there was *something*. The silence was not absolute.

Saul walked quietly down the hall into the west wing, listening to his own breathing, slowing as he neared his daughter's room. He had a strange feeling that something was not right. *Maybe it's the lack of Mataphin.* The air itself seemed strange; it felt damp. His skin felt clammy.

Standing outside his daughter's door, a terrible thought occurred. He listened. There were no sounds from inside, no gurgling, no monster snores. No mindless babbling like when she found the strength to play with her fingers. Saul stood outside the door, feeling his clammy skin, wishing for his Mataphin. There was something going on; he could *feel* it. Maybe, he thought, trembling, maybe this is the feeling you get when someone in the house has died.

Oh, my God, he thought. Maybe she died?

Saul reached out to open the door but hesitated, freezing. What if she *was* dead? What would he do? Hundreds of pounds of dead daughter lying there, impossible to move, impossible to . . . to what? What would he do? Stand there and stare at her? Start crying? What if he couldn't cry? He'd have to find Mirro and with dry eyes tell her that their daughter was dead. Mirro would blame him—maybe even accuse him of killing her. He had been wanting his daughter dead for over fourteen years, and here she was, dead, and Saul not crying, not even sad . . . only guilty. How could he possibly face Mirro?

Saul put his hand out and touched the smooth surface of the door with his fingertips, slid them down to the handle. This is ridiculous, he told himself. Getting myself worked up like this . . . there's nothing wrong. How could I know something's wrong? And even if there is, even if she's dead, I can go to a sink and *apply* some tears before I go find Mirro.

Saul pushed the door open and stepped in.

There his child lay, puffy, bloated, freshly changed and fast asleep, her head tilted back on a self-adjusting pillow that kept her weight from breaking her fragile neck. Her mouth was open, and a healthy river of drool ran down the side of her face. With a mixture of relief and sadness Saul turned around and left the room, closing the door behind him.

His Mataphin license, he remembered, was on his bed stand. Saul remembered it with a surge of disgust—why had he forgotten? Where else would he have put it? Letting out an angry grunt, he walked down the thickly carpeted hall toward the master bedroom; the door was partially closed, and he pushed it open while silently cursing himself. Why did I leave without it in the first place? he wondered. Why didn't I pick it up when I got my money-card?

Saul was halfway across the room before he noticed his wife and Vicky. He stopped in mid-stride, his mouth dropping open, his face feeling hot as it flushed red. He felt like running, felt like getting out of there and hiding before they could see him.

Saul didn't move. He stood and watched, his breath caught in his throat. The two women were oblivious; they didn't notice him at all. Saul didn't know what to do, what to think. He didn't know how to react. He knew his wife was bisexual; he knew she'd been seeing an awful lot of Vicky lately—she had never bothered to keep it a secret. Saul had even come to think of it as necessary considering his stunted libido. But to see her like *this*? With his assistant from work? They weren't even facing each other! This was making love? *Love?*

Saul crept across the room to his bed stand while holding his breath, his feet padding silently on the carpet. There was his Mataphin license, a plastic rectangle with a laser-encoded strip and a holographic head-and-shoulders shot of himself. He bent down and lifted it off the smooth wood, moving slowly, slipping it into his shirt pocket. He was so careful about being quiet that every movement hurt. He turned and crept back toward the door, stepping easily, watching the two lovers to make sure they didn't see him—

—and suddenly Vicky opened her eyes and was staring directly into his, hers growing wide, her motions coming to a dead halt. Mirro's gasping slowed and stopped; her eyes flickered

61

TRAVELS

open, and she turned and looked at him, gaping, motionless.

Saul ducked his head in shame and embarrassment, treading quickly out, shutting the door behind him. From there he ran through the house to the garage, pulling the charge cord from his personal car and yanking the door open. He threw himself in, switching it on, and accelerated out of the yard. Saul drove like a maniac up the coast to a drugstore, where he rushed in and bought his Mataphin, immediately tearing open the package and swallowing a triple dose.

11. Television

IT WAS THE THIRD OF JUNE, BUT IT WAS BEGINNING TO LOOK A LOT LIKE Christmas. Dodd expected advertisements to start saying, "Only twelve more shopping days until the Second Coming!" So far no one had dared, but he thought it was only a matter of time. The United Church urged its followers to celebrate the Second Coming the way they did with Christmas, with an exchange of joy, goodwill, and presents. There was a lot of emphasis on "presents." Dodd wondered if June 15 was going to replace December 25, or were they going to keep both?

That morning he awoke early, finding himself alone in bed again. Sheila was still at the television—he could hear Travels down the hall. This is getting psychotic, he thought. He'd called the cable company yesterday morning to have them send a man out and physically disconnect Travels from his apartment. They had promised a man would be there that day, yet when he got home from work Travels was still going.

Dodd sat up in bed, yawning. He rubbed the sleep from his eyes, then turned and looked over at the bedroom phone. The cable company offices wouldn't be open yet, but he could leave them a message. He swung his legs off the bed, moving over so that he could reach the handset. He pushed the button for mail, watched the screen light up. He opted to use the transcription feature even though it was slower; as he spoke, words appeared.

TO: **Cherokee Cable Data Co.**
DATE: **6/3/42**
FROM: **Dodd Corley**
SUBJECT: **Disconnection**

This is regarding account #2834737–838–73726459–28374627B. Yesterday I had ordered a physical disconnection of your Travels service from my apartment, and you promised me it would be completed that day. It was not completed, and you did not notify me of the reason for delay. Today I expect the disconnection, and I expect that you will have reimbursed my account for yesterday and today's connection time to Travels.

He sent the mail off with an angry jab of his right index finger, then stood up and walked out to the front room.

Sheila was asleep on the couch. She looked like hell, and she smelled. She obviously hadn't taken a bath in a couple of days. "I'm getting worried about you," he said to her. She snored quietly in reply. He bent over the video components and turned off the power.

While he showered and shaved, the kitchen fixed him breakfast. He ate while he was drying, and when he was finished he walked naked down the hall to the bedroom where he put on his work clothes. On his way out of the apartment he gave Sheila a kiss on the forehead. She didn't stir.

Halfway to the subway terminal someone came out of the bushes and ran toward him. Army-trained reflexes took over, and he turned and prepared to lash out. The figure stopped short, smiling at him. It was Savina. "Hi," she said brightly.

Dodd dropped his fists and took an embarrassed step back. "What in the hell are you *doing*?"

"You shouldn't be so tense. It's only me."

"Why aren't you in school?"

"I'm on my way to school."

"Aren't you going to be late?"

"No. It's early for me." She tried another smile out on him.

"What are you doing out *here*?" he asked. "This isn't the way to your school."

"Don't you want to see me?"

"What?"

"You're acting like you don't want to talk to me."

"Of course I want to talk to you. I'm just surprised, that's all." He looked at her suspiciously. "Talk to me about what?"

"We haven't talked in a long time."

"We talked just the other day, over at your dad's house."

"We said hello to each other, then you found out about the Second Coming."

"Is that what you want to talk about?"

"Yes."

"Well, we don't have much time. I'm on my way to work."

"I know." She came closer and began walking with him.

"You'll be coming over to dinner tomorrow night with your parents."

"I know. But that would be with my parents."

"Oh, I see."

"So, what do you think about the Second Coming?"

Dodd smiled at her. "I don't know."

"You think it's real?"

"I don't know what to think. I think it's . . . I don't know. I'm afraid of it."

"You do think it's real!"

"I think that if it's real, it's not going to be what the Church is telling us. I think we're all in a lot of trouble if Jesus comes back."

"You've been reading old Bibles."

"Yes, I have. They're translations from documents dating back to the days of Christ. The United Church Bible was written maybe eighteen or nineteen years ago. You tell me which one is authentic."

"The Church claims that the new Bible is from even earlier translations."

"I don't believe that."

"How come?"

"Because they've been translating from old manuscripts for a thousand years, and none has ever differed as radically as the United Church's. They've mixed in Mormon philosophy, Eastern philosophy, popular philosophy, and quantum physics. It is *not* a translation of something two thousand years old. No way."

"Then why does the Second Coming frighten you?"

"Because the Pope received a revelation. I don't like it, but he's the closest thing there is to a Catholic pope nowadays. I don't necessarily believe in his revelation as much as the fact that this does sound like the end times in the old Bibles."

"According to the old Bibles, we've been in the end times since Jesus died."

"I know."

"So why worry?"

"Are you sure this is what you sneaked out here at dawn to talk to me about?"

"No, not really."

"I knew it. There's something wrong. What's wrong?"

"Well, I have a friend who's in a lot of trouble."

"A friend?"

"Yeah, her name's Lamissa."

"Okay."

"Lamissa has a boyfriend who she has been . . . sexually active with. They both have access to the pill, but he said he was on it, so she, well . . ."

"I have the feeling you're about to tell me she's pregnant."

"Yes."

"How old is she?"

"Seventeen."

"Lamissa will have to get an abortion."

"Yeah, but they'll sterilize her."

"Yes, they will."

"She doesn't want that."

"It's the law."

"She doesn't care."

Dodd stopped walking, turned to face her squarely. His face was grim. "This friend of yours, 'Lamissa,' she wouldn't happen to be you, would she?"

"No!"

"Are you sure?"

"Lamissa's my best friend. She and I go to school together."

Dodd sighed. They resumed walking. "I understand the predicament your friend is in," he said, "but I can't see any way out of it. She's trapped by stupid, outdated laws that are set in granite. There is no legal way out of her situation."

"I've *got* to help her out, Dodd."

"Tell her that being sterilized is not the end of the world. She can still have a clone baby."

"Where is she going to get forty million dollars?"

"Four million."

"Might as well be forty million!"

"When she's eighteen she can marry someone who's rich. Are you sure we're not talking about you?"

"Yes, I'm sure."

"I'm not so sure."

"I told you, her name's Lamissa."

"Okay. You're a big girl now, if you don't want to tell me, that's okay."

"What if it *is* me, Dodd?"

"Then we have a serious and complicated problem." Dodd was beginning to feel uncomfortable about their conversation. This was his friend's daughter, after all. She was his friend, too, but that only made it more complicated. He hoped to God that she wasn't pregnant. Abortion and sterilization were such horrible wastes, and he couldn't bring himself to let it happen to such a sweet young girl who had a whole lifetime ahead of her.

"It's me," she told him.

Dodd sighed and put his hands over his face.

"I'm sorry," she said. "I'm too upset about this to think straight. I couldn't just blurt it out; I didn't know how you'd react."

"I was hoping you really had a friend named Lamissa." He wiped at his eyes, which had teared up.

"I wish I did, and I wish it was her that was pregnant instead of me."

"Yeah, I bet." They reached the subway terminal, and Dodd stopped and faced her. "Your parents don't know yet, right?"

"You bet they don't!"

"Okay."

"You're not going to tell them, are you?"

"No." Dodd shook his head. "That's your responsibility."

"Thank you."

"Just don't let them find out that I knew before they did, and didn't tell them. It would ruin the friendship between your father and me. I mean, I've never kept a secret from him in all the time we've known each other."

"I know."

"As far as your problem goes, I don't know what to do. But I'll think about it, okay? How far along are you?"

"A couple weeks."

"Well, you could still lose it naturally. I would wait a while before telling your folks."

"Yeah." Her voice was sad.

"I'll start making some phone calls to see if there's any loopholes as far as sterilization. I may be able to find a doctor who'd perform an old-fashioned abortion and lose the records."

"You think so?"

"I've heard of them. I don't know how safe it is. I've got to talk to some friends who would know."

"I knew I could count on you." Tears were leaking, running down her cheeks. "I love you," she said, and hugged him.

He hugged her back, feeling sad. "I'll help if I can," he said in a hoarse voice as they were hugging.

"Thank you," she whispered back.

They parted, her tears on his shirt.

Dodd trudged down the steps into the terminal and pushed his way through the crowd toward the loading ramp. He stood in line at the gates, feeling upset, waiting for his chance to insert his moneycard and have the fare deducted from his account. He'd known Savina since she was a baby. She was the closest thing he had to a child of his own. It hurt him that she was in so much trouble, and he felt guilty that he was helping her without consulting his best friend, her father. Maybe I should tell him, he thought.

The line moved forward, and he gained access to the loading platform. His train had yet to appear from the tunnel. God, he thought, this is hell. He caught the scent of brotone—an acid-based etching paint—and heard a faint hissing sound. Turning, he saw a dirty-clothed teenager defiantly painting words on the terminal wall. He was directly under a security monitor.

BEWARE THE ANTI-CHRIST AI!
THESE ARE THE LAS

Dodd pushed through the crowd toward the boy as he was finishing the last line. "What do you mean by that?" Dodd asked.

The boy jerked his head up, stared at Dodd suspiciously with wide, drugged eyes. "Beware the Antichrist AI!" the boy shouted at him. "Just what the fuck it says!"

"What is the Antichrist AI?"

"You'll see it on the fifteenth."

"Well, what is it?"

"Fuck you, man!" The boy spit on his shoes and took off running as a police drone appeared in the terminal. The drone, a long black oblong floater, hovered above the crowd with hardly enough room to move. It watched as the boy ran, probably computing his path and relaying it to other drones on the surface. It was still there when Dodd's train came; he boarded with relief, watched out the window as the station slid out of sight.

At work, Dodd looked around for Bob Recent during the slack time before he had to log on to his forklift. He was either in a meeting that no one knew about, or he was late. I'll bet he's late, Dodd thought. Maybe that's my problem, I was never late. You can only get into management when you're habitually late. Otherwise, you're too valuable where you are.

Dodd climbed aboard his forklift and turned it on. The little screen came on with his morning assignment. "Okay, let's go," he told it, tapping a few commands on the grimy keypad. Coffee in one hand, he and the forklift went racing across the yard.

Three and a half hours later, Dodd spotted Bob's little white cart, and he had the forklift inform the central computer that he was taking a break to talk to his supervisor. It confirmed his request was okay, and Dodd took manual control, sending the 'lift speeding over. Bob was looking at tags that hung from giant valves. He looked up at Dodd with a neutral expression.

"Hi, Bob. Haven't been answering your telephone lately."

"No, we seem to miss calls for some reason. I think our phone's ringer is broken."

"Oh, well. I've been trying to invite you and your wife over for dinner."

"Dinner?"

"Yeah, you know. Dinner. Toby and his family are coming over tomorrow night, and I'd like to have you and Denise over. That's if you have nothing planned."

Bob shrugged, looking anywhere but into Dodd's eyes. It was like he was trying to come up with a reason to say no. "What time?" he asked.

"Around five-thirty."

"Well . . . well, okay. We'll be there."

"Good! We're serving up a feast, you won't be sorry. See you later." Dodd backed the forklift away, pointed it in the right direction, and let it take over driving. Bob dwindled out of sight.

• • •

The hot June afternoon stretched on and on until Dodd thought the day would never end. He watched the last ten minutes of work count down with glacierlike slowness. When the whistle blew, he hurried out of the plant, hoping for a seat on the subway. It was a dream, to actually be able to sit on the way home. Dodd made it to the subway in record time only to find it already jammed with people. His train came hissing in, and there was no room for him to get on—he and a hundred other people were forced to wait another twenty minutes for the next train, and even then he didn't get a seat.

Stuffed in the train, body to body, it seemed incredible to Dodd that scientists and engineers were building faster-than-light starships—yet no one had ever come up with an adequate ventilation system for a subway car. The wind rushed past the windows with a roar, but there wasn't the faintest of breezes inside. At his stop, Dodd emerged gasping for air, sweat soaking his clothes so that it appeared he'd just climbed out of a pond. The walk from the station to his apartment in the open air was a vast relief.

As he reached the apartment building, he saw a man emerge from his apartment and climb into a utility truck. It was the guy from the cable company. He finally had come to disconnect Travels, and that made Dodd's day. It hadn't been a terribly good day, with Savina's problem and dealing with Bob and the hellish ride in the subway, but having Travels removed from his place made things seem a whole lot brighter. Before Dodd had a chance to thank the man, the van pulled away and went speeding down the street.

Dodd went up to the front door and let himself in. As soon as the door opened, Dodd was enveloped in Travels music. Sheila was sprawled across the couch, staring at the screen with glazed eyes. She didn't notice him come in.

"What in the hell!" he exclaimed.

Sheila blinked and pulled her eyes away from the screen. "Hi, Dodd," she said in a soft, relaxed voice. She slurred the pronunciation of his name, her tongue in between her teeth.

"What is Travels doing still hooked up?"

"What?"

"Travels! The man here, didn't he unhook it?"

"I told them there was a mistake," she said. "We didn't order Travels disconnected."

"Yes, I did! I ordered it to be disconnected!"

She stared at him, not understanding.

"You told him not to disconnect it?" he said.

"Yes."

"Oh, God," he said, sighing. "Sheila . . ."

"What's wrong?"

"I was the one who called to have Travels disconnected. *I* want it disconnected!"

"It's okay. I told him it was a mistake. It's still connected."

"That's . . . Sheila, that's not what I'm saying!"

"What?"

"Listen to me. I called to have Travels disconnected. It was *not* a mistake. *I* was the one who ordered that man to come here and disconnect Travels. *Me.* Understand? Travels is *supposed* to be disconnected. Okay?"

"Okay?"

"Sheila, are you awake?"

"Yes."

"Did you understand what I just told you?"

"I'm awake."

"Yes, but did you understand?"

"Yes, I'm awake."

"Are you sure?"

"Yes, I'm sure." Her eyes drifted back to the screen.

"Sheila."

"Hmmm?"

"Sheila."

"Hmmmmm?"

Dodd turned to the television components and shut off the power. "Sheila," he said, turning back to her, "this is not healthy. Your mind is being sucked out of your body." 73

"Why did you turn off the television?"

Dodd looked up at the ceiling. "Jesus, she wants to know why I turned off the television."

Sheila looked up at the ceiling. "Who are you talking to?"

"Jesus," Dodd said to the ceiling, "she wants to know who I'm talking to."

"You're talking to Jesus?"

"He's coming back to Earth on the fifteenth, right? You do remember that, don't you?" Dodd's voice was dry, sarcastic. He was exasperated and felt he was losing control. "Jesus is coming back, so what's wrong with talking to Him? I mean, He's the Savior, right? He can hear us, right?"

"I guess so."

"I'm turning to Him for help because nothing I do seems to work."

Sheila nodded vaguely. She looked like she was lost in the conversation and was making a real effort to figure out what they were talking about.

"I'm going to pray to Him about you, Sheila," Dodd told her.

"Why?"

"You know what you said to me yesterday?"

"What?"

Dodd switched to a quavering falsetto voice. "'It's weird, Dodd, but I could swear you just left for work and here you are coming home again.' You said that."

"Yeah," Sheila said, her voice and expression brightening. "That happens a lot! Did you notice that time passes really fast—"

"Yes, I've noticed! Don't you understand, that's what I'm trying to pound into your head! *All* your time is passing really fast!"

"Dodd, why are you so angry about it? I think it's great."

"Great? Losing entire days is great? *Don't you enjoy anything else?*"

"What do you mean?"

Dodd stared at her for a moment without saying anything. "I

mean, isn't there anything else you'd like to do besides watching television?"

"I like watching television."

"You want your days to go by in a blur? Is that all you want out of life?"

"I enjoy life."

"You enjoy television."

"Yes."

"Your life is television."

"Yes."

Dodd looked up at the ceiling again, making a silent plea for strength.

"What?" Sheila said.

"Nothing." Dodd turned and walked back to the television components. He turned the power on, and as Travels filled the room Dodd walked down the hall to his bedroom. Sheila did not follow. "Jesus, I give up," he said with a glance at the ceiling. He stripped off his clothes and collapsed on his bed, sighing, wondering what to do.

After a while the phone rang, and Dodd answered it without turning on the video pickup. "Yo, Dodd. Where are you? I can't see you." It was Toby, seeming to peer in at Dodd through the screen.

"I'm in a state of undress," Dodd told him wearily.

"Ah, I see. I've got some bad news. We are not going to be able to make it to your dinner party tomorrow night."

"Why not?"

"Something very bad has happened. I'm afraid my daughter's been raped."

"What?"

"I don't know when it happened, but the boy turned himself in. He saw the error of his ways."

"When did all this happen?"

"I just got the call from the police today. We have to take Savina in tomorrow afternoon for a pregnancy test."

"Oh no."

"It is a sad thing."

"What's going to happen if she's pregnant?"

"They'll have to abort it. She's underage, and who's going to pay for a rape-child anyway?"

"They won't sterilize her, will they?"

"They have to, it's part of the abortion."

"No, they don't have to! It's not necessary, and it's not fair—not if she was raped! Why punish *her*?"

"It's the law. What can we do?"

"We can fight it!"

"We can't fight it." Toby shook his head, a troubled expression on his face.

"You can do something, make some sort of appeal—go to the Church, maybe they can help."

"No. They told us to take her to the Medical Authority Center tomorrow at five. To do anything else would be to break the law."

Dodd was at a loss. "I'll be off work by then. Do you want me to go with you?"

"No, it would not be appropriate."

"No?"

"I appreciate the concern, but no."

"Okay."

Toby nodded. "I'll call you tomorrow." He rang off.

12. Robot

"I'M NOT GOING. I WASN'T RAPED. I ALREADY KNOW THAT I'M PREGNANT, and I want to keep it. I don't care what the law says, I am not going to let them take it from me. This is my decision, and it is final." Savina's face was full of firm resolution as she gazed at herself in the mirror. Her parents were downstairs watching a sermon while they readied themselves to go. Monotone voices drifted up to Savina from the television, chanting the Beatitudes from the United Church Bible:

> Blessed are the poor in spirit,
> for theirs is the kingdom of heaven.
> Blessed are those who mourn,
> for they will be comforted.
> Blessed are the meek,
> for they will inherit the Universe.
> Blessed are you who hunger now,
> for you will be fed.
> Blessed are the merciful,
> for they will be shown mercy.
> Blessed are the pure in heart,
> for they will meet God.

A hymn burst forth from a choir, "The Celebration of the Homecoming," a hundred blessed voices accompanied by the popular beat-feet rhythm. It was a hymn to which people could slam dance if they so chose. Savina thought it was ridiculous.

There were footsteps coming up the stairs. Savina turned and faced the door, her heart pounding loud in her ears. The door opened, and her mom stepped into the room. "Are you ready to go, child?"

"I am not . . . I am not going," she said in an unsteady voice. "I wasn't raped, and I am not . . . and I already know I'm pregnant and I don't care . . . I don't care what the law says, I am not going to let them take it from me. This is my decision, and I am not going to back down."

"Is that so?"

"Yes."

"Why did not you tell us this before?"

"I . . . I was thinking of how to break it to you."

"And why now has this boy turned himself in for raping you?"

"I don't know. I guess he thought maybe it would help. Help take the blame."

"Ah, now." Her mother sighed. "I'll tell this to you straight out, Savina. You cannot have this baby. It is not right, it is not ethical, and it is not possible. Do you understand?"

"Well . . . I'm not backing down, Mom."

"Is that so?"

Savina nodded.

"Child, you are too young to have a baby."

"Mom, I'll never have a baby if you take me to the MA!"

"That is nonsense, Savina."

"Mom!"

"They do not sterilize you unless it is a voluntary abortion."

"Where did you hear this?"

"I just happen to know it."

"You're lying, Mom. That's a cruel lie."

"Sterilization is the penalty for giving up a child you do not want, Savina. That is what the sterilization is for. They do not punish people with medical problems or young girls who are not making the decision for themselves."

"Are you *sure*?"

"Yes, now you get ready to go." She turned and left the room, and Savina heard her calling her father's name.

Savina didn't know what hurt more: her mother out-and-out lying to her like this, or the possibility that her mother knew something that everyone else didn't. Even if they weren't going to sterilize her, she didn't want to give up the child. She had never once thought about getting it aborted; she had concentrated all her energy on finding a way to keep it. It was strange, but she already loved the baby. The realization brought on a wave of sadness, and Savina sat on her bed and cried.

There were heavy footsteps coming up the stairs—her father coming to get her. Savina rolled herself in blankets and hid her head under pillows. She didn't want him to see her crying, she couldn't stand the thought, but it only made her cry harder. She heard him enter the room, felt him sit on the bed beside her. "I love you," he said. "I'm sorry."

Savina remained hidden.

He pulled the pillows away, caressed her cheeks. "We have to go," he told her. "If we don't go, they'll come here and get you. We can't have that, now."

She opened her eyes and saw his sad face, saw her mother behind him. "Let's pray," her mom said. Mother and Father bowed their heads, closed their eyes and were silent.

Savina felt angry that they were praying. If they wanted to help her, they'd *help* her, and not submit meekly to the Medical Authorities. Praying would accomplish about as much as sleeping as far as she was concerned.

"Come on now, it's time to go." Her father pulled Savina to her feet. He had to shove her out the door and drag her down the steps. Savina was determined not to go willingly. When they had herded her outside, she had to squint to see; to Savina's amazement, it was a bright, beautiful blue-sky day.

They walked several blocks to the subway station, then stood on the platform for ten minutes waiting for the train. On one of the walls of the station was a large advertisement:

There was a realistic painting under the words showing Jesus smiling with His arms spread out in greeting, His head outlined by a colorful halo. Under the poster the caption read:

WATCH HIS GLORIOUS RETURN LIVE ON JTV!

There was a warm rush of air, and their train came hissing out of the tunnel; it slid to a smooth stop and opened its doors. Since the rush didn't start for another hour, there were empty seats available. Her parents guided her into the train and down the aisle to a seat away from the exits. She sat down and stared at her hands as they lay numbly in her lap. They had put her next to a window, blocking her in with their bodies. It was like they expected her to make a break for it. Savina hadn't even thought about it. There was a long hissing sound, and the train slid forward, accelerating into the dark of the tunnel.

The train ran underground for nearly an hour, the only evidence of motion the occasional light flashing past only centimeters outside the window. Then the train emerged on the outskirts of the Depopulated Zone, raising up to race across the open valley on a concrete trestle. Savina gazed out at the open farmland that passed in the distance, and the square kilometers of green crops dotted with autonomic farm machinery, and found herself wishing she was out there, out away from the endless city and all the people and all the public surveillance cameras.

The Depopulated Zone seemed to go on forever; it was the largest area of reclaimed farmland in the region, certainly the largest in California. It passed out of sight as they reentered the city and the train dipped back below the surface of the earth. In the tunnel Savina felt worse than ever. She felt trapped. I can't just let this happen, she thought. I've got to do something. I've got to get away.

They reached the Medical Authority Center just before 5:00 P.M. Savina's parents coaxed her to her feet. Savina felt in her back pocket for her moneycard—she had over a thousand in her bank account, enough for her to get by on her own for at least a little while. She felt a thrill as her resolve strengthened. She was going to run. She was going to do it.

Her father must have sensed this. He kept a strong grip on her arm as they stepped out onto the platform and held firm all the way to the lobby of the main building. Savina didn't have a chance to break away.

Her mother filled out all her forms at one of the terminals at the registration desk, then they waited a long while before a human attendant, a police academy medical intern, came to lead Savina away. The intern was a thin and feminine man with a sway in his walk and subdued—but still startling—punk-resurrection-style orange hair. "So," he said, "your admission says that you already know you're pregnant."

"My mother put that on the form?"

He nodded. "You came in here voluntarily?"

"Not quite," she said, her voice sullen.

"Well, your parents know what's best for you. Through here, please." He directed her into another hallway.

"Am I going to be sterilized?" Savina asked.

"I'm afraid so."

"Even if I was raped?"

"It's a part of the process. It's a shame, really, but it doesn't mean you can never have a baby. You can have a gamete made from your genes. That's how lesbians accomplish it."

"I'm not a lesbian."

"I didn't say you were." They reached the end of the hallway and entered an elevator. It was all shiny metal inside and looked very sterile. "Floor seven," he told the elevator, and the shiny metal doors slid shut. The elevator lurched into motion.

"Are you going to do it?" she asked.

"The abortion? No. I'll be there, but this sort of routine procedure is handled automatically by the table."

"You mean a robot is going to kill my baby."

"Yes." He looked at her with no sympathy whatsoever.

The elevator stopped, and the doors slid open. The intern led her down a narrow corridor to a small dark room; he touched a switch and lights came on. Instruments began beeping and whirring. One whole wall was made up of computerized equipment, several dozen modular components mounted within a set of black-steel racks. In the middle of the room was a robotic operating table with four highly articulated surgical arms. Across the table was draped a white hospital gown.

"You'll have to take off your clothes and put that on," he said, indicating the gown. He turned his back and began fiddling with buttons and peering into readouts while he waited for her to change.

Savina slowly kicked off her sandals, staring down at her feet. She felt helpless, a doll moving to rigid programming, no free will at all. She slipped off her blue jumpsuit and tossed it across a chair in the corner, then dropped her panties around her ankles and stepped out of them. She used her toes to pick them up and drop them on her sandals.

"You don't have to worry about your bra," the intern said, his back still turned.

Savina snatched the bit of cloth that passed for a gown and pulled it over her arms, fastening the tabs at the back. "Okay," she said. "Now what?"

The intern glanced over his shoulder. "Get on the table and put your legs through those supports. Watch out for the arms, one has a steel blade."

Savina reclined on the cool, soft table, reluctantly spreading her legs and resting them in the supports that would hold them open. There was a draft; her vagina was exposed and aimed at the intern. Turning, his face preoccupied, the intern touched a button and watched as all four of the surgical arms twitched and pulled back, resetting themselves. They made tiny electric whines as they moved.

"You ever had an operation before?"

"No," Savina said.

"Don't worry, it's simple. These tables don't make mistakes. I'll be here watching carefully throughout the entire process." He stepped across to the side of the table, fumbling with controls.

Savina noticed lenses on movable stalks mounted at various angles on the ceiling, and miniature electric eyes on the robot arms themselves. She felt on display. The intern picked up a headset and held it in front of her. "This is a neural-induction set, very simple. I'm going to put it over your forehead and turn it on, and the next thing you'll know the whole thing will be over and you can go home." He opened up the headset and made a motion to put the device on her head, but she reached up and caught his arms.

"Wait a minute!"

"What?"

Savina swallowed nervously. "Aren't these the sets they use in euthanasia centers?"

The intern scoffed. "They don't use these in euthanasia centers."

"I heard they put a headset on you, and it stops your heart."

"No, no, they inject an overdose of Msunginol into your jugular vein, kid. Nobody produces a headset that kills."

"Are you sure?"

"Yes, I'm sure. This just puts you into a deep sleep and blocks pain. It's a sedative."

"I'm sure that's what they tell you in the euthanasia centers."

"Have you ever been in a euthanasia center?"

"No. Have you?"

"No. Look, this has nothing to do with euthanasia."

Tell that to my baby, she thought. "I don't want you putting that thing on me."

"I have to put it on you."

"You're not going to. It gives me the creeps."

The intern gave her a funny look, as if he thought she might be up to something, but then he sighed, and said, "Look, I'll show you how it works. You see this knob over here? I can adjust it so that it only makes you feel relaxed at first. Then, when you're nice and calm, I can sink you slowly into sleep." He tried once more to put the headset on her head, but she still held him back with trembling hands.

"Please," she said. "It scares me."

The intern had a disgusted look now. "Believe me, it's not going to hurt you. I'll put it on myself—see?" He clamped the headset onto his forehead, right behind his temples. He touched a button and gave her a pleasant smile. "There—see?—it's on low. I'm not twitching. My heart hasn't stopped. I'm fine. It's great, in fact . . . In fact, I'm totally relaxed."

The intern didn't say anything more for several seconds, just stood there with a dreamy smile and a faraway look in his eyes. Savina, holding her breath, moved her hand toward the little gray knob.

"Yes," he said, "this is really nice . . . We used to play around with these at the academy." He licked his lips, slowly, and then his eyebrows dropped in sudden concern. "Something like this can be quite addicting. If we were to—" He broke off, sighing, his eyes rolling up into his head. His legs gave out, and he sank to the floor, half sitting and half lying against the base of the table, the headset still firmly clamped against his forehead.

Savina pulled her hand back from the control knob, staring down at him. The knob was at full power, and as far as she could tell there was no timer. The man would be asleep until someone found him.

She slipped off the table, stepping gingerly over the intern, pulled the hospital gown off, and began dressing. The room was full of video pickups, but none of them looked like a security monitor. She had no idea if the building's security AI was watching or not. In some places the AIs watched every monitor at all times, while in others the AIs only watched part of the time. If one was watching now, she wouldn't get off the floor without being intercepted. She squirmed into her undergarments and slipped on her jumpsuit. Patting her pocket, Savina checked to make sure she still had her moneycard, then opened the door and strode as calmly as she could into the corridor.

Savina took deep breaths, relaxing her muscles, calming herself. Security monitors could sense tension even better than they could see. In order for them to completely ignore you, you had to remain calm, avoid direct eye contact, and refrain from quick movements. Every schoolkid knew that. There was a monitor right outside the door, pointing straight at her. She turned with a fluid motion and walked calmly down the corridor toward the elevators. Ignore it, she told herself. It's not interested in you.

"Excuse me, are you lost?"

Savina whirled around, staring, her heart pounding. A male security nurse in a white-and-green uniform, with graying hair and wrinkles around his eyes, stood staring at her. He must have seen her walking out the door. "Yes," she told him, stepping up to him. "I always get off on the wrong floor. Which floor is this?"

"You're on the seventh floor, sweetheart. Which floor do you want to be on?"

"Pediatrics?" It was the first thing to enter her head.

The old man looked at her quizzically. "You've got more than your floors mixed up. You're in the wrong building!"

Savina shrugged. "I'm new here."

"Oh, you *work* here?" He was looking at her suspiciously now.

"Not exactly. I'm a volunteer."

"You're a social worker?"

"Uh, yeah, you guessed it."

"Aren't you a little young for a social worker?"

"I'm older than I look. You can imagine the trouble I have buying drinks."

The old man's wrinkled brow relaxed, and he laughed. "My granddaughter's got the same problem. She's twenty-three and doesn't look a day over fourteen. It's the new inoculations, I think. I wish they had been around when I was young."

"You're, what, forty?" Savina asked.

The nurse was tickled. "Forty! Oh, sweetheart!" He laughed. "I'm ninety-seven, almost a hundred years old."

"That's amazing! You don't look anywhere near that."

"Are you married?"

"I'm engaged."

"Rats."

"Sorry." She shrugged.

"Oh well," he said. "Anyway, the elevator's right down that way. You want building five for pediatrics, which is two over from the left after you're through the main exit."

"Thanks."

"No problem, sweetheart. You take care." He turned and walked away.

Savina felt like she was going to die of a stroke at any moment. She tried not to rush as she walked down the corridor toward the elevator, but she couldn't help it. At the elevators she pressed the DOWN button and stood waiting directly under the unwavering gaze of a security monitor. She fought to control her breathing and heart rate, but it was no use. The old guy had startled her, and now she was out of control. Standing there under the monitor she felt naked and vulnerable.

The elevator was taking forever to arrive.

Savina glanced at the button to make sure it was green. It was. Her call had been registered in the elevator's queue. It was on its way. Savina stood waiting, feeling the sweat break out on her forehead. Where is it? she wondered. Come on, come on! She jabbed at the button again, suspecting that the security system had shut the elevator down. She looked back down the corridor for a stairwell, but saw none. She wondered fleetingly if she should go looking for one.

She pressed the button again. It went *click* just like last time; it still glowed green. Maybe it's broken, she thought, and pushed it several times more. There was a low, quavering sound, and she jumped. It was the elevator arriving. The doors to her left opened to reveal a beautiful woman in a white smock who smiled at her. She was blond, wore thick makeup, and had very red lips. "Hi," she said to Savina, her voice pleasant. "Going down?"

86   "Yes," Savina said, smiling back. The woman had the badge of a full administrator, and inside Savina was quivering with nervous energy, her legs twitching and wanting to run. Any stories of being a social worker wouldn't pass with this one; she had a headset disguised as a headband, and there was a thin trail of ribbon running down with the woman's hair. It was an antenna. She was wired directly into the MA computers and could check a fact with the merest thought. Savina got into the elevator with her and pressed the button to take her to the lobby. "Nice day today," Savina told her.

"Yes."

"It's hotter than yesterday, isn't it?"

The woman nodded, not in the mood to talk. Thank God, Savina thought. The elevator stopped on the second floor, and the administrator got out, saying a pleasant good-bye. Savina was amazed. If she acted like she had a right to be there, nobody questioned her at all.

When the elevator doors opened again she was in the lobby. She peered cautiously out of the elevator and spotted her parents, both sitting in the huge round waiting area with the television screens in the center. There were numerous screens showing numerous stations, and her parents were in front of the JTV area—of course. Their backs were to her. She slipped out of the elevator and walked around the waiting area toward the main doors, keeping a curved row of plastic plants between her and her parents when she was in their line of sight.

A loud undulating tone blared over the PA system, startling Savina, and a computer voice announced, "Security report to floor seven. Security report to floor seven. Code three-nine-three." *They found the intern!* she thought. Time to throw caution to the wind. Savina bolted out the door. She leaped over a low hedge and disappeared into the throng of pedestrians filling the sidewalk, heading away from the MA complex as fast as the foot traffic would let her.

13.Bulu Road

SAUL WAS ON THE BEACH WITH HIS CREW, SITTING IN HIS FOLDING CHAIR between sequences, listening to the screeching of the seagulls and the babble of the people around him. It was pleasant, relaxing, all the sounds blending together to form a white noise, the ocean waves crashing, the breeze blowing in fresh and cool. Then from somewhere behind him there was a long, drawn-out cry of anguish, and instead of the beach Saul found himself rushing down a road with cars coming straight at him, their panic-horns blaring like a chorus of screams. Saul found a wheel in his hands. He was in his Mitsubishi Electric ReRun 550 with a woman passenger beside him, and she was clawing at the dashboard in terror.

There had been a moment, a flash, when both things were happening at once—Saul was on the beach *and* in the car, with the anguished wail from behind blending and harmonizing with the squeal of terror beside him—then the beach was gone, and Saul was pulling the steering wheel hard to the right to avoid the oncoming traffic. Brakes locked and tires skidded, but no impact occurred. Cars passed to either side of him. Gasping, frightened out of his mind, Saul waited for a break in the traffic, then brought the car to the side of the road and stopped.

Beyond giving him a dazed, bewildered look, the woman beside him said nothing. Her eyes were red and swollen, her makeup streaked from tears. After making sure everything was safe, she turned back toward the passenger-side door and resumed her crying. Saul himself was utterly at a loss—he had no idea who she was. He had no idea where he was driving. How had he gotten there?

"Excuse me," he said to the woman. "I don't think I'm well."

She paid no attention to him; she was too busy crying. Saul turned to his onboard computer for a clue. It answered immediately, transparent words forming in red letters on the windshield in front of him, shimmering:

OUR LOCATION IS BULU ROAD, 1.4 KILOMETERS FROM CAMERON COVE

Cameron Cove? Saul thought. Where is Cameron Cove? The answer came to him slowly, like the sun rising: Cameron Cove was where he lived. He set the destination into the autopilot, which should have been driving in the first place, then turned to consider the woman beside him as the car pulled itself back onto the road.

The woman, while he could not place her, did seem familiar. It seemed he should know her. She glanced up to see him staring, and said in a choked voice, "I'm okay. Just let me get the shock out of my system."

It's finally happening, Saul thought. I'm going insane. "Okay," he told her. "We'll be home soon."

She nodded, turning away. She looked familiar, so very familiar, but her name escaped him. It seemed, possibly, that he worked with her. That he knew her.

The car pulled into a large beachfront villa and parked itself in his garage. The woman got out and, without waiting for him, went inside. She didn't even look behind to see if he was following her. He wasn't, because Saul did not recognize the villa—he knew he owned it, it was *his*, but he could not remember ever being there.

Saul knew he'd been there—he lived there!

What's happening to me? he thought. How can I forget that I live in a house that I know I live in? How can I forget who that woman is—? I *must* know her. I have to know her. Think, think, who is she? What's her name?

Saul drew a blank—a total black void. It must be brain damage, he thought. The Mataphin is eating my brain. Or have I always been this way? I can't remember.

I can't remember!

Saul forced himself to get out of the car. He made his way over to the door that led to the kitchen—he knew it led to the kitchen, and when he opened the door there was indeed a kitchen. Totally unfamiliar, but a kitchen nonetheless.

He hesitated a long time before entering because it occurred to him that this might not actually be his house. Perhaps he only thought it was his house—how could he know for sure? Maybe it belonged to the woman whom he'd just brought here? No, the car was his, and it was the car's autopilot that had driven him here, to *his* home. Saul took a cautious step through the door. Just as it closed behind him, a beautiful blond woman rushed into the room. It was his wife, Mirro. She looked at him gravely. He recognized her without a problem, knowing everything about her—and at the sight of her he felt a surging rush of affection.

"She's okay, Saul," Mirro said. "I gave her some NoBluze, and now she's calmed down. She's resting."

Saul looked at her helplessly.

"I'm glad you called me," she told him, a curious edge to her voice. It sounded uncomfortable and apologetic. "This is a big blow to her. She loves her son very much. Her ex-husband wouldn't have been much of a comfort to her even at a time like this." She paused, licking her lips, and took a deep breath. "This was very . . . this was very sensitive of you, Saul. I didn't think you . . ." She trailed off, staring at him. Then in a rush she crossed the room and grabbed him, kissing him on his numb lips. Letting go, she turned and strode out of the kitchen, back into the depths of the house. The unfamiliar house.

Is it possible, Saul thought, that this is the way normal perception is *without* Mataphin? Everything like this? Jumbled? Confusing? Unfamiliar? It seemed like it now, now that Saul was thinking about it. Yes, he thought. Mataphin makes things *clearer*. It's the only thing that helps me put everything together in a way that makes sense.

Saul reached into his shirt pocket, pulled out the dispenser, and took four. Then he walked out of the kitchen into the unfamiliar hall, past the dining room and beyond. His wife, he had to find his wife. She had gone down here somewhere. At one point he found a door, opened it, and peered inside. A bathroom. Empty. He stared at it for a long time, his mind blank. What was it I was going to do? he asked himself. He stepped in, kneeled impulsively beside the large white tub, and started the bath cycle. The temperature control blinked and Saul set it for a hundred degrees Celsius. A buzzer went off somewhere; the control blinked again. Bubbling, hissing water came sputtering out of the jets, splashing him. He jerked when the water touched him, he had no idea why. What was going on? He was just reaching down to stick his hand in the tub when someone from behind Saul grabbed his arm.

"Saul!" his wife exclaimed. "What are you *doing*?"

"What?"

"You want to cook yourself? What are you doing?"

"I don't understand."

"You have boiling water coming out of that tap!"

"Boiling? It's only . . ." He stared at the temperature readout in shock: 100 degrees Celsius. "How in the hell did that happen?" he exclaimed.

"Saul, are you feeling okay? Vicky says you nearly drove into oncoming traffic on the way over here." She tugged on him, pulling him to a standing position. He wavered on his feet, staring down at the tub.

Mirro bent over and shut off the water, set the tub to drain. Saul, watching, realized the tub was familiar, as was the entire bathroom. Then he thought, Why *shouldn't* the bathroom be familiar? What a stupid thought! What is wrong with me? And the house—why shouldn't my own goddamn house look familiar to me? And that woman, Vicky . . . poor woman, it's such a rotten thing about her son. In jail for rape! Facing a long sentence and sterilization. How awful.

I wish I'd been sterilized. I wish we'd had our kid aborted.

"I know that, Saul," his wife said in a low voice. Saul realized that he must have been speaking out loud. "But we have her," she told him, "and we can't change that."

He said nothing, feeling embarrassed and ashamed.

She stood in front of him and peered up into his eyes. With one hand she reached out and felt his forehead. "You look pale. Are you sick? Please tell me."

"I'm fine," he said, pulling away from her. He strode out of the bathroom and back toward the kitchen, knowing that he lied, knowing that there was something terribly wrong with him. He had the kitchen fix him a fried steak, watched the robot arms with bleary eyes. It could be the Mataphin, he thought. I've been eating it like candy.

And, in a flash of clear thought, Saul realized how disoriented he'd been, how frighteningly disjointed the whole afternoon was—ever since Vicky had been called by her ex-husband with the bad news. But then he wondered, Was the day really like that, or is it just the way I remember it?

He had no idea.

14. Euthanasia

SHEILA DIDN'T HELP HIM IN PREPARING THE MEAL. SHE REMAINED IN THE living room, trapped. He'd managed to get her to shower and dress up, but having done so she was right back at the television, the Travels sphere reflecting in her blank eyes. Dodd had given up trying to get it disconnected—now he was thinking of getting rid of the television system altogether. What is she *escaping* from? he wondered, as he and the robot arms stirred and mixed the dinner. Some ancient sorrow she hasn't told me about? A bad experience? Or is she escaping from life itself? Too complicated and too much effort; she doesn't want to deal with it, and instead of checking into a euthanasia center, she simply turns off her mind.

Suicide is a sin, he thought. Watching Travels is not.

Letting the robot arms take over completely, Dodd walked into the living room and stared at the television. It was interesting, it was colorful, and the images and the music drew him in—

He turned abruptly away, angry. It had almost gotten him. Averting his eyes, he walked to the video components and, instead of turning off the television, he changed the channel. Here's an experiment, he thought. Would Sheila even notice?

He had tuned into the Politico Network, but it was playing a commercial patterned very closely to Travels. A man folded a piece of paper into an airplane and tossed it out what looked like a two-hundredth-story window; it flew through various landscapes, lush and colorful, then zoomed straight up into space at a terrific speed. The announcer, speaking in a rich and mesmerizing voice, said, ". . . with our exclusive tachyon carrier-wave systems, we can get your data *anywhere*, faster than *anyone*, with clarity and power that nobody else can match. We're Global Telesis. We invented faster-than-light technology. We're on the leading edge of tomorrow . . ."

There was perhaps three seconds of blank screen with a low, hollow-sounding tone, then a man's face appeared, his features rough and timeworn like a weathered old skull. It was the president of the United Americas, Dodd realized. "New Millennial Marxism has spread throughout most of the world, but Capitalistic freedom has infiltrated it. People in Marxist countries are freer now than they have ever been before—"

"What *is* this?" Sheila said, her voice betraying shock and panic. "What happened? Who is that man?"

"That's our president," Dodd told her.

"What's he doing on Travels?"

Dodd shrugged. "I don't know! Maybe we're at war again?"

"Oh no!"

Dodd felt guilty at the panic-stricken look on her face, but then again, was she panicked because of the possibility of war or because she might lose her Travels channel? The president continued, and as it turned out it was a commercial for his political party, the Free Exchangers. There was a quick blurb for the famous *Free Speech Forum* show, and then a Politico Network station identification.

"This isn't Travels!"

Dodd made an astounded expression. "No! It isn't! Hey, that was weird, huh?"

"Yeah!" She made a motion for the channel changer but Dodd beat her to it.

"Let's watch the *Free Speech Forum*," he said. "It's on next."

"What?"

He smiled at her, but said nothing. Let her figure out what I said, he thought. Thirty seconds ticked by.

"Dodd, change it back," she said.

"What?"

"Change it back."

"Change what back?"

"Change the channel back to Travels!"

"This *is* Travels."

"It is not."

"Yes, it is. This is Travels."

Sheila's expression was that of a person who'd just experienced a spontaneous lobotomy. Dull confusion and pain. Struggling to make sense of small words. "This isn't Travels," she said, unsure.

"Yes, it is."

"It is?"

"Yes, they changed it. It's going to be a talk show from now on."

Thoughts passed like anemic, dying sparks behind her eyes. "This is the Politico channel!"

"It is?"

"Yes!"

"Amazing!"

The doorbell rang.

"Well," Dodd said, "the guests are here. Time for the TV to go off anyway." He shut it off, and reached behind to pull out a few signal cables just in case Denise mindlessly walked over and tried to turn it on. Sheila made protesting motions that Dodd ignored. He answered the door and welcomed the Recents inside, smiling and happy. They walked in like robots, motions stiff and uncomfortable. Denise's skin was a ghastly pale. She immediately went to the television to turn it on, and the giant screen filled with static.

"What's wrong?" she said, concerned. "Did I push a wrong button?"

"No, it's been acting up. I've got to have a repairman out here, huh, Sheila?"

"What?"

"First it would change stations at random, and now it doesn't pick anything up at all."

"Oh yeah," she said vaguely.

"How *awful*," Denise said, with feeling.

"It was a mess," Dodd told her. He was staring, shocked at how thin she looked. *Sickly thin.* He walked over to Sheila and took her by the arm, leading her to the dining-room table as Bob and Denise followed. He had it all set up with his finest bone china, made in the American state of Brazil, and had the gold electroplate flatware arranged perfectly on the thick, white, cloth napkins. No one complimented him on his table, they just sat down, bored expressions on their faces. They didn't even notice that there were no places set for Toby and his family. Dodd had to point it out to them, and explain what was going on. They muttered regrets automatically, on cue, but showed no real concern for Savina. Dodd let it pass.

"Dinner's going to be ready in just a minute or so," he told them. "I'll be right back." He turned and walked into the kitchen, dodging the robot arms and checking the condition of the food. Rabbit Rizzo in white cream sauce, with cheese vegetable and baby potato rehydrated in the finest grade ersatz soy butter . . . It smelled delicious.

"Is it done?" he asked the kitchen control. It indicated an affirmative, so he and the robot arms began dishing it up. He brought it out to the table with two shades of wine on a rollaway tray, served everyone, then sat next to Sheila to dig in. Dodd was pleased to see the rich flavor bringing everyone to life. See! he thought. See, you morons, there's more to life than Travels!

"This is really good," Bob said with food in his mouth. He looked surprised, as did the two women.

Dodd glowed. "Glad you like it."

"This is really good," said Denise.

"Why, thank you."

"This is really good," she said again, not being able to get over the shock.

"It tastes better than Travels?" Dodd asked.

"What?"

"Are you sure it's not too rich? I put in extra butter and cheese."

"No, it's really good."

Bob gave him a funny look. He had caught the remark about Travels, but didn't say anything about it. "So, what do you think about this Second Coming?" he asked Dodd.

"It's going to be the end of the world." Dodd took a bite of the potato—yes, yes it was good. He had outdone himself.

"How do you mean?"

"What?"

"You said 'end of the world.'"

"Oh, exactly that. I think that if the Savior returns, then the world will end." He smiled at their decidedly blank expressions. "What do you guys think?"

"I think it's a crock," Bob said, dismissing it. It was obvious he was sorry he had brought the subject up.

"I think it's a crock," Denise said.

"Really?"

She nodded, stuffing more food in her mouth.

Dodd turned to Sheila. "How about you?"

Her eyes were brightening, as if atrophied brain tissue was struggling back to life. "I think it's exciting."

"Do you really?" he said, encouraging her.

"Yes, it could be . . . it could be a whole new beginning."

Dodd was proud of her for having a thought all on her own, despite its simplicity. "What good things might come from a new beginning?"

She pondered this. "They can get rid of the euthanasia centers."

Now Dodd was really proud of her. She was recovering! "Is euthanasia bad?"

"Yes, Dodd, you know it is."

He smiled at her.

"That would be a good thing," Bob said, pausing with a fork before his mouth. "I hope that comes about."

"Really?"

"Yes. It's not right. The planet's not overpopulated anymore. Why are they still around?"

"I don't know," Dodd said, urging him to continue. "You tell me."

"Well, it's too convenient. The courts send prisoners there, it's easy for them to do. People kill themselves there without someone to try to talk them out of it." He put the fork of food into his mouth, chewing thoughtfully.

Denise was looking back and forth between Dodd and her husband with an anxious expression. "I think it's wrong, too," she said.

"Why do you think it's wrong?"

"Well, you know."

"Do you think it's wrong for a person to decide not to live anymore?"

"Yes, it's . . . Yes."

Dodd leaned forward. "Why?"

Denise's face twitched. She looked away from him, down at the plate, around the table. She couldn't come up with an answer.

"A person is given a life," Bob said, coming to her rescue. "It's a shame to waste it; you only have one."

"They're getting very close to being able to back up all the knowledge in a person's brain," Dodd said. "If you could back up your brain, Bob, and store it on a computer, then load it into a new body when yours gets too old to continue living, would that new body be you or would it be your child?"

"It would be another body."

"But it's cloned from your DNA. It has your memory RNA in it. Your memories are fed into it, your attitudes, everything you know. It will think it is you. Will it be you, or not?"

"It would be another body."

"So you would have died?"

"Well, no, I guess not. Maybe it would be me. Why are we talking about this?"

"I personally believe that this new body will not be you. I think that death is death, and I agree with you about those euthanasia centers."

"Oh." Bob shrugged, but Dodd could tell he was pleased to have someone agree with him. Dodd wanted to encourage that, because he wanted to keep everybody talking. All of them, the Recents and Denise, seemed to have forgotten how to talk to each other in just a short period of time. It was only now, with all of them at the table in the same condition, that Dodd finally realized it was more than his imagination. *Something is happening to these people.* It frightened Dodd. They were all growing mentally weak, and Denise was physically so.

The end of the world, he thought. Here was proof. He wanted to broach the subject to them even though he knew it would ruin the evening, but before he had a chance the phone rang. It was Toby.

"Hello, all," he said through the screen to everyone. "Dodd, I need your help."

"What's wrong?"

"Savina got away from the Medical Authorities. My child ran away."

"What!"

"For some reason she is protecting the boy who raped her. She told us a story about not being raped, said she was pregnant and knew it. I do not know what to do, Dodd. Will you help me?"

"Sure I'll help! When did this happen?"

"Just now. They found the intern unconscious, and their security computers spotted her leaving the hospital."

"She knocked out an intern?"

"Yes. That is what they tell me."

"Are you still there?"

"Yes."

"And this just happened, what, a minute ago?"

"About five minutes, yes."

"Did the police ask you for the number of her moneycard?"

"No, they did not."

"Well, they will. I don't know if she knows it or not, but most fugitives are caught when they use their moneycard in a cab or a restaurant."

"Savina is smart. I think she will know."

"Then I bet you that the first thing she's going to do is try— she'll want to get cash from her account before the police put a trace on it. Find out from Information where the nearest bank is around there, and I'll meet you there. Maybe we can find her before the MAs do."

"Okay. I knew I could count on you!" Toby rang off.

Dodd dialed Information himself, searching for the spot to meet his friend.

• • •

Savina had walked a couple of kilometers before she felt safe enough to slow down and catch her breath. She was exhausted. Just ahead there was a subway terminal with a throng of people, the last wave of the rush hour, the entryway choked with bodies entering and exiting. She ducked off the sidewalk into the alcove of an old building, leaned up against a rail of some low steps, and stood there thinking. Her excitement was a physical thing, an electricity running up and down her legs and arms. Freedom, she thought. Freedom is an incredible feeling. She put her hand against the lower part of her stomach, feeling the firmness. "You're going to be okay," she told it, the little spirit forming down there. "Mama's going to take good care of you."

Pedestrians passed by in herds. Cars and autocabs buzzed and honked. Savina looked up and down the street and into the air for any sign of a police drone, then slipped back into the crowd. An autocab came by in cruising mode, searching for customers; Savina hailed it and jumped in, pulling out her moneycard and slipping it into the slot. "I need to go to the nearest branch of any bank," she told it as she keyed in her secret code.

Accessing information, it replied, glowing words on the little screen above the keyboard.

Location determined, plotting course.

Course plotted. Approve?

The screen showed a section of city map with a plot determined through the streets. Savina approved and the cab took off, pulling into traffic with arrogant machine confidence. Savina watched their progress carefully, ready to pop the emergency door and jump out if it veered off toward, say, a police station. She didn't think they could have gotten her card number into their system yet, but there was no way to tell until it was too late. She had to risk getting to her money or she would lose access to it.

The bank was only another kilometer or so away. It was right next to a euthanasia center, which gave her the creeps. Already she could see it looming over the skyline. There was always at least one in sight.

There was motion in the corner of her eye, and she turned to see a police drone hovering above the traffic. It made its way past Savina's cab, passing about three meters overhead, and continued on down the street. Her cab turned left, veering off. Savina let out her breath. Police drones were a common enough sight, but the appearance of this one had caused her heart to stop.

The cab cruised down the wide, clean street for another half kilometer, then pulled over to a stop, the screen flashing the same message that its electronic voice announced: "You have reached your indicated destination. $14.30 has been deducted from your account. Please remember to take your moneycard as you exit. Thank you for your patronage!" Savina grabbed her card and stepped out of the cab. She was right in front of the euthanasia center, the bank a tiny little building squeezed in next to it.

Savina looked up.

The euthanasia center was impossibly tall, its sharp white lines stretching up and up into infinity as if God had reached down, taken hold of the top, and pulled, stretching it like a piece of taffy into outer space. It filled Savina with a dreadful fascination, made her feel infinitely small and lonely, a germ on the floor. She couldn't look away. It was like an eternal monument; it was there and always had been there and always would be there, and in comparison Savina was a quick little spark, her entire life nothing more than a second in passing. The sight inspired hopelessness, defeat; this was a place people ended up when they discovered it was all too much, that existence was overwhelming, and they just could not handle it. People were put to sleep like sick animals; the poor, the hungry, the weary, the anguished, the crippled, the insane—even criminals. As Savina stared, wanting to look away and yet unable to, people passed around her in a hush, saying nothing, taking light, quick steps and not looking up.

Somebody grasped Savina by the shoulder. "It's an illusion," said a warm, deep, throaty woman's voice.

Savina tore her gaze away from the building and looked at the woman. She was shaking her head at Savina, her long, straight, black hair swinging back and forth. The woman was tall, and her skin was dark, but not quite the same shade as Savina's. She appeared to be Native American, or at least seemed to have a lot of it in her blood. "You don't want to go in there," she told Savina. "That won't solve anything."

Savina realized she was surrounded by ragged-looking people, dressed in shabby, ill-fitting clothes with wild, long hair. Anarchists, Savina thought. "*I'm* not going in there," she said.

The woman's brown eyes bored into Savina's, calm, peaceful eyes with an awesome sense of presence. "This building was designed to induce the feelings you were experiencing. It's only two hundred meters high, and the top fifty meters are hollow. The rest is a hologram."

"I knew that," Savina said, intimidated.

"Don't ever be sucked in by it. Illusions never deliver what they promise."

"I'm just going to the bank."

The woman nodded. "You were distracted. Part of the building's purpose is to lure. You felt the lure, didn't you?"

Savina stared into the woman's eyes. "Yes, I did."

"The image robs you of hope and inspires thoughts of mortality. To those without hope, it brings a sense of peace. They feel that if they surrender to it, they become part of it." The woman shook her head. "It's a lie."

Savina nodded, not knowing what to say. The woman was strangely magnetic.

"You look troubled," the woman said.

"I'm . . . I . . . I've got to get to the bank."

"Okay. Just don't go into the euthanasia center. Don't ever go into the euthanasia center."

"I don't intend to," Savina said, edging through the other anarchists. Weird, she thought. Too weird. She got by them and made her way past the white tower, very consciously not looking up at it, then entered the bank and got in line for the autotellers. Savina had known that the anarchists hung out at euthanasia centers; they were famous for talking people out of suicide, were even heroes in some circles. The tall woman with the intense eyes didn't seem like an anarchist, though. There was too much to her, some sort of gestalt power. *Intense* was the word that came to Savina's mind.

There were security monitors everywhere inside the bank. Savina was rattled because of the woman anarchist—she hoped it wasn't to the point where it would trigger the interest of the bank's security AI. She stood in line, waiting with everyone else and refraining from making eye contact with the monitors. As she stood there, she realized she had gotten into the slowest line. Figures, she thought.

I wonder if I should splurge and get a room for the night? Tonight I can give Dodd a call, ask him for help. Maybe I can get him to come and stay with me? Savina smiled at the unlikelihood of the thought.

She moved up in the line. Hers was still the slowest—she

couldn't believe this always happened to her. Today was the worst, and it was the worst time for it to happen. If the police had inserted her number into their system, then the autoteller would call them as soon as she inserted her card. If she took the safe way out, stayed away from the bank, she would be destitute. Is it worth it, though? she wondered. I'm free *now*. What good will cash be if I'm going to prison?

She was two people away from the autoteller, and the old man at the front was now verbally arguing with the machine. You might as well argue with a wall, Savina thought. To either side of her the lines were moving smoothly. God, she thought, why this now? Now of all times! She hid her face in her hands, keeping her frustration in. Yelling at the old man would only attract the attention of the security AI.

The old man, hunched and gray and slow-moving, gave up and got out of line. The woman in front of Savina stepped up to the autoteller and opened her purse, dumping the entire contents onto the stainless table used for signing vouchers. She began digging through the contents for something, probably her moneycard.

Savina leaned casually over toward her. "Excuse me, I'm in a hurry. I was wondering if I could take care of my business really quick while you're——"

"I beg your pardon," the woman said, "I'm in line here before you; I waited just as long."

"I'm sorry," Savina said. "Never mind."

"I think you're a very pushy, rude child. Who do you think you are to just go pushing in line. Think your business is more important than mine?"

"Look, I didn't mean anything. I'm sorry." Savina was beginning to sweat because the security AI was surely looking at them by now. "Go on with your business, never mind me."

"Oh, never mind you, huh? Like it's me who's doing the wrong thing. Don't you try to make it out like it's my fault that——"

"Lady," a man behind Savina said, "this girl says she's sorry, and we're all in a hurry here."

"What, are you her boyfriend? Now you're going to push me out of the way? Let me tell you something, you—"

"Lady, just shut up and finish," the man snapped at her.

"Shut up? You're telling me to shut up?"

"He's telling you to shut up, and I'm telling you to shut up," said another person behind Savina, a tall woman with a green punk-resurrection hairstyle. "It's late, and we're all in a hurry. How long do you want to stand here?"

Shouted down, the woman in front of Savina turned and pointedly ignored them, taking her own sweet time in finishing up her transaction. I'm living a nightmare, Savina thought. Her imagination told her that every security monitor in the bank was focused on her. She closed her eyes and tried to pretend she wasn't there.

Finally, the crabby lady finished and walked away with a stiff neck. Savina took a breath and stepped up to the autoteller. She inserted her card and punched in her code with shaking fingers. There was $1322.70 in her account; she instructed the machine to give her all of it. The screen blinked as if taken aback, and two large words appeared:

PLEASE WAIT

Wait? Wait for what? This had never happened before. Then again she had never pulled all the money out of her account before. There was a humming noise, and Savina thought, This is it.

The crabby woman had been standing at the rear of the room rearranging things in her purse and was just now opening a door to leave. There was a loud click and a dull beeping. The doors were locking, and the one that was open—the woman, startled, was standing against it—began to push its way closed, forcing her back into the bank. Savina stared about wildly. It was happening; it was really happening. She turned and bolted for the door, sliding through as the woman unintentionally held it open for her. She hurtled down the front steps three at a time, and at the sidewalk came to a sliding halt: Her father, Bob Recent, and Dodd Corley were no more than thirty meters away, walking slowly toward her.

All three of them were looking up at the infinite white tower of the euthanasia center.

There was a narrow alley between the bank and the center, a space for the autonomic garbage-collection trucks to pass. Savina ran for it, up several steps, then over a railing, dropping two meters to the smooth concrete of the alley. She threw one last glance behind her before she was out of sight, and found a whole group of anarchists standing and watching her. She continued running, pounding the ground hard with her feet, flying headlong down the alley to find it was a dead end.

15. Sidewalk Rule

DODD HAD MIXED FEELINGS ABOUT FINDING SAVINA. HE WANTED HER SAFE, but he wanted her to have what she wanted. He also wanted to help Toby, who was worried sick about his missing daughter. Either way, he was betraying someone he cared about.

Bob had volunteered to come along, which had surprised Dodd. Bob was almost eager to go. He was alive again, awake. Wonders could happen during a crisis. People showed their true colors—even Toby was back to his old self. All three were gazing up at the specter of the white tower when there was a muffled shout accompanied by banging noises. Dodd pulled his eyes down from the dizzying sight and looked over at the bank. There were people inside, and the doors were closed. The people were all looking out, some calling for help, some banging on the windows.

"Something's happening at the bank," Bob said.

"There's people locked inside!" Toby exclaimed. "Look at that."

They hurried up the steps toward the closed bank door, and a hand reached out and gave Dodd's sleeve a tug as he passed. Dodd paused, looking back. It was a familiar face, a half smile nearly invisible in a scraggly beard. "Dodd," the face said, "what's up?"

"Danny," Dodd said, surprised. He looked back at the other two, who had reached the bank door, then turned back to his anarchist friend. "Danny, did you see a young black girl around here, about so high?"

"She was pretty," Danny said.

"You saw her?"

"I saw a young black girl. She came running out of that bank just before it locked up. The police are going to be here any second."

"Where did she go?"

"Why? I'm not turning anyone in."

"Danny, this is me! Where did she go?"

Danny shrugged. "She ran into the alley, but that doesn't lead anywhere."

Dodd stood looking into his friend's eyes for a moment. "It doesn't go anywhere?"

"Nope."

"Okay." Dodd thought a moment, struggling with his conscience. "Don't tell anyone anything."

"I'm oblivious," Danny said, grinning.

As Dodd started up toward his friends, they turned and came trotting back down.

"She was here!" Toby said. "You were right!"

"These guys said they saw her running down that way," Dodd said, pointing down the street. "It was hardly a minute ago."

"Let's go!"

"You two go, I'll cut through here in case she's going around the block." Dodd pointed at the alley.

"Okay!" Toby went trotting down the street with Bob tagging along. Dodd made his way into the alley, which went around the building and ended. There were solid locked doors and concrete walls ten meters high, and right in the middle was a large black trash Dumpster with the lid closed. Everything was glaring light, white concrete and white building walls, white doors to the building. The blackness of the Dumpster was a harsh contrast, sucking in light like a hole.

Dodd walked up to the Dumpster and raised the thick plastic lid. Savina stared up at him, half-buried in shredded computer printouts and used silicon drinking cups. "What in the hell are you doing?" he asked her.

"Dodd, help me!"

"I sent your father racing down the street on a wild-goose chase. He's never going to forgive me for this."

"Dodd, the bank ate my moneycard! It tried to lock me in."

"I saw."

"You've got to help me!"

"You are in over your head, you know that, don't you?"

"Yes."

"Why are you running away?"

"To save my baby!"

Dodd sighed. He couldn't imagine a better reason to run away. "I can't believe I'm doing this," he said, more to himself than to her. "You stay in here for now, I'm going to go talk to one of my friends in that group of anarchists around front. If you get away, you call me. If you get caught, swear to me that you won't tell them I tried to help you. Your father will kill me, and I mean that. He will rip my fucking arms off and beat me to death with them. Do you understand?"

Savina nodded.

"The guy's name is Danny Marauder. He has a beard, red hair, and a broken front tooth. If he tells you to do something, do it. He saved my life at least twice back in the war."

"I love you, Dodd."

"Well, I'm *pissed* at you." Dodd closed the lid.

He walked around to the front, where quite a crowd was gathering, and looked up and down the street for any sign of Toby or Bob. Bob was way, way down on the corner of the city block, searching the passing pedestrians for Savina's face. Toby was nowhere in sight. The group of anarchists was still spread around the wide entrance to the euthanasia center, keeping their distance from the bank. Dodd looked at his watch. Police drones would arrive any second.

Dodd spotted Danny Marauder standing next to a tall, dark-haired woman who looked Native American. "I've got a favor to ask," he said, walking up to Danny.

"You've got at least one coming," Danny told him.

"That girl I was asking you about, she's hiding in the Dumpster behind the bank. She's pregnant and underage, wants to keep the baby. Her name's Savina."

"She means a lot to you," the woman said.

Dodd looked at her, distracted. "Yes, a lot. I'd like her to get away."

"Your kid, huh?" Danny said, smiling.

"No, I'm kinda her uncle . . ." Dodd trailed off, realizing what Danny was implying. "No, it's not my kid! I'm not the father; it's one of her school friends."

"Sure," Danny said.

"He's telling the truth," the woman told Danny. She turned to Dodd. "We'll help her get away. We'll take care of her and her child."

Dodd looked from her to Danny and back. "Uh, well, thanks." There was something strange about the woman. He instantly liked her.

"Don't feel guilty about your friend," she told him. "You did the right thing." She gave Danny a little push, and he patted Dodd on the shoulder and made his way off through the crowd.

"I'd better, uh . . ." Dodd indicated the direction that Toby and Bob had gone.

"You go. We'll take care of Savina."

"Thanks." Dodd turned, feeling a peculiar reluctance to leave. He forced himself to trot off toward Bob, who was still at the corner. As he ran he felt he had thrown all his emotions up into the air, and they were raining down around him willy-nilly. He felt bad, he felt good, he felt guilty, he felt like a traitor. Bob spotted him coming up the street and waved.

"The alley was a dead end," Dodd said. "Where's Toby?"

"He went off that way, toward the subway," Bob said. "I'm here in case she doubles back."

"If you see Toby, tell him I went this way," Dodd said, pointing in the opposite direction Toby had gone. He waved and trotted off down the city sidewalk, avoiding other pedestrians and hoping to get himself utterly lost. He didn't care where he went, he just didn't want to be found again.

The end of the world, he thought. The end of the fucking world.

• • •

Inside the Dumpster it was hot and smelled of moldy coffee grounds. When Dodd had opened the lid, the rush of cool air had revitalized her, but now that it was closed again, the oven effect was back. Her blue jumpsuit was becoming soaked with sweat.

Savina waited, as Dodd had told her. She knew he'd help her, she just knew it. She loved him more than anyone in the world at that moment. A woman's voice from outside the Dumpster spoke her name. "Savina, we're going to help you. I'm going to throw a shirt and a hat in. I want you to put them on before you come out. The shirt is overlarge, so you can wear it like a dress."

The top opened only long enough to let in a rush of air and a few cloth items, then it was closed again. Savina stood, lifted the lid just enough to peek outside. It was the Native American woman.

Savina struggled out of her jumpsuit in the cramped box, then put on the shirt and the wide-brimmed felt hat. The shirt hung almost to her knees. She opened the top and self-consciously pulled herself out of the Dumpster, dropping to the ground next to the woman.

"My name's Evelyn Sunrunner," the woman said, closing the lid. "We have to hurry." She led Savina down the alley toward the street.

"Are you a friend of Dodd's?"

"Yes. Don't be frightened, but I'm going to get jumped. Get ready. Someone's going to grab you, but it's a friend."

They emerged from the alley right into the line of sight of two police drones. They were ugly oblong floating bugs about two meters long and painted black; scanning receptors swung back and forth like the antennae and legs on a insect. Savina was so close she could hear the servos whirring.

Two men jumped from the crowd and tackled Evelyn to the ground. She screamed at the top of her lungs, and the men swung their fists, smacking theatrical blows. Arms grabbed Savina from behind and pulled her back. A large redheaded man with a beard stepped in between Savina and the fight, blocking her view of the drones.

"Help!" Evelyn screamed. "Oh, help me! Rape! Rape!"

"Eeeyaa!" one of her attackers yelled.

The red-haired man and Savina backed away slowly, very slowly. Both police drones moved to hover over the fight, and a mechanical voice issued a command to cease and desist immediately. The second drone pulled back, moving around to scan the growing crowd. Rocks flew from nowhere and pelted it, drawing it away as it searched for the source. One of the wavering insect legs was a stunner gun; it began zapping indiscriminately into the crowd. The other drone was busily spraying down Evelyn and her attackers with an aerosol paralysis gas. Within seconds they were limp.

Savina and the red-haired man had made it to the outside edge of the crowd. "Walk," he told her. "Walk calmly. Never run. I'll be behind you."

Savina turned and walked slowly down the sidewalk. She couldn't stand it, she had to run, but she forced herself to walk, trusting the man because Dodd had told her to, biting her lower lip and feeling that all eyes were on her. Every footstep was an agony, every yard she gained an eternity. She doubted she would get as far as the corner.

Her imagination put one of the police drones right over her shoulder, following silently, scanners looking right into her mind, into her thoughts. Just following, knowing she would not be getting away—any sudden moves and it would be a hiss of gas and she'd drop to her face on the pavement. She hoped to God the footsteps right behind her belonged to the redhead. He wasn't close, but he was pacing her.

Straight down the street in front of them came a manned police cruiser, racing through the air about four meters over the street traffic. It was heading right for her. "Don't run," the red-bearded man said to her in a conversational tone. "Look right at them, watch them as they approach. If you avert your eyes or break your stride, you'll catch their attention."

"I thought if you look at them, then you catch their attention."

"That's if it's an AI program watching you. These are people in an air launch, they're used to people looking at them. They're always watching for people who don't want to be seen."

The police cruiser passed practically overhead, and she turned and watched. They ignored her completely. The cruiser lowered to the ground, and two sharply uniformed women jumped out, stun pistols in their hands. One began questioning the people in the crowd about what had happened, and the other began accessing the intelligence in the drones. When she finished with the first drone, it rose up into the air and began drifting toward Savina. "Oh shit," she said.

"Don't get nervous, it's just scanning. Let's turn and walk away."

The man put an arm around Savina, and they continued to walk down the street. They reached the corner and turned left, walking around the block. Ahead, on the other side of the street, stood Bob Recent. "He knows me," Savina said to her companion.

"He knows me, too. Damn." He glanced over his shoulder, saw that the drone was still heading in their direction. "If we double back, we'll catch that fucking thing's attention."

"I'll stand on this side of you," Savina said, crossing to his other side so that he was between her and Bob.

"It's not going to do much good."

"Did he see me?"

"I don't know. He's seen me, he's coming this way."

"Marauder!" Bob's voice called out. Savina felt stupid hiding behind this man. Bob was going to see her anyway. "This is it," Danny Marauder said to her in a low voice. "You're going to be on your own now. Go for the old college in the Depopulated Zone. Stay away from security monitors if you can."

"What old college?"

Danny didn't answer. Bob had reached them, and he saw Savina. "Hey," he said. "You found her."

"Found who?"

"Savina!"

"That's not Savina," Danny said, and punched Bob in the stomach. Bob gasped for breath, looking very confused. Danny hit him again, very hard, and Bob fell to the ground. Danny took off running, and the police drone came rushing after him. He swung on it, a gun in his hand from the inside of his shirt. There was a deafening concussion, and part of the drone disintegrated in millions of flying shiny pieces, like glitter, and the machine began spinning in midair. It made a noise like a wounded animal, bleeding smoke and parts, spinning faster and faster as it rose up into the air. Its spinning quickly reached a terminal velocity and it flew apart with a startling bang. Danny, running again, disappeared into an alleyway. Another drone seemed to come from nowhere and went hurtling after him. Both disappeared from Savina's view, and there was another loud concussion, then silence.

Just walk away, Savina told herself. She put one foot in front of the other, took a step, felt herself moving. It all seemed so unreal. She was walking away, she was just walking away, and more police drones were flying in from all directions like giant angry wasps, buzzing in the air, crowding into the alleyway where Danny Marauder had gone. She walked away, down the street, muscles taut and spine stiff, but she was walking away, just walking away.

Behind her, Bob Recent struggled to his feet just as a drone swept down over him and sprayed him with gas. He fell again, paralyzed, confused, as the drone stated his rights in a clear voice and repeated them in a dozen languages. He could see Savina walking away and tried to point, but he couldn't move his arm, and his voice was the croak of a frog.

She walked into the distance, out of sight.

16. Psychopath

VICKY HAD ELECTED TO SPEND THE NIGHT AT SAUL'S HOUSE. SINCE SAUL HAD problems enough with one woman, he was not invited to bed with the two of them. Saul and Vicky didn't even really like each other, and having sex with her, especially failing in sex with her, would be more humiliation than he could stand. It was bad enough that she was sleeping with his wife. Saul ended up spending the night huddled in blankets on the reclining chair on the back porch.

Morning broke, and with relief Saul found it stable and whole. Reality was back, and the night was gone. The night had been terrible.

There had been no refuge; the lights savagely attacked him, and the dark hid enormous threats. Inside the house he could hardly breathe; outside there was too much air. The silence of the house roared at him, and on the porch the ocean would growl— it was horrible, *horrible*. The world pulsated, his imagination taking over, every whim of his subconscious taking matter and form, appearing in front of him and lurking behind him. When he fell asleep there was no respite—vivid and overwhelming nightmares plagued him, waking him up but not stopping, continuing on as he clutched at his head, his knees tucked up against his chest, his breath rasping and shuddering.

Now it was over. The sun was shining, and the surf sounded friendly. Saul crawled out of the blankets and stood on the porch, stretching. He found he had slept in his clothes.

I need a nice warm dip in the pool, he thought. Then he remembered about Vicky, that she and Mirro were in the bedroom where the pool was. His bedroom. Oh, *hell*, he thought. I ought to go in there if they want me or not. If I interrupt something it's their problem . . .

Then he thought: Vicky's son is in jail. She's upset, and I have to make allowances.

Christ! It wasn't fair. He had to suffer——him——just because some jerk kid went and raped a girl, then was stupid enough to turn himself in. Not only did Saul have to put up with Vicky openly replacing him in the bedroom, but now he couldn't even go into his own bedroom to use his own pool. And, he thought, I'm the one who decided to buy this house because of that pool!

From deep inside came a terrible thought: He envied Vicky. He envied her because she was able to satisfy Mirro, and he envied her because her kid was locked away, gone, out of her life.

Shuddering and feeling ashamed, he suppressed the revolting thought and pretended it wasn't there. He settled for taking a shower in the west-wing bathroom, the one in which he'd nearly scalded himself the night before, but after the shower Saul still needed to get into the bedroom for a fresh change of clothes. Resigned, he knocked on the closed door and waited. Mirro answered, putting her finger to her lips. She was naked.

"How's Vicky doing?" Saul whispered.

"Fine. She's sleeping." Mirro held the door wide open; Saul could see Vicky's head and bare shoulders protruding from a pile of wrinkled sheets. She was on Saul's side of the bed. "Come on in," Mirro whispered, "just be quiet."

Saul tiptoed around, gathering clothes. Mirro followed him into the bathroom and stood with him as he slipped out of his old underwear, put on a fresh pair, and began dressing. "Saul," she said, "I'm really proud of you for how you're accepting all this."

Saul shrugged. "Tell Vicky not to bother coming into work today. I can spare her. But I'm going to need her tomorrow, or the day after at the latest. She'd better get her things with her lawyer done fast. We've got this Jesus thing coming up, and I'm going to need her."

"Saul, are you sure there's nothing to that?"

"To what?"

"The Jesus thing."

"No, there's nothing at all to that. It's a stunt, a fraud." Saul laughed, pulling up his pants. "Even if the Savior was returning to Earth, if this was really happening, I'd still have my job to do."

Mirro smiled. She picked up his slipover scarf-tie and put it over his head. Then her arms slithered around him, and she was kissing him, using her tongue and the rest of her body, pressing herself up against him the way she used to do—the way she hadn't done in years. Saul felt—with elation!—his penis growing erect. Mirro felt it, too, and redoubled her passion.

A long, terrible scream sounded, echoing throughout the house, jarring both of them and waking Vicky. It's the baby, Saul thought bitterly. His daughter, with her usual bad timing. His desire evaporated quickly, followed by his erection, and, after a sorrowful few moments, he and his wife drew apart.

Saul finished dressing and left for work.

At the Telcron Systems building, company security people were standing around looking pissed off and eyeing everybody with suspicion. Saul had arrived late because he'd allowed himself the luxury of a quiet breakfast at an out-of-the-way coffee shop. Also, in case the Mataphin problem got out of hand, he'd stopped off at a pharmacy near the office and picked up a package of DeTox, a multispectrum neutralizer. One of the security men found it and looked it over inside and out as Saul was being frisked inside the front door. They were searching everyone coming and going.

"What's going on?" Saul asked, as the security man handed him back his DeTox along with his Mataphin dispenser and a few other objects.

"Security has been tightened."

"No shit," Saul said. "I want to know why, and who ordered it."

"Lisa Schemandle ordered it. There was a security breach last night."

"Security breach?"

The man nodded and began frisking the next person through the door. Saul stood there a moment, wanting to know more, but he was being pointedly ignored. He turned and headed toward the elevators, thinking that he probably didn't want to know about it anyway. Probably a shootout between network spies. The elevator came and carried him upward, and he exited on his floor, looking to and fro in case Lisa was waiting for him. She was nowhere in sight.

Saul entered his spacious office, and there she was, brooding over her coffee at his desk. His terminal was on; she'd been going through all his files again. "Saul," she said. "You're late."

"I know. Good morning to you, too."

"I heard about your assistant. You give her some time off?"

"Yes."

Lisa nodded. She was heavyset, with short black hair on a big, strong head. She had a rough, windburned face from years of riding a motorcycle. Her eyes were small, perpetually red, but very, very sharp. "Her son is up for seventeen years in an undersea prison. The parents of the girl are pressing for maximum penalties."

"It's a shame."

"I think the little prick should be castrated, but that's just me. I feel sorry for Vicky. Anyway, that's not why I'm here, Saul."

"I know."

"You've done a great job raising the AHL, but goddamn it to hell, Kalman, we're still losing viewers. You know what those JTV bastards just did to us? They broke in here and stole copies of our top animators, our best AIs! Then they tried to kill off our backup copies."

"Our backups?" Saul felt all the strength in his arms and legs suddenly vanish. He almost fainted.

"Saul! Are you okay?"

"They killed our backups?" He sank to a chair, all the color drained from his face.

"No, they tried, but they didn't get them all. We've got copies in New York on a one-way data line. They couldn't touch them. Updated last night, didn't miss more than a few hours."

Some of the color began seeping back into Saul's face. He sighed. "Thank God," he said. He had a massive headache, and his fingers were itching for his Mataphin dispenser.

"My guess is that they're going to use our AIs, *our* fucking artificial intelligence programs, to make their descent-from-heaven scene."

Saul heard the rest of their entire conversation before it actually happened. It was so predictable. "You want me to intensify the AHL even more?"

"Yes! Exactly! Dammit, we gotta glue their fucking eyes to the screen. I want 'em so wrapped up in Travels they forget to eat. We've got to keep 'em! Hold them down by their fucking short hairs!"

"What about my AIs?"

"Copies of the backups are being sent over right now from New York. They'll be on-line and working before you're back from the field today."

"What about viruses? What if they left viruses behind in the computers? What then?"

"Don't worry about that, Saul. We're bringing in all brand-new equipment. Sterile chips, sterile operating systems. No viruses."

"We're going to have all new equipment installed and the backups running by the time I get back from the field?"

"Yes. They almost hurt us, Saul, but they failed. Those bastards. You know what I'm doing now? We're retaliating, Saul. I've got hired assassins after those JTV hackers right now." She laughed, slapping the desk with her hand and spilling coffee. She continued, not noticing. "We're *killing* those fuckers, Saul! We're having them assassinated! That's right, every single one of them, dead by tomorrow." She grinned in angry triumph.

She's serious, Saul realized. She's a psychopath. What's she going to do to *me* if I ever let her down?

"I'm not going to take up any more of your time, Kalman," she said, standing up. "You have your job, I've got mine. Time's wasting. We're going to see this thing through. We're going to do it—right?"

"Right," Saul said automatically.

She nodded approvingly and turned her thick bulk on one heel, striding out of Saul's office and leaving her spilled cup of coffee on his desk. Saul stood up, looking after her. He felt dizzy, he realized, and discovered he'd gone into hyperventilation. Mataphin, he thought. I need it.

He fumbled desperately in his pocket for the dispenser, brought it out. He hesitated, trying to stop himself. Two tabs fell out onto his open hand, and he told himself that two should be enough. Then he relented, and let two more fall out.

Saul ended up taking six.

17. Depopulated Zone

SAVINA HAD SPENT THE NIGHT IN A CHURCHYARD, SHELTERED BY THE LARGE
silvered satellite dish pointing up at the JTV star. She slept maybe
twenty minutes all that night, awaking with a start to discover she
was not at home in bed. She was out in an unfamiliar neighborhood, a fugitive from the police, sleeping in the open with nothing
but a shirt and a hat for warmth. It was a warm night, at least. It
only got cold at dawn.

In the morning she was starving. She wanted desperately to
call Dodd, but without a moneycard she couldn't even place a collect call on a public phone terminal. The loss of her moneycard
was a bad blow.

No food, no transportation. No phone. No clean clothes, no
shower. Was this worth it? There was a strange stubborn streak in
her that refused to let her answer that. Just take it as it comes,
she told herself. Once I get to the Depopulated Zone, there's
food for the picking.

Without access to the subway or a cab she was hopelessly far
away from her destination. Without a map she could only guess
which direction it was. She began walking, ignoring the hunger and
trusting that she would find food along the way; someone, anarchists maybe, would give her a meal and ride.

The sunlight and harsh shadows of the early morning made
everything seem lonely. She walked east until the sun was straight
up and people were everywhere, but no anarchists. Exhausted
and weak with lack of sleep, dizzy from hunger, she leaned up

against the corner of a building and began asking everyone who passed for spare change. Not many people carried cash anymore, and even fewer were willing to part with it. One lecherous-looking old black man eyed her and gave her enough for a vender meal and asked her if she wanted to come home with him. She almost accepted.

The money bought her a sandwich and a protein bar, which she washed down with water from a drinking fountain. It was only after she'd eaten that she realized she could have used the money to buy a call to Dodd. She cursed her stupidity, but had to admit she felt a lot better for having eaten. She continued walking, trying to stay in the shade of trees and buildings as the June sunlight beat down with physical force. She began to look at everything with a tired sense of wonder. Her situation seemed very heroic to her, and the sense of freedom suddenly came back to her. Her spirits climbed, and she began smiling at the people she passed. She collected a few dollars more before the pedestrians began to thin out. By the time the sunlight was at a definite angle, she was in a run-down little neighborhood made up of old rectangular apartments surrounded by large oak trees. While the area was clean, it was not well maintained; all the buildings were in need of fresh paint, the old peeling away; there were mowed lawns, but the edges weren't trimmed, and grass grew along cracks in the sidewalk and even into the street itself. Small white children wearing ill-fitting, faded clothes played with battered electric tricycles thirty years old. Beyond the neighborhood was a fenced-off area; the fence was temporary and in ill repair, big plastic sections fitted together and bolted, but some bolts were missing, and sections were torn out entirely. She crossed through.

On the other side, Savina found more apartments and some houses, but most were empty frames and others had been half-consumed by fire. The trees and plants had gone wild, spreading without check and turning the area into a jungle. This was an area zoned for leveling—the edge of the Depopulated Zone. After the area was leveled, the fences would be moved back and the people evicted. Thus the Depopulated Zone was enlarged.

It was very quiet, the hot afternoon air thick and still. The angled sunlight filtered through oak trees, casting streams of light. Speckled lizards ran along the ground, taking cover while she passed. Ahead were crouched figures, young boys about twelve or thirteen years old, stalking each other with toy guns. One of them spotted her, and they followed along behind her, making her nervous, but she managed to keep well ahead of them. After a while they grew bored and resumed their pursuit of each other.

Savina began noticing signs of habitation in the area; some of the old houses had been cleaned up, haphazard repairs being made on the deteriorating wooden structures. This was a different area of the Depopulated Zone than Savina was used to—the ruins she had explored with Greg were far south of here, an area that had once been the center of a city before all the cities had merged. The atmosphere there had been different, full of noise and teenage adventure. Here the atmosphere was solemn and serious. People *lived* here; this was their territory. This was not a place for city people to spend summer afternoons letting loose out of sight of public security systems. This place seemed to have its own security system, its own unspoken codes and morals. Savina had the feeling she was trespassing.

There were occasional tree houses in the giant gnarled oaks; some were very simple—no more than a scrap-wood platform nailed among the branches—but some were multistoried and complex, with rope and counterweight elevators, glass windows, and satellite dishes protruding at odd angles. People peered down at her through windows and branches, their expressions suspicious. A few half waved at her. "Do you know where there's an old abandoned college?" she yelled up at one.

"Yeah."

"Is it close?" she asked.

"Not really."

"Where is it?"

"North. Up that way."

"How far is it?"

"Don't know. Never been there." The man smiled at her.

Savina continued on her way, heading vaguely east.

The trees thinned out, and the ruins of the old houses turned to foundations with partial walls, nothing more. Eventually she found herself walking through tall, dry weeds that hid details of old, rusted, gasoline cars, getting stickers in her sandals. She stumbled upon a clearing in the grass, a hidden spot with an old ratty mattress sitting on a slab of concrete. Savina eyed the mattress longingly but decided against lying down—she didn't want to be caught sleeping by the lovers who must use this spot.

Savina looked across the vast stretch of farmland to the mountains beyond, then gazed to the north, along the perimeter of the zone. The field was unbroken to the horizon. To the south it was the same way.

She turned north.

She walked for a kilometer or so along a dirt road that crossed occasional aqueducts and wound back and forth along the perimeter; she passed more rusted carcasses of the old gasoline-engine cars, some stacked on top of each other like big neglected toys. There were also piles of large concrete blocks that looked like they marked something, but she couldn't figure out what. To her left she passed a caved-in ruin that had a sun-bleached, eroded fiberglass statue in front. It looked like some sort of clown.

When the sun was just settling to the horizon, Savina spotted a small group of deserted metal structures, just big boxes of rusted corrugated steel. It looked like a good shelter for the night, but before she could reach them she had to get across one last aqueduct, and this one didn't run under the road. There was a long, narrow plank that served as a bridge. She decided to crawl instead of doing a high-wire act. The plank wobbled and shook as she crossed, but she took her time and reached the other side. She paused there, staring into the water. The concrete sides were green with algae, but the water was crystal clear. She scooped some with her hands and tasted it. It was sweet, and after her first mouthful her body realized it was thirsty. She drank for several minutes.

Sated, she turned to the metal buildings—which looked like old aircraft hangars—and sneaked up on them in case they weren't as deserted as they looked. She almost hoped to find someone because she was getting hungry again; maybe two dollars would buy her a meal out here in the new wilderness.

The place was silent save for the calling of birds and the rustle of wind in the oak trees. Inside the building she scared a few pigeons—they flapped and jumped to new perches where they could keep an eye on her—but other than the pigeons, she owned the place. It was just as well. Her weariness outweighed her hunger, and she was content just to find a pile of old rags in a corner and collapse.

Another night on my own, she thought. I'm going to have a lot of stories to tell Dodd. A giant yawn escaped her, taking with it most of her energy. She lay there, staring up at the dark, oiled timbers supporting the corrugated roof, eyes half-closed, heart beating in her ears. It seemed like she could hear the blood rushing through the veins in her head. The rags smelled musty, but she was beyond caring about that. The sky outside deepened in color. The pigeons flapped restlessly in the rafters, nervous of her presence; she tried to see them, but it was getting too dark, and she could only make out dull gray blobs.

She remembered another time she had spent lying in a quiet old ruin, felt the ghost-memory of Greg's hand running lightly up her bare thigh. Involuntarily she hugged herself, remembering Greg hugging her. Loneliness welled up, mixed with a feeling of emptiness and frustration. Turning her head to one side, Savina began to cry. For a while her tears flowed freely, but as the sky darkened her whimpers grew softer, then faded out altogether, replaced by slow, rhythmic breathing. Later, when the sky was completely black, the deserted building echoed with the sharp rasping sounds of snoring. Savina was in a deep sleep all night, a sleep without dreams, and in the morning she awoke in a patch of dawn sunlight that streamed in through a gaping, glassless window. Her muscles were stiff, sore. Her stomach was a gaping, empty pit.

I'll pick up breakfast at the vendor on the way to school, she thought. Then she realized where she was. Images of a quick, neat breakfast died in the black pit of impossibility. She felt a longing for home, where food was not a problem.

She stood up, stretched, and pulled twigs out of her hair. Looking out the window, she saw fields of wheat. Bread was made from wheat, she thought. If she had a phone, she could access the school library and find out how wheat turns to bread. It had something to do with grinding it, but that's all she knew. Somewhere out there was a form of food she could eat without preparation, there had to be.

The pigeons above her cooed, and she looked up to see them staring down at her. She'd heard of squab, but never tried it. She might be able to hit one with a rock, but . . . what then? Savina had never been the kind to carry a pocketknife, and she had no idea how to clean and skin a bird—or any animal, for that matter. On the rare occasions that this problem would come up at home, the kitchen autochef and its robot arms would take care of it.

She walked outside, looking around to make sure she was alone, then picked her way to a secluded clump of bushes and disappeared among them for a while. There were no public toilets out here. When she was finished she went to the aqueduct and washed up as well as she could, then moved upstream a ways and drank. When she looked up she saw a ground squirrel racing across the open toward its hole, pausing for a moment to look at her before diving in headfirst. I guess that's edible, she thought. If it's not diseased or something.

Not only did she not have a knife, she didn't have a lighter either. How would she start a cooking fire? Rub sticks?

Savina was beginning to feel hopeless.

The morning was bright and cloudless, the air clear. Savina

limped along with stiff legs down the path she'd followed the previous afternoon, still heading north, gazing hungrily off to the east and looking for something, *anything*, besides wheat. Then she stopped. It wasn't because of something she saw; it was something she smelled. Burning wood and roasting meat. Spices. Her mouth started watering, and she spun around, sniffing, trying to figure out where it was coming from. It seemed to be from the west, back toward the city.

Savina followed the scent into the ruins of the perimeter.

There was a large building that had burned and crumbled away over the years to form a small mountain of rubble; on its slopes grew skinny trees and tufts of brush. In the shadow of its west side, amid oaks and gutted brick dwellings, was a man sitting in a folding chair next to a large barbecue. On the barbecue was what looked like a rabbit turning on an automatic spit. The man was wearing a business suit with rips in the legs and dirt matted into the material; on his lap was a small portable terminal with a cable leading to a headset on his head. Beside him was a large hole in the ground. Every second or so a mass of dirt came flying out of the hole, landing to the other side away from the man in the chair. In the background were a pair of tents and a truck, the kind sold with a water-conversion engine. Savina pulled the two dollars out of her hat and walked out into the open, heading toward the man in the chair.

The man smiled at her. "You owe me money?"

"I want to buy some breakfast off you."

The dirt abruptly stopped flying from the hole, and a black-haired man with a beard peeked over the edge. "What the hell?"

"We have a visitor," the blond man said.

"Kid, this isn't a restaurant," the bearded man with the shovel told her. He climbed out of the hole and pulled a rag out of his pocket. He used the rag to wipe the sweat off his brow.

"I don't eat much," Savina said. "I'll pay for what I take."

"Put your money away," the blond man said. "You can have some when it's done."

"Wiley," the bearded man said.

"Oh, relax. She's hungry. We can share some food."

"Are you alone, kid?" asked the bearded man.

"Yes."

"Are you sure?"

"Yes."

"You're traveling pretty light."

Savina nodded. "That's the way it turned out."

"Do you live out here?"

"For now, yes."

"Been out here long?"

Savina shrugged. "A while."

The blond man was still smiling. "You're a runaway, aren't you?"

Savina began to feel defensive. "Not necessarily."

"Not necessarily?" The blond man laughed.

"You look like one," the bearded man said. "I'm thinking that someone wants you to look like one."

"Who?" Savina asked.

"Don't listen to him," the blond man said. He took off the headset and stood up, putting the computer on his chair. He unfolded another chair and offered it to Savina. "My name's Wiley, and his is Aaron. Here, sit. Go ahead."

"Thank you." She sat. "My name is Savina. I'm really glad I found you guys out here. What are you doing? Camping?"

"Let's set some ground rules," Aaron said. "You don't ask us what we're doing here, and we won't ask you what *you're* doing here. Fair enough?"

"Sure. I'm here for breakfast."

Wiley laughed. "You want something to drink? Got some real cow's milk, not that bacteria stuff."

"Real cow's milk?" Savina made a face.

"Everything else we've got is a little too strong for breakfast, especially for someone as young as you."

Savina shrugged. "I'll try some cow's milk."

"I'll go get us some. How about you, Aaron?"

"Don't let her in the tents."

"Yeah," Wiley said. "You better wait here, Savina. Aaron, did you want one or not."

"No. I want some coffee."

"It should be ready by now. I'll take my turn when I get back." He walked off under the trees toward one of the tents.

"What are you digging for?" Savina asked.

"None of your business."

"Oh, okay. Look, I don't care, I was just curious."

"Don't be curious. You're here for breakfast, that's all."

"Yes, absolutely." Savina eyed it, wishing it was done.

"Who are you working for?" Aaron asked her. He was watching her closely for her reaction.

"Nobody," Savina told him. "I'm unemployed."

Aaron brushed dirt off his clothes, which were all black. Black short-sleeve shirt, black pants, black socks, black shoes. He even had a black belt. For the first time she noticed he was wearing a gun in a black holster. "What are you looking at?"

"You seem to like the color black. You ought to wear light colors in the summer, it's much cooler."

"Yeah, I suppose."

"Why do you think I'm working for somebody? You think I'm a spy or something?"

"That's what I was thinking."

"What are you doing that—No, forget I said that. I don't care."

Aaron eyed her silently.

Wiley came back with a tray of cups with a stand. He set it down in front of them and offered Savina the milk. There were plates, knives and forks, and napkins.

"Amazing, you brought civilization to the Depopulated Zone," Savina said.

"He's got to bring everything with him," Aaron grumbled, taking his coffee.

"Certain things are nice to have, being that we're stuck out in

"Been out here long?"

"Longer than I'd like to think about."

"Do you know if there's an abandoned college up north?"

Wiley's expression froze. He glanced at Aaron, then back to her.

Aaron said, "What about an abandoned college?"

"I'm supposed to meet someone there, but he didn't tell me where it was."

"Why didn't he tell you where it was?"

"He was, well . . . he was in a hurry."

"That's odd. That someone would tell you to meet them at an old broken-down college and not tell you where it was." Wiley sipped his milk.

"Who are you supposed to meet there?" Aaron asked.

"A guy named Danny Marauder."

"Marauder!"

"We know Marauder," Wiley told her. "Really short guy with a bald head?"

"No, this guy was tall and had red hair and a beard." She watched them as they glanced at each other again. "He was with a group of anarchists outside a euthanasia center. One was a woman named Evelyn Sunrunner. Do you know her?"

"This is too much," Aaron said. "You stay there, Savina. If you're some sort of police probe, you're getting yourself in a hell of a lot of trouble." He walked over to one of the tents.

"What's going on?" Savina asked Wiley.

"Don't worry. He's going to check on your story."

"You guys do know Danny, don't you?"

"Maybe. You haven't even tried your milk. Go ahead, try it. It's so much better than that mass-produced crap. *Smoother*. Go on, try it."

Savina took a sip. It had a funny, animal taste to it, but she thought that could be her imagination. It was actually very much like the milk she was used to, but heavier, smoother—just like he'd said. As she drank it down, Wiley pulled the rabbit off the spit and began carving servings.

Aaron appeared out of the tent and walked toward him. "She checks out. They want us to keep her with us for now."

"Really?" Wiley said, surprised.

"Who wants what?" Savina asked.

"I just talked to Sunrunner at the enclave. She wants me to tell you that she's glad you made it out here okay. She also thought you'd like to know that Danny got away from the police."

"You have a phone out here?"

"Yeah, in a way."

"Can I use it?"

"Uh, no," Wiley said. "Here, eat your breakfast." He handed her a plate.

"I want to get a message to someone," Savina said. "He helped me get away—I've got to at least let him know I'm okay."

Wiley looked at Aaron. "Can we send a message?"

"Give me the message and the number, and I can send it. But it's going to be anonymous, so make sure he'll know who it's from without you having to tell him."

"Just tell him I'm okay, that I'm doing okay, and I can't wait to see him again. He'll know who it's from." She gave Aaron the phone number, and Aaron went off to the tent to send it.

Savina devoured her food. When she was finished, they handed her a shovel and asked her to take a turn in the hole. She looked down into it, curious. It was about seven feet deep. "What am I digging for?" she asked.

"Anything that's not dirt," Aaron told her.

Savina shrugged, climbed down into the hole, and sent the blade inexpertly into the soil.

18. Hackers

IT'S THOSE WORDS AGAIN, DODD THOUGHT. HERE THEY COME. "ALMIGHTY Jesus, please help us in our time of need . . ." The words left his lips feeling hollow, like bubbles of vacuum. He was saying them in unison with Toby and his wife, their relatives, and a trainload of their church friends. Dodd said the words exactly the way everyone else said them, but the others sounded sincere to him, and he knew *he* was faking it.

Secrets and lies were foreign to Dodd; he was not skilled at handling them. He felt a niggling little guilt that told him he had betrayed his friend. It pestered him in the night when he was trying to sleep, it caused him to bang his head against walls when no one was around to see. Right above his hairline was a nasty bump caused by a moment when he'd almost convinced himself he'd done wrong. It wasn't successful, Dodd still didn't regret it—he wanted Savina to have her baby. But watching her father worry and suffer made it very hard on Dodd.

The prayer broke up after a silence, and it was time for more cookies and punch. Dodd, already up to his eyeballs in cookies and punch, excused himself to go to the rest room. Someone had beaten him to the downstairs one, so he went upstairs. When he was through, he stepped out into the hallway and into Savina's room to use her phone.

He dialed his home number and waited, wanting to make sure Sheila had eaten dinner. The phone rang and rang, and finally Dodd's house computer answered to take a message. Dodd dialed in an access code and got a computer menu, chose the option SNEAK A PEEK and activated the video pickup on the phone in his kitchen. The dinner he'd programmed for Sheila had been prepared and was sitting untouched in the warmer, drying out and hardening. He couldn't see the living room from any of the phones, but he could hear the Travels music. Dodd gave up, exited out of SNEAK A PEEK, and brought up the messages menu. **Messages: 00 Mail: 01**

He called the mail up onto the screen:

TO: **Dodd Corley**
FROM: **Some Humans**
DATE: **6/5/42**
SUBJECT: **Your Friend**

Someone wants you to know that she is okay, she's doing fine, and that she can't wait to see you again. You're supposed to know who she is.
Beware the Antichrist Al!

He cut the connection and blanked the screen. It would have been just wonderful if Toby had walked in and seen Savina's message. Dodd straightened up and stepped back from the phone. There was just enough light in the room to see the frills on the bed and young female knickknacks on little shelves and across Savina's desk. She gave up everything she knows, he thought. She did it. My God, how brave children can be.

Savina's not a child anymore, he thought. I'll be damned if I don't admire her. She made a decision and she stuck with it; she's doing something she believes in despite the entire world.

Dodd smiled. He felt better now. It was good to know he wasn't going through all this for nothing.

He left her room and walked downstairs. Another prayer was going on; they were praying for the soul of the boy Greg, the one who'd turned himself in for raping Savina. "... may the Lord be with him in his punishment, and guide him from wrong to right . . ."

Why did the kid turn himself in? Dodd wondered, standing on the side of the group and listening with what he hoped passed for a respectfully bowed head. Did he think it would help Savina? Didn't Savina tell her parents that she wasn't raped? That's right, she did. But Toby hadn't believed her.

Dodd frowned. Somebody's going to have to clue Toby in so that he drops the charges. But it can't be me, or he'll want to know how I know. What can I tell him? I can't tell him *anything*—as far as he knows, I only know what he's told me.

I'm guilty of aiding and abetting a fugitive. If Toby found out I helped Savina, he'd turn me in, press charges against me. Savina's going to have to be the one to convince Toby.

Several more prayers went by, and they all shared the Spirit of Jesus in song, everybody except Dodd, who felt left out. He ended up leaving before everyone else, excusing himself to go home to feed Sheila. Toby understood, and shook his hand at the door.

"I'm sure you're going to at least hear from her anytime now," Dodd said. "Have you been checking your messages or anything?"

"Constantly."

"Is that kid still scheduled for sentencing this week?"

"Yes. In a few days. We are pressing for the full penalty."

"All the way, huh?" Dodd said. He had intended on asking if Toby was considering being lenient on the boy.

"What's wrong? You don't think he deserves it, now?"

"He did turn himself in. I just thought that Jesus would want . . ."

"Jesus will send him to hell," Toby said vehemently. "What that boy did was a deadly sin."

Dodd nodded. "Yes. Well, I'll be praying that she comes back to you. Good night."

"And if you see your friend Marauder, you better have him get hold of me. I still think he helped Savina get away."

Dodd froze. "Danny said that girl wasn't Savina, and that Bob said something to her that pissed him off."

"I don't think so."

Dodd shrugged. "He's never lied to me."

Toby gave Dodd a strange, suspicious look, but let it drop. "Good night, Dodd. God be with you."

"And also with you." Dodd shook Toby's hand awkwardly and turned away, walking down to the sidewalk and turning toward home.

• • •

It was a hot afternoon, and Savina had been without a shower for days. No shower and no change of clothes . . . I bet I smell pretty ripe, she thought. So this is what it's like to be an anarchist. No, pardon me, a Mutualist. *Anarchist* is a term imposed upon us by others.

She grinned.

There was a nice spot along one of the canals not far away, with a shade tree and some bushes to provide a tiny bit of privacy. It was better than being naked out in the wide open. The water was beautiful, so clear and cool; it made her feel wonderful. The only problem was that the current was so strong she had to swim constantly to stay in one place. If she stopped for a moment, she was pulled dozens of yards downstream and had to swim like hell to get back to her clothes.

Swimming on her back, looking up at the large oak tree above her, she saw a branch hanging out over the canal that would be perfect to tie a rope to. If she had a rope hanging down, especially with a large loop at the end, she could put it over her arms and just lie there with the water rushing under her.

"Hello, Savina." It was a woman's voice. Savina looked over to the bushes and saw the tall Native American woman, Evelyn Sunrunner, standing with a large bundle in her hands. "I brought you some clothes."

Savina couldn't pull her gaze away from the woman's eyes. They were like magnets. "Uh, thanks," she muttered, forcing her eyes away. She swam to the edge and carefully pulled herself up the rough concrete.

"You're starting to get a little tummy," Evelyn said.

Savina looked down at herself. Her stomach was poking out a bit. "Wow, I hadn't noticed." She laughed. "There's not many mirrors out here, and I haven't tried to squeeze into a pair of pants for a while."

"Just wait until your last month," Evelyn said. She was smiling, too.

"Have you had children?"

"Oh, no. But I've got sisters upon sisters with children." She handed Savina the clothes. "I am just passing through, and I brought these for you. They're all real loose; they should fit you fine."

"Where are you going?"

"I have business to attend to."

"You can't stay a while? I've only got these two hackers to talk to, and half the time I can't understand what they're talking about."

"I'll be back before long. Then you can come with me. Oh, and by the way, Dodd got your message, and he's thinking about you. I have to go now. Take care, Savina."

"You talked to Dodd?" Savina was excited.

Evelyn shook her head, a half smile on her face as if Savina was missing something. "See you later," she said.

"Oh . . . okay. Bye."

Evelyn turned and walked away, back toward the city. You're a little bit strange, Savina thought, but I like you. As if she'd heard the thought, Evelyn turned and gave her one last smile and waved. There was something about the woman's eyes, but Savina couldn't pin it down. Power, she thought. Power eyes. It was almost as if they were lit up with electricity.

The woman disappeared among the oaks. Savina looked down at her new clothes, which were mostly denim. It all looked too heavy for this summer-afternoon heat—even standing in the shade with wet naked skin, Savina was burning up. She could imagine what she was going to feel like with a denim skirt and a vest over a thick cotton blouse. She spread the clothes out and found a long thin pullover dress and chose that, putting it on, hoping it wasn't see-through because she was not putting on anything else, except shoes. She gathered up her new wardrobe and made her way back to the camp.

Wiley saw her from down in the hole and came out, eyeing her. "I like it," he said, indicating the thin white dress.

"You can see right through it, can't you?"

"Wellllll . . . yes."

"No wonder you like it. I'll put on something else if it bothers you."

"Doesn't bother me at all."

Aaron poked his head out of the hole. "Whoa. Doesn't bother me either."

"Don't you guys get any ideas. I'm dressed like this because of the temperature of the air."

"I hope it goes up a few more degrees," Aaron mumbled, then disappeared back into the earth. Wiley was sitting on the edge, grinning at her.

"If you don't stop, I'm going to put something else on."

"I'll stop, I'll stop. Evelyn tells us you're pregnant."

Savina was ready to be angry. "I don't need you making any remarks about that."

"Oh, I'm not. I was just wondering why you didn't tell us. I hope the digging didn't hurt you or anything."

"No, just gave me sore arms."

"Well, you're not doing any more. If you want, you can pull out a cot and lie down here in the shade."

"Why? I'm not sick or anything, I'm just pregnant."

"You haven't been sick in the mornings?"

"Only a little. That doesn't happen to all women." There was a strange light coming out of the hole, flaring. It lit up Wiley's face from below, making him look like an old flat-film monster. Blue smoke drifted up in a plume. "What's that?" she asked, stepping forward.

"Just a laser."

Savina peered down into the hole, squinting. There was an exposed length of thick cable that looked like a black pipe a foot wide. They had clamped something on it where it was completely exposed, and it was pulling a pencil laser around the surface, cutting into it. "What's it doing?"

"Cutting off the insulation. We have to get to the fiber optics without damaging them, so the laser is only cutting down to the surface of the optics."

"Whose cable is that, anyway?"

"Remember, this is a secret."

"I'm one of you now, remember?"

"Oh, tell her, Wiley," Aaron said without looking up. He was facing the cable with a pair of goggles held up to his eyes.

Wiley looked down at him in amusement. "That was a one-hundred-eighty-degree turn of the heart there, Aaron."

"I like the way she looks in the dress," Aaron mumbled.

Wiley laughed.

Savina stared at Wiley for a few silent seconds. "Well? Are you going to tell me or not?"

"You can't tell anyone about this, Savina. It's very important that you don't tell anyone, not even your friend Dodd."

"I won't tell anyone at all. I'll forget the moment you tell it to me."

"Okay. This line down here," he said, pointing at it, "this is the secure line for data communications between La-La Land and Sacramento, owned by the United States Food and Materials Corporation. This is an A-one priority secure line."

"Oh, so you're going to sell stolen information."

"No. We're tapping into it because it's the line JTV uses to send backup information between their two big mainframe computers."

"JTV? Why are you guys interested in them?"

Aaron looked up, smiling evilly. "We're tapping their hot line to God." He and Wiley laughed.

Savina didn't know if she should believe them or not. Finally, she decided it didn't matter; if they weren't going to tell her the truth, that was fine with her. It had nothing to do with her anyway. "Are you tapped in now?" she said.

"No, we're just preparing it. If we tapped in now, they'd know it. If they catch us doing this, well, uh . . . we'd be in it up to our necks."

"Right to jail, huh?"

"Jail, nothing," Aaron said, looking up at her. "They'd just kill us and bury us in this hole."

She looked at Wiley. His expression was serious. "They'd kill you for this?"

Wiley nodded. "And you, too."

"JTV kills people?"

"No, Savina, not JTV. The USFMC—they control JTV."

Savina looked back and forth between them. They were serious. "How do you know all this?"

"Have you ever heard of CoGen?" Wiley said. "Your friend Dodd, if he was in the war like you say, with Danny, he'd have heard of it. It was the AI program that controlled the bombardment from orbit. Well, Aaron and I wrote the basic engine of that program, and Aaron designed a lot of the hardware."

"What does that have to do with any of this?"

"We know the USFMC computer network inside and out," Wiley said. "And we happen to know CoGen is still alive."

"Yeah," Aaron said, "but he's got a new job." The two of them found this very funny and laughed as Savina stared at them in bewilderment.

19. 230,000 Volts

THERE WERE TWO GROUPS OF ANARCHISTS AT THE EUTHANASIA CENTER that night, one coming and one going. It was like a shift change at work. Dodd had been watching them for fifteen minutes and hadn't seen a sign of Danny or anyone he'd ever seen with Danny. He was hoping to at least run into the Native American woman. The only woman in this group was thick and short, and looked mean.

Savina hadn't contacted her father at all yet, and Dodd hadn't received any more messages. That day at work he'd decided to come out here and try to get word to her about Greg. In the back of his mind, he was hoping he would get to see her. This didn't seem likely.

The anarchists had spotted him and knew he was watching; they gave the occasional suspicious glance, eyes betraying subdued hostility. This was not the way they usually reacted to people; it was like they suddenly had something to hide, like they had an enemy. You're not supposed to act like this, Dodd thought. Anarchists are friendly people who are disillusioned. You're out to save the world. Why are you paranoid now?

The slogan ran through his mind: *Beware the Antichrist Al!*

Is it this Second Coming? he wondered. Has that got them all upset? Well, it sure has knocked my world around.

The two groups lingered together, talking, then the off-shift abruptly walked away, heading west. Why are you waiting? Dodd asked himself. You're not afraid of them, are you? Dodd got up from the bench he'd been sitting on and crossed the street, wearing what he hoped was a friendly expression. He walked up to the group standing in front of the euthanasia center. To his surprise, they immediately surrounded him.

"Hey," he said. "Take it easy. I'm a friend of Danny Marauder."

"Who?" a tall blond kid asked him. He had a five o'clock shadow; his hair was thick and long, and a bit tangled. "We don't know any Danny Marauder."

"He looks like a Narco," said someone from behind Dodd.

"I'm not a policeman," Dodd said. "I'm a war vet, I drive a forklift. I'm just looking for a friend of mine who was here the other day."

"You mean he went in there?" the blond kid said, pointing toward the center's doors. "I don't think you'll be seeing him again!"

"No, he was out here. He's an anarchist. Come on, you guys know Danny Marauder."

"I'm afraid we don't, Narco."

"I just need to get a message to him."

"Can't help you."

Dodd turned around, trying to look in their eyes. They really had him surrounded. "Come on, one of you has to know him. He helped a girl named Savina get away from here Tuesday last week. I need Danny or someone to pass a message through to Savina."

"Do we look like mailmen?" one of them said.

"Yeah, Narco," said another. "Go use a terminal."

"Look, her parents are pressing charges against her boyfriend for rape, and if she can't at least call to convince her parents that he's innocent, he's going to remain in jail."

"The Narco thinks he's clever," said the blond kid.

"I told you, I'm not a—"

"Nobody but a Narco comes out to a euthanasia center to ask an anarchist a favor!" the kid shouted at him. He placed an odd emphasis on the word *anarchist*. Dodd cursed himself; he was using the wrong word.

"I'm sorry," he said. "My mistake. I'm not asking an *anarchist* for any favors. I am asking a Mutualist for a favor . . . please, get this message through." He looked the blond kid straight in the eyes, pleading with him. The kid's expression of aloof hostility didn't waver. He flexed his long muscles and made his shirt change shapes.

"Good-bye, Narco," the blond said.

"Listen, come on now——" Dodd was cut off as they rushed him.

He swung out in reflex but hit nothing. Two dozen hands had him, holding him tight, pulling him and pushing him along, his feet not touching the ground. It was a nightmare sensation, paralyzed by strong grips and moving along without walking, caught in an irresistible force. They twisted one arm to near breaking to stop his struggling. "Over here," he heard one of them say. They were taking him around the building, down the same alley where he'd found Savina. He saw the lid to the black Dumpster swing up, and then he was propelled up and down into reams of shredded paper. A lid slammed over his head. There was the slide-*clunk* sound of a bolt being thrown.

With a sense of unbelieving horror, Dodd realized they had locked him in the same trash Dumpster Savina had been hiding in over a week before. Locked in! He yelled in panic, pushing up on the lid, but the lid would only lift a few centimeters. "Hey! Hey wait! Goddamn you, listen to me! Come back here! Hey!" His yelling became more frantic, and his language deteriorated to the vilest curses he knew.

He stopped, regaining control of himself. All was silent. The group was gone. I'm in here for the night, he realized. Angry again, he began pounding on the side with his fists and kicking with his feet, banging it like a drum. After thirty minutes no one had heard him. He propped the lid open with wadded shreddings so that he could get some fresh air, then twisted about to make himself comfortable, thinking he might as well relax. All this, he thought, just because he was trying to do Savina's boyfriend, or ex-boyfriend, some kid he didn't even know, a favor. So much for bleeding hearts, he thought. So much for the brotherhood of man.

• • •

Using a faked Idex, Danny had shown up at the United States Food and Materials Corporation Annex in the heart of Sacramento and checked out a delivery truck. He was surprised by how easy it had been; he had thought this would be the hard part. Security was lax, depending too much upon software to detect things out of the ordinary. If I worked here things would be different, Danny thought, driving out of the Annex yard with a big grin on his face.

He drove to an old warehouse and backed the truck up to a loading dock. No one had paid any attention, not even thinking that the warehouse was abandoned and that the people loading the truck were "anarchists"—they were in costume, normal clean clothes—and no one even suspected that the large technical-looking piece of equipment they were loading was a hand-wrapped superconducting EMP cannon. It weighed about a ton and looked like an anonymous piece of factory equipment. Danny grinned.

He drove around all day, aimlessly wandering, then around quitting time for the boys and girls at the Annex he returned to check in the truck. He sweated, praying they didn't check in back. No, they didn't even think of it. They will from now on, Danny thought happily as he parked the truck in a space where the tail end more or less pointed toward the fifty-story USFMC building across the street. Hello, JTV, he thought. I've got a surprise for you.

There was no one in sight as he climbed out of the truck and hooked up the recharge cable. Not even the security AI would be able to see that the recharge connection had been rewired to send the current to the device inside. Regardless, Danny's heart was beating like a mad drummer, a beat-feet musician who'd had too much Mataphin. For a moment it felt like his heartbeats were ringing like pistol shots, *KaPow KaPow KaPow!* He opened the back of the truck just wide enough that he could crawl in. This, for sure, would cause a security AI to flash an indicator to some guard . . . if, of course, a security AI was watching him. Danny had seen no obvious video pickup within sight. He locked the door shut and waited.

No guards came.

He set the alarm on his watch and tried to get a few hours' sleep. Images drifted up to him, images that had haunted him for years. The deep purple flashes that he was never sure were actual light or just some strange afterimage of something he couldn't see . . . the ruined villages, the dead people, the dead animals, the dead trees, the dead ants stopped in their tracks at the entrance to their dead anthill. Danny remembered the propaganda and the real thing, and the difference between the two, which had twisted his soul out of shape, nearly killing it, forever crippling it.

Unlike Dodd, Danny had seen action. One firefight. The enemy had been armed with vintage Arabian machine guns that did nothing but jam. Danny and his sergeant had wiped out the entire enemy squad with five blasts from their rifles. One of the enemy, mortally wounded, managed to hit Danny in the arm with a rock.

It wasn't a world war. It wasn't even a war against nations. It was a bank action, a foreclosure on a loan. The entire South America Coalition, buried under the impossible debt owed to the world banks, had banded together and declared their debts null and void. The global economy collapsed. The United Nations were angry—the world as they knew it was ending. Strike back, they said. The world banks and corporations said, Foreclose! Repossess! Russia made verbal protests yet sent aid to American troops. International conglomerates acquired tracts of land equal in size to most European nations, including Russia's NCCTZ Corp., and all this made possible by the grace of America's Freedom of Business laws. For once everyone was working together to save humanity, but the price . . . No, they didn't acknowledge it, nobody acknowledged it, and nobody really knew except for those poor souls who'd actually been there when it happened, and for those poor souls to whom it had happened.

Danny dozed for a while, then his alarm went off. It was 10:00 P.M. He touched a button on the side, silencing it, then said good-

144   bye to it. He threw a switch, and the EMP cannon began a relatively low-power emission, warming itself up and conveniently scrambling all the security monitors within the Annex—or so Danny hoped. That's what they told him it should do, anyway. He unlocked the door and slid it open, jumping out and walking quickly across the yard to the Annex itself. There was a buzzing sound, and the large double-wide doors to the mechanics' garage were going *thud-thud* as the locks opened and closed to the beat of a EMP-affected circuit. Danny looked at his watch; it was flashing and scrolling a parade of garbage characters.

In his pocket he had a lockpick kit he didn't need. He waited for the door lock to thud open and pulled it up before it locked again. The door slid up into the wall, and Danny entered.

The recharge system for the delivery-truck fleet was to his left. It was little more than a large transformer hooked to the building's fusion generator. Danny quickly undid the wing nuts holding down the panel and shut the system down. A loop of heat-resistant superconducting cable hung around his neck; he removed it, cut it into a straight length, and then short-circuited the charge cable leading to his truck with main-line voltage straight from the fusion generator. He looked at the large switch that would send the current down the line, and thought, I'm not throwing that with my bare hands. He had to hurry because now that no power was going to the EMP cannon, some or all of the security monitors might be working. Somewhere in the distance he heard a bell ringing. He looked around the garage for a broom or anything that had a long wooden handle. There was nothing.

I can't throw that switch with my bare hands, he thought again.

Right beside him was a folding plastic chair. Yes, he thought, that will work. He folded it up and placed one leg against the switch, ready to push it down. He closed his eyes. He took deep breaths. When 230,000 volts arced down that line and hit that cannon, it was going to be one hell of a show.

He opened his eyes and checked to make sure the leg of the

chair was in firm position to push down on the switch. It was—all he had to was push down on the chair. Danny closed his eyes again, took a few more deep breaths. The bell was still ringing in the distance, and he thought he could make out shouting voices. He took another deep breath, and once more peeked to make sure the chair leg was positioned right. Christ, he thought, just do it. Just *do* it.

Okay. He put his free hand over his closed eyes. The chair was light in his other hand. He gripped it tightly, and pushed down.

There was lightning in the room. He saw it as a bright red flash through his hand and closed eyelids. The building rang, the metal bending and twisting. Plaster rained down on him in sudden darkness. He felt it hitting him and wondered what it was. He was dizzy and vaguely nauseated.

Danny wandered out of the garage in a daze, looking up into the night sky and seeing stars. All the yard lights were off. All the lights in the skyscraper across the street were off. The only lights in sight were the merry flames flickering up from the burning delivery truck. It was warped all out of shape, like a toy made from wet clay, bent, twisted, and compressed.

Danny was impressed.

Fighting his way out of the daze, he walked quickly, then broke into a run, heading for the inner fence, which, he hoped, was not electrified. He jumped, grabbed the edge at the top, and swung himself over, dropping to the ground on the other side. He landed on his left leg at a bad angle, and it collapsed under him. I'm not young anymore, Danny thought, landing on his butt. He sat there a moment, dealing with the pain.

The fence made a snapping, sizzling sound. Lights started blinking on. Danny stood up and fell back down again, half because of his leg and half because he was dizzy. He tried again, unconsciously reaching for the electric fence for support. Realizing what he was doing at the last moment, he pulled his hand back and let himself fall over again. Danny rolled away from the fence and tried one more time.

The shouting he'd been hearing was getting loud now. Danny made it to his feet and limped over to the outer wall, which was tall and made of brick. Running feet pounded the cement on the other side. Gates were being pulled open by hand, and men and women in uniform were rushing into the Annex yard. They headed for the fire equipment.

Trying to be inconspicuous, Danny jumped up and caught the edge of the brick wall, pulling himself up and peering over the edge. People were coming out of the building across the street like a swarm of mad bees. Danny pulled himself over, swinging down and hanging a moment before dropping. He landed on his good leg and started limping away.

A hand grabbed him by the arm. "Hold it!"

Danny suppressed his reflex to strike out. "There's a fire!" he said.

"What were you doing on the wall?" It was a uniformed security guard with dark features, frightened eyes.

"There's a fire! Listen, there's a fire, what do you want me to do, burn up?"

"A fire?"

"See the smoke! A fire!" Danny pointed.

"Oh, okay, sorry." The guard ran off to help fight the fire.

Danny limped away.

• • •

Wiley had his laptop sitting on his knees, screen open and displaying a page in the USFMC on-line distribution catalog. The page was titled: **Silicon Garbage Bags, Unit Prices and Sizes,** and had a list of figures below. Aaron and Savina sat on each side of him in folding chairs, watching the screen. They were silent, waiting. A moth flew around in the tent, banging again and again into their lantern.

"Would someone please kill that bug?" Wiley said.

Suddenly the screen on his little laptop computer filled with garbage: jumbled letters, numbers, and symbols with no pattern whatsoever. Wiley keyed a couple of times, and the screen cleared, then filled again.

"Is that here or there?" Aaron asked.

"It's not us. It's coming in over the link."

"That's it, then. He set it off."

"Okay, let's cut."

"What happened?" Savina asked. "What did Danny do?"

"He scrambled the Sacramento mainframe so that we can tap into the data line while they're too busy to notice." Wiley tapped on the laptop's keyboard. "Okay, your program is up, Aaron. It's now or naught."

"Now. Let's do it."

"Okay." Wiley set the program running.

Savina watched, waiting. Nothing seemed to be happening. "Is it working?"

"We don't know yet," Wiley said. "The tapper has to warm the optic cable to a certain temperature before it splices in. It has to warm up, cut through with the megalink, and bond itself without screwing up the alignment of the individual fibers. That's fifty thousand fibers at least. If just one of them gets so out of alignment that the megalink can't burn a channel through, they'll not only be able to tell their line is compromised, but they'll also know *exactly* where we are."

"In other words, if this doesn't work, we have to get out of here fast," Aaron told her.

"When will we know?" Savina asked.

Aaron glanced at Wiley. "Good question."

"Yeah," Wiley said. "And one we've been asking ourselves for quite some time now." He glanced at the screen and pointed out blinking words to Savina. "It's burning channels through now. This is going to take about ten minutes. JTV in LaLa Land is trying to reestablish contact with Sacramento, but Sacramento is down. If Sac goes back on-line before the megalink is done, they might know we're here. Or . . . they might think they're still having trouble because of Sac's problem."

"We want them to think the EMP blast in Sacramento was a terrorist attack," Aaron told her. "We don't know if they'll assume that or not."

Savina didn't ask what an EMP blast was—it sounded awful. "What else would they think it is?"

"A diversion, which it was."

"In which case," Wiley said, "they'll be looking for exactly this kind of thing."

"Oh." Savina was beginning to understand.

Minutes passed. Wiley, watching the screen, said, "Uh-oh."

"Sac's back?" Aaron said.

"Yes. They recovered fast. Our AI kicked in."

"You guys have an AI?" Savina asked.

"Small one, not conscious. It's for programming, mostly. Right now it's attempting to simulate an out-phasing."

"A what?"

"It's trying to convince LaLa and Sac that they're still having problems." He looked tense. So did Aaron.

"Savina, we've got a job for you," Aaron said. He motioned for her to follow.

They stepped outside the tent and walked by starlight to the truck. He opened the back hatch and rummaged around, pulling out a pair of military-grade spotters. He held them out to her by the strap.

Savina took them, put the strap around her neck. "What should I look for?"

"Anything. Anything that's coming toward us at all. Can you climb one of these oak trees?"

"Sure."

"Okay, be careful. Let us know if you see anything."

Savina nodded, and watched as he turned and walked toward the tent. He assumes I know how to use these, she thought, holding the spotters. Maybe it's because I didn't ask. She liked their feel; they were light and fit her grip. She turned them on and put them up to her eyes, looking toward the stars. The stars were so bright it was startling. The spotters began picking out the man-made objects it could identify, and locked in on certain ones so that even when her hands wavered, the image held true and steady. One image changed from a star to an oblong sliver object. Glowing letters identified it as an O'Neal cylinder. Jeez, she thought, this one's a lot more powerful than Dad's.

Savina climbed one of the bigger oaks near the tent, pulling herself up branch by branch until she was up near the top and clear of most of the leaves. Putting the spotters to her eyes, she looked to the north, toward Zone Sacramento. She saw a pretty view of distant lights, but nothing was coming at them. The lights sparkled and shimmered like candle flames.

She looked to the west, toward her home zone, and thought about Dodd. Somewhere out there amid all those lights was Dodd's apartment building. One of those lights was the streetlight on his corner. I'm sending you a psychic message, she thought. Can you hear me, Dodd? I hope so! I love you!

She smiled. Oh, the thoughts I've been thinking about you. You would be shocked!

She looked to the south, scanning slowly. The spotter picked out all moving objects with brackets, indicated the direction of travel and, occasionally, identified the actual object. Suddenly a whole cluster of objects flashed. It indicated they were coming dead-on.

Wiley called up to her. "You can come down now," he said happily. "The tap is complete, and they didn't notice a thing."

Savina told him about the lights. "There's five of them, and they're coming at over Mach four."

Wiley cursed and started yelling for Aaron. Savina continued to watch. In the enhanced view, she could see amazing details. A new readout in red stated ETA 00:03:47 and was counting down. She yelled out the new information, which agitated the two hackers even more. Aaron was starting up the truck as Wiley threw equipment into it. The engine sputtered and rattled for a moment, then settled down to a low rumble.

"Has it identified them?" Wiley yelled up.

"It says, 'CT-969 Military transport and four Spinner 522 wing-less fighters.'"

"Holy shit! Savina, get down here, we've got to be out of here now!"

Savina began her climb down. She was frightened, but there was no sense of panic. She grasped every limb and made every foothold secure, being careful, keeping in mind that a fall might not kill her but could easily abort her child. There was a tightness in her stomach and electricity running through her veins, and it felt good. Four Spinner fighters would be strafing this area and troops would be dropping by parachute, and she had less than three minutes to get away. I'm having fun, she thought. This is fun. She couldn't believe it.

She dropped from the last limb and landed lightly, then ran and jumped into the truck. The truck tore off to the west, heading for more cover. Two minutes later they pulled to the lee of a gutted house and stopped. Wiley took the spotters from Savina and jumped out.

"Are we safe here?" Savina asked.

"Not really," Aaron said. "They can track us by the warmth of our tire tracks. It's just that they'd be less likely to strafe an area this close to the city."

"I see 'em," Wiley said. "They're not slowing. They're not losing altitude."

"Are you sure?"

"I'm sure about *that*. Who knows what they plan on. They could drop a bomb for all we know."

"We're not out of range of a purple."

"They wouldn't drop a purple around here," Wiley said. "No way. All the damage to the crops? They wouldn't do it." He lowered the spotters, walking back to the truck. He was smiling.

"What?" Savina said.

"We're stupid. We're sitting on a straight line between LaLa Land and Sacramento. They passed right by, heading for Sacramento. We're paranoid idiots."

"Better than dead paranoid idiots," Aaron said, then laughed.

Wiley got back in. "Well, I guess we can celebrate now." He turned to Savina. "If you think it's okay for your little one, we'll pop a bottle of champagne."

"I think the baby could handle a little," Savina said. "Just a sip."

Aaron turned the truck around and they headed back.

• • •

There was a loud *clunk*, and Dodd awoke with a start. There was light, but all he could see was something black, and his eyes wouldn't focus on it. The black opened like a giant door, and Dodd was looking at blue sky. Orange punk-resurrection-style hair and an old, rough-hewn face eclipsed the sky, staring down at him.

"Get out of there!" the man yelled indignantly. He was dressed in a union janitor's jumpsuit.

"Uh, yeah," Dodd said, climbing out. His muscles were all stiff. He felt like he was dreaming. "Thank you," he muttered.

"I was about to throw a ton of trash in on you, you nut."

"Thanks again," Dodd said, to the janitor's disgust. He wandered away, searching for a phone to call in sick to work.

20. Last Day

THIS IS IT, SAUL WAS THINKING. THIS IS THE LAST DAY. HE HAD TO KEEP repeating it to himself.

Saul had the feeling he was spinning out of control. It was a strong physical sensation, almost strong enough for him to doubt his eyes, which were telling him he was traveling in a straight line. The ball rolled in front of him, bouncing grimly along, being controlled by his crew. They controlled his floating chair as well. I'd hate to think what would happen if I had to control it, he thought. I would send myself spinning into a tree.

A cable ran down from the socket in his skull to a fortune's worth of cephalic hardware on board the chair. His crew monitored the images being recorded. Just as people needed a waking life to inspire dreams, the Travels animator AIs had to have raw images to build the broadcast; Saul was using experimental techniques to raise the AHL in his raw images so that it would be superfuel for the AIs. More and more he found he had to do things himself. No one else had his talent.

I'm not spinning, he told himself firmly. I am not.

He was holding on to the arms of the flying chair with a death grip, his mouth set in a grimace. He was starting to hallucinate. Occasionally he would catch a glimpse of an enormous chasm off in the ocean, the water pouring down into mist . . . or it would be right on the other side of a grove of trees, a gaping red hole kilometers across. The breeze that tossed his thinning hair went unnoticed, along with the shout of the seagulls and the crash of

the ocean waves. He took slow, deep breaths, patient breaths. He   **153**
was sweating in streams.

He could see the edge of the chasm coming closer. He was
crawling toward it like an ant approaching the Grand Canyon. The
force of all his superiors at Telcron Systems was at his back, all
the board members and advertisers, all pushing him forward.
The ground at the edge of the chasm was suddenly crumbling at
his feet, he could feel it. He could look down and see it. There
was no way to avoid going over; he already *was* over. He reached
out and grabbed for something, anything . . . He caught the edge
and held on.

His crew watched the raw images with amazement. The
sphere was running along the edge of a bottomless canyon,
almost tumbling over . . . but not quite. An angled rock here, an
outcropping there . . . just when it looked like it was going over it
would bounce away. The AHL reading was high on the scale. What
an imagination Saul had! What a master of the Mataphin! Mes-
merized by the raw images coming in, they failed to hear his
mournful cries for help.

All that was left between him and the fall was one weak, tenuous grasp on the bare face of the rock. The drop spread out
underneath him vividly, all Arizona reds and grays, old sandstone
bluffs and arid sand. The sweat from his hand was making it slip-
pery.

Just do it, he thought. Push yourself off with a yell. Let go, let
yourself fly. Then you'll have all the weight of the push behind you.
Everything will be behind you. You can do it, just let yourself.
Come on, if you can let yourself go over then you can let yourself
do anything. Just do it. Just let go.

Saul held on anyway. He held on despite what he was telling
himself. One tenuous grasp held him, and he clung.

His crew watched as the AHL went up yet another digit.

Saul gripped his chair, kept his eyes open, and kept up his
slow, even breathing. This was killing him, he could feel it. The
chasm gaped like an open mouth ready to swallow him. He hung

on, desperate, knowing full well it was futile. How in the hell can I keep this up? he wondered.

Easy. Let go.

I'm just one person, damn it! How can I compete with Jesus Christ? How can I make His followers abandon Him? To them He is God! Who am I? I am a small and unhappy man who has burned his brain with drugs, who has produced mutant offspring, who has lost his wife to another woman—who has placed himself in a position where he must do something that he *cannot do*.

You *can* do it. You can do it if you let go.

I cannot!

You have no choice.

I will fight it to the end, he thought, and willed himself back over the lip of the chasm, back onto flat ground.

The Travels sphere went bouncing off away from the chasm, off onto a flat, featureless plain. The rolling slowed but did not stop; it rolled on, lost, tired. Saul's crew watched in dismay—the image had nothing to do with the reality, had nothing to do with the ball they were controlling for Saul's eyes. The AHL meter dropped to almost zero. Saul's eyes were closed; he'd fallen asleep.

"Saul? Saul?"

Saul opened his eyes. A voice was calling his name from the armrest. He touched a panel and said, "What?"

"Why don't we call it a day, Saul. We've got some fantastic material, best stuff anyone here's ever seen. We're all tired, and we know you must be. We're going on twelve hours now."

"No," Saul said. "No, not yet. Give me a minute, I'll get back on track." Just today, he told himself. I only have to get through today. This is the last day before Jesus comes; He'll be here tomorrow.

Saul pulled a Mataphin dispenser out of a pouch on his harness. Hold back, he told himself, and was proud that he only took two. He could feel himself spinning again, careening out of control toward the edge. He dug in, held on. Rocks fell away under his feet. It *can't* be Jesus, he told himself. The only reason I'm thinking He's real is because of the pressure. It's the pressure that's getting me.

There would be no pressure, his own voice said in his ear. There would be no pressure if you let go.

Shut up!

This time the crew heard it—his fearful, angry cry. They looked up, watching him sadly. After a moment they returned to their work, guiding the ball and Saul's chair, processing the raw images. The AHL began climbing again. Saul was back on track. It was amazing. They didn't know how he could do it. Those who really understood what it took to get images this dense from a human mind regarded him with a mixture of reverence and horror.

Finally, three hours after sunset, Saul and the crew finished. Now Saul had to take all they had produced back to Telcron and hover over the technicians and their computers while the animator AIs processed it for broadcast. By tomorrow it would be on the air, and Saul would know by noon whether or not he had accomplished his task.

21. First Day

DODD STEPPED OUTSIDE INTO THE MORNING AIR, STANDING IN FRONT OF THE door and letting it close behind him. He took a deep breath and faced the morning as if it were a thing in front of him to contemplate. Nothing down at the plant had led him to believe he had the day off, even if the Second Coming did occur. He had always worked alternating Sundays; it was part of his original contract. Unless Jesus Himself changed things, Dodd figured that would continue as always.

If Jesus really does come, he thought, today could be the end of the world. It made the day seem physically different to Dodd as he strode at his normal pace toward the subway terminal. The air around him seemed charged, as if there were going to be a lightning storm. The morning sunlight seemed different; the light was richer, more golden. Not a cloud was in sight.

The streets and walkways were much quieter than usual, even for a Sunday. There were only a few other people at the station, one a young woman. From behind she looked like Savina. She turned and glanced at him; she was older than he'd thought, at least in her mid-twenties. She smiled at him, then shyly turned away.

Dodd wondered about Savina. Where was she? Was she with Danny? Was she with the Native American woman? He hoped to God she was still okay. He hadn't heard anything since that anonymous message. He found himself missing her.

I hope your baby is beautiful and perfect, he thought. He tried to picture it in his mind, and for some reason it looked a little like himself. On Savina's face was that big wide grin of hers, proud of the child, holding it casually, then looking up at Dodd.

Dodd quickly put that out of his mind, thinking of something else.

While waiting for the train, Dodd struck up a conversation with the woman who had reminded him of Savina. No, she told him, she wasn't sure she believed Jesus was coming back. It was too convenient, she said. It was all happening during a period where JTV's ratings had fallen to an all-time low.

"Where'd you hear that?" he asked.

"The Politico Network," she told him. Her voice was sweet and soft.

Dodd nodded, his expression thoughtful. "Do you ever watch Travels?"

"No."

"Have you ever?"

The woman shook her head. By her expression it seemed she considered Travels beneath her. "I hardly ever watch television," she said. "I read. And if I do watch television, it's either the free speech program on Politico, or some of their editorial hours, or pornography on one of the broadcast networks." With the last comment came a teasing smile; then she was off, her train had come, and she stepped aboard and it rushed away.

Dodd looked around, his hands in his pockets. He was now the only one in the subway station. That had never happened to him before, not even on the rare occasions when he was getting off the train in the middle of the night. When his train came hissing out of the tunnel, Dodd was startled. It buzzed to a halt in front of him, and he stared at it with no desire to get on. The doors slid open, beckoning.

I could call in sick again, Dodd thought. I can just go home and call in sick. But then I'd have to fight with Sheila to gain control of the television . . . Hell, I'd rather go to work.

The doors remained open, waiting. They would close any second. He had to make a decision. He thought that he could go somewhere other than his apartment and watch the Second Coming, but that thought made him mad. He told himself that he was *not* going to miss a day at work just so he could watch a goddamn TV show. He put one foot forward, followed by the other, forcing himself to enter the subway car. The doors closed right after he got on, as if they'd been waiting specifically for him. The train hissed and made a clicking sound. It smelled freshly cleaned, even antiseptic. Dodd looked up and down the car, not knowing what to think. He was the only one aboard. With a gentle nudge, it began moving, gaining velocity, rushing on out of the empty station and into the black of the tunnel. Dodd had an eerie feeling that he shouldn't have boarded.

He walked slowly down the blue-carpeted aisle to the rear end of the car and peered through the glass doors into the next. It, too, was empty. He opened the separating doors and stepped through, hearing for a moment the outside rush of air. He walked swiftly though the next car to the trailing end and peered through the glass doors into the last car on the train.

Empty.

Nervous, Dodd made his way forward, going from car to car, until he was in the front right behind the robot engine. He was the only person on the train. The only one. That had never happened to him in a lifetime of riding the subway.

There was a long, low beep over the loudspeakers, and the onboard computer announced the next stop. Holding on to the railing as it decelerated, Dodd watched the windows, looking for something, anything. The red-tiled station slid into view. The train came to a stop and opened its doors. Dodd could see no one in the station, and no one boarded the train.

Nobody is out there, he thought, amazed. Bits and pieces of his King James Bible came to him, and he fought it because it scared him. The Rapture. The Rapture, which was not included in the United Church Bible, but here it was. The Rapture which took all those who were faithful to God away from the Earth to spare them from what was to follow. They would disappear into thin air, and then the world would end. The Earth would stop turning, the sun would be blotted from the sky. The stars would fall from the heavens. The air would turn to poison. Those left behind would suffer beyond their worst nightmares until God came to judge them.

It's happening, Dodd thought. It's really happening.

And I'm still here.

There was a hissing and a click as the train doors closed. The train pulled out of the station and back into the darkness of the tunnel. Dodd looked away from the window. He felt like he was living a nightmare. I shouldn't have gotten on this train, he thought. Somehow I failed God. I went to work instead of watching for Him to arrive . . .

Dodd made his hands into fists, clenching them tightly. I'm working myself into a hysteria, he thought. Why should God care if we don't sit around watching for Him on TV? Jesus isn't going to arrive until noon, anyway. But according to the King James, those who would be Raptured would be gone *before* Jesus returns. So, then, what happened to those sitting around waiting for Him to appear? Were they already gone? If so, who would see him arrive?

No, this is dumb, he thought. Dumb! Nobody is on the train because everybody is at home watching JTV. They're all staying home. That must be it! This Rapture stuff is nonsense; it's not real.

Regardless of what he told himself, Dodd was frightened. Being the only person on a normally crowded subway train would be enough to unnerve most people all by itself, but on the day of the Second Coming, it seemed especially weird. Dodd was so used to standing on the subway that—despite having a whole train to himself—he was still standing, holding on to the rail.

At the next stop Dodd was relieved to see several people on the platform. A few boarded his train. One, a woman with curly gray hair and a puffy face, stepped into Dodd's car. The way he was staring at her must have made her nervous; she looked away from him and took a seat at the far end of the train. This doesn't prove anything, Dodd thought. These people, like me, could be Left Behind. This doesn't prove there wasn't a Rapture. Not to me. Not while I've got the goddamned idea in my head.

The world was not the same that day. Whether the Second Coming was real or not, the world was different. JTV had created an illusion with its announcement, made it vivid with publicity, penetrating and infecting the world with it—and now Dodd no longer knew what was real.

When he reached the Honda Aerospace plant he saw a vast, empty, unmoving space beyond the chain-link fence. A notice attached to the main gates announced that since so many of the employees had called in sick or had simply not shown up, they had closed down the plant for the day. In the yard, even the autonomic machinery was silent. It was as quiet as a graveyard. Dodd turned away, shuddering, and walked back toward the subway station.

Now what, he thought. I don't want to go home. I don't want to go to Toby's, either. It was hard for him to face Toby anymore. The whole thing about Savina, and about Savina's boyfriend going to prison . . . Dodd just couldn't handle it. Not that day.

Dodd reached the railing around the entrance to the subway and stopped, leaning against it. The morning was so alien, it was getting to him. He felt sick to his stomach, and he kept getting the impulse to cry. It's my nerves, he thought. The things running through my head. Second Coming, the End of the World, Beware the Antichrist AI, the Rapture, the Rapture, and you've been left behind . . .

He reentered the subway station and boarded the first train that came in. It had four people on it, and none of them seemed to want to talk. Dodd rode, not caring where he was going, and got off at a stop that was near Bob Recent's place. It was perfect; he could talk to Bob about this—he found himself really wanting to see Bob and Denise. Dodd stepped on the moving walkway that brought him into the enormous complex and rode until he reached Bob's building. Bob and Denise had a penthouse up at the top, a place much nicer than Dodd's. Dodd could have afforded such an apartment had he not been saving for a kid.

It seemed to take forever to get to the top floor. The elevator was done in pastel plastics, very nicely textured and void of graffiti. The carpet was short but soft—barefoot carpet—it continued out of the elevator, the same color. Dodd watched it pass under his feet as he stepped out and walked down the hall to the Recents' door. Here and there were crushed streaks where heavy robots regularly trod.

Dodd reached the door and pressed the button, smiling up at the Recents' electric eye and waiting for their computer to announce his presence. He waited a full minute, and then pressed the button again. What, he thought, is it broken? He pushed again, waiting.

They're gone, he thought. They're Raptured.

He pushed the button again and added a loud rap on the door. Raptured my ass, he thought, they're watching Travels. He pressed his ear to the door, listening carefully. It seemed to be ... yes, it was. Racing, sparkling music, the Travels sound track. They had Travels on and were so deep into it that they couldn't hear the door. A wave of anger rose through Dodd, and he pushed down hard on the doorbell button, kept ringing it over and over, and then began pounding very hard on the door with his fist, thumping it like a drum. Then he kicked it, yelling.

No response.

He kicked at the door a few more times, scuffing the textured pastel surface with the steel toes of his work boots. All in vain. Bob and Denise were trapped in the world of Travels, just like Sheila, and they were not coming out. Dodd tried the door latch, but found it firmly locked. Had there been an exposed window, he would have broken it. Finally, he gave up. He stormed back to the elevator and pushed the down button, standing and waiting.

Where *now*? he thought. He still didn't want to go home or over to Toby's. Then an idea struck him. Why not go to a church? Surely they'd have a TV turned on, and he could watch the Second

Coming. Why not? It was as good a time as any to start going to church.

Still, deep inside he was terrified that no one would be there. He kept having wild thoughts about the Rapture, which was the real reason he didn't want to stop by Toby's house—he was certain that Toby and his wife would be gone, vanished. If he'd found Toby's house empty, it would be too much to take.

Stepping into the empty elevator and watching the door close behind him, Dodd felt utter loneliness. The sinking feeling as the elevator descended matched the feeling inside of him. Where I really want to be, he thought, is with Savina.

"Yeah," he said aloud in the empty elevator, "I'm a dirty old man."

The elevator continued to sink.

22. Coverage 1

ON THE SUNDAY OF THE SECOND COMING, THERE WAS AN AVERAGE OF twenty-four thirty-second advertising spots per hour on JTV, with an average price of 1.5 million dollars per second. All the advertising time was bought and paid for in advance, some at an even higher price as the last few spots were auctioned off to the highest bidders. On this one Sunday, the network stood to make more profit than during its previous five operating years combined. All in all it was a very good day for the network.

One commercial, sponsored by the Off-World Immigration Commission, costing 45 million to make and 90 million to air, showed wholesome and happy people working and playing among awesomely imaged panoramas of alien landscapes; great virgin forests of autumn-leafed trees, green-green-hued hills towering over a small and open settlement; and, prominent in the last shot, taking the fullest advantage of television's 3-D effect, a large sprawling United Church temple set behind an ultramodern VTOL orbital shuttle. The temple had a sixty-foot brass cross planted in its courtyard, supporting a handsome transparent figure of Jesus hanging in glory. Underneath the cross was the inscription:

HE IS RISEN. HE IS EVERYWHERE.

The commercial faded to blackness. The blackness lasted perhaps two seconds, then a pair of JTV newscasters appeared on the screen, their expressions excited, their eyes wide and sparkling. Both were almost unisexual, but upon closer inspection one could be seen to be a woman; she had breasts pressed flat under a plain white shirt, and her hair was slightly longer than her companion's. Her voice was low but feminine, while the man's voice was high but well modulated. They were both designed to appeal to male and female viewers, hetero- or homosexual. It didn't matter; the two were so neutral they couldn't offend anybody.

"We have the Good News," the man said.

"Our Lord Jesus Christ is arriving," the woman said. "The moment we have been waiting for is here."

"Exactly three minutes ago, a visual anomaly was spotted in space above Jerusalem by Alan Soigne, United Space Workers Union member and also a Saved Christian." The male newscaster smiled. "Telescopes aboard the InterStel Corporation shuttle *Mary Lee* were turned upon the anomaly, and it was determined to be an unexplained optical distortion above the atmosphere. About a minute ago, a bright light and figures were sighted within the optical distortion."

The female newscaster smiled. "For live coverage we now turn you over to Norman Shire at the JTV bureau in Jerusalem."

On the screen in sharp 3-D detail appeared bright lights and moving dots, all within an odd-looking setting of wispy clouds. It was confusing at first; there was nothing to look at for a sense of perspective. Then the scene pulled back to reveal stars and the blue-and-white crescent of Earth.

"What you are looking at," said Norman Shire in a heavy, authoritative voice, "is a live picture being sent down directly from the InterStel Corporation shuttle *Mary Lee*. What it looks like—and Reverend Juan Krishni here with me in the studio agrees—is an actual opening in the fabric of space. A dimensional warp, I might say, as in what is created by faster-than-light spacecraft."

"It looks very much like a hyperspatial hole, yes indeed," added a quavering, excited voice.

"That was the Reverend," Shire's voice said. "He and I are

here in the Jerusalem studio, as I've said, watching this spectacular shot beamed down to us from orbit. Can you make anything out of this, Reverend?"

"No, not as yet," the Reverend said. He had a slight East Indian accent. "I don't really, I mean . . . I have no way to know what those moving things are, though I would hazard a guess that they might actually be, um . . ."

"Could they be angels, Reverend?"

"Oh, yes, they very well could be. Did I say that right? Well-could-be? Could-well-be? I guess that's right. They could be angels."

There was a moment of silence, then Norman Shire's voice muttered: "I wish we could get a better close-up. Hmmm. Oh, hold on . . ." He paused. "I've just been informed that the *Mary Lee* is maneuvering closer, but the pilot is anxious . . . They don't want to take the shuttle too close."

"They do seem to be getting closer."

"Ah, they're zooming in again . . ."

The lights and mist grew bigger on the screen, filling it so that the Earth and stars were no longer visible. Thin as it was, the mist glowed with its own light. The bright white lights that showed through seemed to be from a long, long ways away. After staring at it a long time, the illusion of an opening in space became clear; the inside of the opening was solid white. The moving figures were just on the verge of being recognizable shapes; they clustered around this opening, moving in patterns that suggested playfulness. The view shook violently for a moment, then stabilized.

The Reverend chuckled, his voice giddy with excitement. "What was that? Somebody bump the camera?"

"I . . . no, I've just been told that that was a jolt from the *Mary Lee*'s thrusters. They're maneuvering to within four kilometers."

"Praise the Lord!" the Reverend said, delightedly.

Norman Shire dutifully echoed him.

The scene, as it stood, looked a bit like gnats swarming in slow motion around a porch light. It changed very little over the next few minutes, and finally the space shots were replaced by two figures in the small studio; Norman Shire, a thick-bodied, square-shouldered man with a large, handsome grin, and the Reverend Juan Krishni, smaller in stature, a ruddy timeworn face, graying hair, and squinting eyes; both sat together in front of a blue studio desk decorated with a simple brass cross and the insignia of JTV. There were wireless earphones sticking out of their ears. "Since we have a pause in the action," Shire was saying, "we're going to take a very quick break. But we'll be right back, here on this historic, glorious Sunday."

The commercials flashed past, most of them only five- and ten-second spots. One, a commercial featuring two healthy, wholesome church members, showed them drinking brightly colored PTL Cola with great relish and obvious sexual satisfaction; this commercial was played twice in succession, probably for effect. A moment later the cola commercials were forgotten, leaving only a sudden thirst in their passing.

Norman Shire's swarthy and well-groomed features flashed back on the screen. As he gave a summary of what had happened so far, the view pulled back to include the Reverend and another man, thin and pale with big eyes and blond hair. Shire announced: "This is Gary DeLeon, technical adviser from the stel . . . sorry, I mean InterStel . . . corporation, whose ship is sending us back live pictures from space. He's joined us to give us an insider's viewpoint as to what is taking place aboard the *Mary Lee*, in orbit above Jerusalem."

"Well, the ship isn't really in orbit," Gary DeLeon said. "It's having a difficult time right now because its having to maintain a stationary position above Jerusalem at an altitude far too low for a geosynchronous orbit . . ." As the technician went on and on about details concerning the shuttle's maneuvering problems, the view switched back to outer space. The lights and the moving figures were closer than before, the white hole filling most of the screen. The swarming figures had become definite shapes; tiny humanoids with spread white wings, soaring about in effortless, lazy circles. Some appeared to be chasing each other. Reverend Krishni broke in and remarked upon this excitedly, then began to mumble a happy prayer.

"Those *are* angels," Shire's voice breathed. "I can't possibly think of what else they might be."

"Oh, this *is* a glorious day!" the Reverend exclaimed in his quavering voice. "Praise the Lord! Praise-the-Lord!"

Shire and DeLeon echoed him dutifully.

● ● ●

After another break for commercials, the view returned to the scene from space, with angels darting around at a comparatively intimate distance. Details could now be seen: Most of the angels were unmistakably children; they were the ones chasing each other. Most appeared to be nude. Other angels, however, were clothed in full, flowing gowns; they were bigger in size, more calm in their flight—probably adults. They caressed each other as they passed, flying with a grace that was hypnotizing to watch. So far Christ was not visible, or at least He was not distinguishable from His angels.

The scene continued for several minutes, with occasional comments from Shire or the Reverend. Then there was another commercial break, featuring an airline company offering low fares on round-trip flights to the Holy Land. When the break was over the scene had not changed, and Shire announced something about the Pope of the United Church having called to say he was watching and that the view from space was "spectacular."

"It certainly is!" the Reverend Krishni agreed.

Moments later something new happened: All the angels spread away from the bright hole in a rush, a few coming quite close to the *Mary Lee*. Then the brightness of the hole intensified, and Shire and the Reverend babbled excitedly as a stream of billowing mist came spewing out of the hole and went drifting down toward Earth. The angels, swooping and spiraling, followed closely behind and to the sides. The mist moved in a dreamlike fashion, with wispy tendrils reaching out before it, curling at the ends, and falling behind as new tendrils shot out. Behind it the hole faded and dissipated like smoke.

"Jesus is descending!" Shire was shouting, overpowering the sound pickups. "Jesus *is* descending!" Beneath the wild sound of his voice, the Reverend could be heard praying under his breath, praising the Lord, almost chanting in his ecstasy.

The picture jerked as the *Mary Lee* maneuvered to follow. The descending stream of mist appeared to be nothing more than a blob against the colorful Earth, the angels too far away to be seen. After about ten minutes, the scene switched to a ground view, looking up, showing blue sky. Burning in the sky, right in the center of the screen, was a blotch of bright light.

". . . this is a shot from right up on the studio roof," Shire was saying, "happening right now, at this very moment. This is, I'm . . . I mean . . ." He trailed off, pausing a moment. "You'll have to excuse me, brothers and sisters, if I keep stumbling over what I'm trying to say. I am literally speechless. This is, this . . . I can't believe I'm here, alive on Earth today, to see this . . . This is undoubtedly the greatest moment in over two thousand years of history. Our God, our Savior, has returned to us . . . is descending before our eyes . . . and I, and I can't . . ."

The view continued showing a bright blotch in the sky. It grew a little in size but that was all. For thirty seconds the view switched back to the *Mary Lee*, still maneuvering in space. Then, shaking a little, the view from below returned to the screen. The scene stabilized, and something else could be seen. A small black dot to the side.

"That's our JTV air launch up there," Shire was saying, having gotten himself under control. "Hopefully, with luck, we will soon be getting live pictures from it. I've been told, however, that at this point the view up there isn't much better."

"How far up is that vehicle?" asked DeLeon, the InterStel technician.

"I have no idea. I have been told, though, that we have a new high-tech air launch on its way—we'll be getting pictures from that, as well." As Shire spoke, the view switched to show him sitting in the studio. His hair had somehow gotten messy. "Until then, as long as the view remains as it is, we're going to take a very brief time-out for a commercial break."

Seven full minutes of commercials blurred past, pacing so quickly and holding attention so intensely that after they were all over it was hard to remember having seen them at all. Then the program continued with shaky pictures from the JTV air launch. The bright blotch had resolved into a large cottony cloud, billowing downward, surrounded by dim pinprick flashes of light.

The scene switched to a closer, more stable view; the dim flashes turned out to be sunlight glaring off the ultrawhite angels' wings as they soared and banked in the air. "Ah, this . . . this is the view from the Mercedes 4000A air launch, graciously provided by Mercedes Aerospace for today's fantastic event." Shire cleared his throat.

"Those 4000As are really slick," the InterStel technician said in a low voice, a side comment to Shire. "Powered by a high-efficiency gravity engine, capable of going into low orbit—"

"Uh, yes."

"They're really safe."

"I'm sure they are . . ."

"We use 'em a lot out in the colonies—"

"Oh! Look!" shouted the Reverend.

23. Coverage 2

THE CAMERA ANGLE HAD SWUNG OVER TO A HORIZONTAL VIEW AS THE MER-
cedes 4000A matched altitude and velocity. The scene was
frightening in its visual intensity—it was taken from quite close,
with the frolicking angels swooping right up to the camera, filling
the screen with glowing, silky wings. They put the cloud into perspective; it was huge, at least fifteen kilometers across, with a
bright glare at the front. The camera zoomed in on this glare, filling the screen with white. Through it motion could be detected,
but no image could be found.

"That may be Him," Shire breathed reverently.

"Yes," the Reverend agreed, his voice humble. "Praise the
Lord. Praise Him. Praise Jesus . . ."

A coloration slowly formed in the glare, a long, stretched-out
rainbowlike effect, but not a rainbow. The view pulled back,
revealing the coloration to be spread in patches, trailing behind,
then dissipating.

The scene switched to the view from the JTV air launch, which
had pulled up level with the Mercedes. The Mercedes drifted in
and out of view: sleek, modern, gracefully sliding through the air.
The Mercedes Aerospace logo was clearly visible on the side.
Beyond was the billowing cloud, with the darting, soaring angels.

The scene switched back to the view from the Mercedes,
then, suddenly, to the view from the studio roof. The cloud, from
below, was round. Its bulk filled the sky.

". . . it's getting close," Shire was saying, "the cloud has blotted out the sun. We can see that though the windows here in the studio. The masses of people, the pilgrims filling the Holy City, are shouting out in excitement, in glory . . . There's a tone, a note, coming, coming out . . ."

"The angels!" the Reverend exclaimed. "It's the angels! They're singing!"

"Yes, they're singing!" Shire confirmed. "They're singing! Can we get that——? Are we picking that up for the TV audience?"

There was a loud thump, as if a microphone had been banged against something. The view, which was still from the roof, looking up, shook a little, then suddenly there was a single note, a distant pastel sound of thousands of choral voices all blending together on a single, heavenly note. It changed slowly, hypnotically. Shire's voice was shaking, muttering, "Beautiful . . . beautiful . . . I can't believe this is happening . . ." He was silent for a long moment—everyone was silent, all listening to the song of the angels—then Shire spoke again. He had regained his professional, modulated voice. "I've just been informed that the cloud is at four thousand meters and dropping, decelerating as it goes. Its speed, as tracked by the pilot of the Mercedes air launch, is approximately two hundred ten kilometers per hour, and slowing."

Nobody had much of anything to say after that, except for occasional cries of pleasure and awe. Masses of pilgrims began singing hymns as the cloud came down, obscuring the entire sky. The view shifted back up to the scene from the air; the angle was from above, looking down at the mist, the angels, and the pastel colors streaming from the bright glow. The scene was switched to the ground view, showing the glow and the cloud rushing visibly downward—suddenly it engulfed the camera and obscured everything in a thick mist, everything except the glow. The scene switched back to the Mercedes, which was hovering above the mist. The angels had vanished, perhaps into the mist.

"I can't see anything!" Reverend Krishni exclaimed. "Can you see anything, Norman?"

"No, I can't."

The singing of the pilgrims had grown to a fevered pitch; the angels had gone silent. The mist spread out and flattened like a cottony blanket over the Holy City, hiding everything. The glow had become golden, dimming in brightness, centering, and drawing in on itself. The mist thinned, becoming translucent. The golden glow continued drawing in upon itself until it solidified, a bright spot of golden light, then it, too, diffused, remaining only a golden tinge in the thinning mist.

There was a sudden, awesome silence.

The view switched to the camera on the roof; it was already in the process of zooming in. There was a golden temple where none had stood before, and on top of the temple stood a white-robed figure, a soft rainbow of light above its head. The flock of angels was nowhere to be seen.

"It's Him," Norman Shire breathed. "God is on Earth." Then he raised his voice and shouted it, his words tremulous and raw with emotion. "GOD IS ON EARTH!"

24. God on Earth

AFTER WATCHING THE JTV SPECTACULAR, THE FIRST THING THAT WENT
through Saul's mind—and he was proud of himself for this—was
that the sales of the Mercedes 4000A were going to go through the
roof. It was only after that, after his professional evaluation, that
Saul wondered: Was that real? Could they have faked that? All that
material?

I'm in the business, he thought. I *know* that can be faked.

But was it?

Was it?

Nobody had shown up to work except for a few apprentice
technicians, so Saul spent the day in the production lab preparing
the next day's Travels from previous stocks of raw images. He had
not done this part of the job for over seven years—four promo-
tions ago. But he fell back into the routine easily enough, working
with conscious AIs was like working with people who already knew
their jobs and just needed you to point them in a certain direction.

Throughout the day, in the back of his mind Saul hid the terrible thought that maybe God had really returned to Earth and that
he, Saul, was working against Him. It kept him on the edge, working in a fevered state—pushing him on with fear, keeping him
going so that he didn't have time to think about it, to consider the
possible consequences.

The AHL was turning out very tight, an insanely rich level. At
57.6 percent it was a full twenty-one points over the old standard,

which used to be considered impossible. It felt to Saul that he'd squeezed juices out of his brain to get it that high. The terrible thing was, he knew it could be higher. He knew he could make it much higher.

Thank God it's over, he thought.

Saul looked at his watch. Enough was enough. The AIs knew what they were doing, they could finish without him. Saul walked around and logged off all the terminals, shutting the monitors down, then locked the room and headed up to his office to relax for a few minutes and let the Mataphin wear off a bit.

His office was dark when he walked in; he could see a little red light glaring on his desk terminal. There was mail waiting for him. Saul turned on the lights and walked over to his desk, bothered by the silence that lay thick and heavy over the room. It was a lonely silence. He sat down with a sigh, keeping his head together, deliberating on whether or not to look at the mail. It could be good news, he thought, trying to be positive. Turning it on, Saul watched the screen light up and tapped a few keys. **Mail: 03** it read. He took a breath, hesitating, but then shrugged and called it up onto the screen.

TO: **Saul Kalman**
DATE: **6/15/42**
FROM: **Lisa Schemandle**
SUBJECT: **Shit**

Saul, I cannot take any of this anymore. The assassins I hired failed, those thieving bastards remain beyond my reach. I watched part of that goddamned program they launched against us and was amazed to find that I fucking believed it was actually happening. So I gave up. I made all my arrangements and turned in my resignation. You know, Saul, you're a damned dependable person. You're the only man I've ever liked.
—Lisa

JERRY J. DAVIS

TO: **Saul Kalman**
DATE: **6/15/42**
FROM: **Terry Liddy**
SUBJECT: **Lisa Schemandle**

Saul, I just received a notice from the Market Street euthanasia center that Lisa Schemandle had herself put to death this afternoon. I don't know what your relationship with her was but let me assure you that I share your shock and sense of loss. But, she must be replaced immediately, and, considering your apparent talent and the successful job you did keeping the ratings from slipping too far over today's crisis, I and the other members of the board unanimously agreed to give you the promotion, effective immediately. I'll be in your office tomorrow morning to go over things with you in detail.
—T. Liddy

TO: **Saul Kalman**
DATE: **6/15/42**
FROM: **Mirro Kalman**
SUBJECT: **Vicky**

Honey, something terrible has happened. Vicky's son was sentenced and we just found out that he elected euthanasia instead of prison. He's gone, he's been gone for days, and they hadn't even told Vicky, they just notified her ex. She's really torn up, and between this and that disturbing JTV broadcast we just can't handle it anymore. I've decided the best thing I can do for her is to take her on a little trip down south so she can take her mind off her son. Sorry to have to tell you like this, but we're going now and there seemed no other way to reach you. Hope you don't mind taking care of the kid. I love you. Bye.
xoxoxo
—Mirro

Saul stared at his wife's name at the bottom of her message, gazing at it a long time but not seeing it. The panic was rising inside him, the feeling of spinning, the feeling his feet were at the edge of the chasm. Without realizing what he was doing, Saul pulled his Mataphin dispenser out and emptied its entire contents into his hand. Twenty pills, twenty tiny orange tabs. Slowly, he raised them to his mouth, then flattened his tongue and used it as a shovel to scoop them in. In a moment they were gone, dry-swallowed. He sat there for a long time, his mind blank, staring at the terminal's screen. Then he reached out, took hold of the terminal, and began pushing it across the cold, smooth surface of his desk, pushing it toward the opposite edge.

No, he thought. No! I will not break an innocent piece of equipment. I will *not* kill the bearer of bad news. That is not done. That is not the kind of thing I do.

Oh my God, how much Mataphin did I *take*?

His own voice spoke to him from behind, like he was standing behind and to the side of himself. His voice was angry and impatient. It said: *You have the power to do anything you want to do. The power is within you. Let go. Let yourself do it.*

No!

Push the terminal off your desk.

No! Saul backed away from the desk, felt the chair catch and tilt backward, teetering. He was on the edge of the chasm. The chasm stretched on and on to either side of him, eternally widening, eternally deepening. Saul fought for balance, spinning his arms. The chair fell backward.

Saul was clinging to the edge of the chasm with a feeble, slipping grasp, his legs dangling into space. His office was gone. The chair had tumbled over the edge. It was still falling beneath him, turning end over end, deeper and deeper into the dull red shadows.

Just let go! he shouted at himself. Let go and it will go away. You will not fall.

Liar! Saul screamed, hanging on, gritting his teeth at the

agony; the bare rock was sliding from his hands, his body was swinging to and fro. The air was thick and humid, hard to breathe. Every time he sucked it in, it was like warm water flowing into his lungs.

I'm small, he thought. I'm helpless. Nothing I can do will change anything.

Let go! You can do absolutely anything if you let your goddamn self do it. Why are you torturing yourself? You jerk!

Above him the sky shone dingy white; he stared at it a long time before he realized it wasn't the sky. He focused his eyes on it and found it was only four meters above his head. It was the ceiling of his office; he was lying on the floor, the chair having tipped over. He pulled himself to a sitting position, grasping the edge of his desk; looking over, he realized he'd knocked his desk terminal onto the floor.

Dammit! he thought.

Saul got to his feet, feeling like he had gears and wires in his body instead of muscles. Every movement had to be calculated. Picking his left foot up carefully, he swung it forward and placed it back on the carpet. Shifting his weight, he followed with his right foot, moving slowly, making his way around the desk to pick up his terminal.

"Mr. Kalman, are you all right?"

Saul looked up. He was in the lobby of the building, facing a night-duty technician. She was about twenty-two years old, with long blond hair and, Saul noticed, sharply defined and gracefully pointed breasts. He stared at them a long moment, breathing quickly, feeling the lust swell up inside him. "I want you," he said to her.

She stared back at him without understanding. "What?"

"I want you," he said. "I want, I want to make love to you." Saul had difficulty getting the words out, he was so out of breath. It felt like he'd just run down twenty flights of stairs.

The woman took her time before answering. She finally said, "I'm married, Mr. Kalman. My wife and I have a child."

"Your *wife*?"

"I'm a lesbian."

Saul grabbed her by the shoulders and shoved her as hard as he could against the wall. Her head hit with a loud smack, but she was not stunned. She made a hard little ball out of her right hand and swung.

There was a flash of light, and Saul found himself on the floor, his head cradled desperately between his bent elbows. "I'm sorry," he said. "I'm sorry I'm sorry I'm sorry I'm sorry . . . I shouldn't . . . I'm sorry I shouldn't . . ."

The technician was gone. Saul was all alone. He sat up and looked around, confused. One of his eyes was puffy and sore.

It's happening again, he thought. My God, how much Mataphin did I take?

The DeTox! I have the DeTox! It's, it's in my car.

Saul stood up and started walking, but the gravity was too light; if he stepped too hard, he knew he'd bounce right up off the floor. He'd fall to the ceiling—he knew this, it seemed to have happened before. Every day, ever since the gravity had changed, Saul had been forced to walk cautiously or he'd fall forward, do a somersault in midair, and land on his back on the ceiling. There he'd lie, helpless, until someone noticed him hanging and helped peel him down.

Careful, he told himself. Step carefully. He noticed that horrible sensation, felt it start to happen. Easy! he thought. Slow down! But the giddy, helpless feeling welled up, and gravity just let go. He felt weightless for about two seconds, then there was a thud, and he was on his back, looking up at the carpeted floor and the lobby furniture and his pale, withered bare feet, which he'd somehow left behind.

No, he was looking down at his hands. They were resting on the table in front of him, beside a half cup of coffee. He'd been there for hours, drinking coffee, waiting for the drug to wear off. God, he thought, this is terrible. This is *terrible*. He moved his shaking right hand over and grabbed the cup, holding it carefully.

"Your Mercedes 4000A air launch has arrived," the waitress told him.

Saul looked up at the human waitress, startled. "What did you say?"

"I said, do you want me to warm up your coffee?" The dark-haired woman stood poised and ready to pour, holding the crystal pot above his cup.

"Oh," Saul said. "Oh, yes, thank you." He watched as she poured, admiring the way she did it, glad that this place still had human servers. Through the window of the restaurant, across the street, he saw the glowing red sign:

TELCRON SYSTEMS, INC.

He had never made it to his car, to the DeTox. He wondered if he ever would. God, he thought, this is going to be a *long* night.

Let go, he told himself.

"I beg your pardon?" the waitress said. "Let go of what?"

Saul looked up into the woman's eyes, which were a warm brown. "I don't know," he told her, feeling like a lost child. "I'm very high right now on a professional creativity stimulant. I've been under a great deal of strain, and I took too much. I don't know what I'm doing. There's some detoxification tablets in my car, but I can't get to them."

The waitress sighed. She glanced around somewhere behind Saul, then back at him. "Where's your car, sweets?"

"In the car park, across the street."

"I can have somebody go get them for you," she said.

"You'll also have to have somebody keep me here . . . I may try to wander off."

"Okay. Just don't get excited. I'll have Ted go get your pills."

A tall man with long curly hair stepped up to Saul's table and held out his hand; Saul gave him the keys and described the car. A moment later the same man was shaking him. Other people were standing around staring at him with alarmed expressions. The man gave him his keys back along with the DeTox dispenser. Quickly, before he could get lost again, Saul popped several of the little tablets into his mouth and swallowed them with lukewarm coffee.

The waitress refilled his cup. "Are you sure you should have taken that many?" she asked. There was a soft, genuine concern in her voice. It kindled a small, warm feeling somewhere inside him, a fire lost in a deep cavern.

"I need that many," he said. When he spoke, he realized his voice was hoarse and that his throat felt raw—it was as if he'd been screaming. The people who had been standing around and staring at him now turned away and resumed their places at their tables.

Saul turned the DeTox dispenser over in his hand, staring at the label with tired eyes. The dosage recommendations read: **Take 1 or 2 tabs as needed.** Underneath, in bold letters, it read:

Notice: Do <u>not</u> use Detox in conjunction with creativity stimulants such as Rhidalf*, Mataphin*, and Sulin-C*.
*Intensification of effect will occur.

Saul let out a cry of panic, dropping the dispenser. The restaurant vanished. He struggled, unable to breathe at all, feeling dizzy and weak and sick to his stomach. He was hanging limp and helpless over the endless chasm, tears streaking his face; he tried to resist, to pull himself back up, but it was no use. It was just too hard. He had slipped too far over the edge.

He gave up his feeble grasp and let himself fall painless and free into the warm, comforting gulf. The enormous weight was gone. The taut, heavy wires that had bound him were severed. The rules had been wiped away.

25. Sheila

DODD WISHED THAT DANNY MARAUDER WOULD STOP BY, OR THAT SAVINA would leave him another message. The Second Coming of Jesus had not brought Savina back to her family despite all Toby's prayers, the prayers of Toby's family, and the prayers of every single member of Toby's church. Dodd was getting very worried about her. He decided it was time to go by the euthanasia center again and see if he could find someone, anyone, who knew about Savina. He didn't care if it meant spending another night in the trash Dumpster.

Dodd was showering after coming home from work. Sheila, pale and thin, was in front of the TV and hadn't moved much from the position she'd been in when he'd left for work that morning. Four days had passed since Sunday, four days that Dodd had watched the world around him with suspicious glares and long, thoughtful looks. There had been no Rapture. There had been no terrible plague. The world had not, as yet, ended. Bob Recent still showed up late for work. Toby still prayed for his missing daughter. Sheila still lay comatose in front of the Travels sphere.

His shower finished, Dodd toweled himself off and walked down the hall to his bedroom, shutting the door to cut off the Travels music. He dressed in clean, nice clothes, deciding not to dress down to the anarchists. That last time he'd tried to imitate them, and that was probably the reason they'd taken him for a Narco.

When he was finished dressing, he used the bedroom phone and called Toby's house.

"Hello?" It was Toby's wife, her face filling the screen.

"Hi. I'm calling to see if you've heard anything about Savina."

"No, Dodd, we have not. But that boy who raped her, now, he's gone to euthanasia."

"What?"

"He's had himself put to sleep, and may Jesus have mercy on the boy."

"He went to the euthanasia center?"

"Yes, Dodd, he chose that over his sentence. I do feel bad for him, now. But we prayed for him, and now it's in God's hands."

"Yes, I guess it is. Well, I'm still praying for Savina. Good night, and tell Toby I called."

"Thank you, Dodd." She rang off.

He killed himself, Dodd thought. I can't believe it, the kid killed himself. He stood up, walked across the room, walked back. He felt frustrated. What was I supposed to do? he thought. Go to the police and turn myself in, and explain to them why I know the kid was innocent? I might have ended up in jail myself.

True. But maybe the kid would still be alive.

Did *I* tell him to commit himself to euthanasia? No. Did I tell him to turn himself in for rape when he was actually innocent? No. Then why do I feel so goddamn responsible?

Dodd abruptly decided he needed to take a walk. He opened the door and walked down the hall, past Sheila in the front room and out the front door. Dodd turned to look at her once before closing it. She looked like absolute hell, dark circles under her eyes as if she'd been punched, stringy hair, wrinkled clothes that she'd had on for days. Urine smell from the couch. Goddamn it, he thought. You're next. You're going to sit there and die.

Dodd stepped back inside, closing the door behind him. "Sheila!" he yelled. "SHEILA!!" She didn't respond.

Goddamn it, he thought. Goddamn it! If I want to go out and save somebody, here's somebody right here in front of me. Dodd walked over to her, standing in front of the TV and looking down at her. What a mess, he thought. You're a zombie. Dodd reached down and shook her violently. Her head lolled to one side, and her eyes closed. She had passed out.

Dodd took a step back, staring at her. Then he turned and went down the hall to the bathroom and started filling the large, round tub with water, using the temperature Sheila had preset for herself long ago. He put his hand into it, swirling it around; she liked it cooler than he did. Dodd contemplated the tub as it filled, then went into his bedroom, removed his clothes, and turned and walked naked out to the front room and turned the television off.

Getting Sheila's clothes off was a little difficult. It was a good thing she didn't wear too much clothing. He carried her limp, nude body into the bathroom and carefully stepped into the tub, then lowered her into the water. She stirred. He stroked her wet skin with a soapy washcloth, washing off her long legs, pelvis, and stomach. She was semiconscious when he reached her breasts, and made a low M sound, "mmmmmmmm . . ."

"Feels nice?" Dodd said.

"Mmmmmm-hmmmmmm."

"Sheila?"

"Hmmmmmm?"

"We have to have a serious discussion."

"Mmmm."

"You've been going days at a time without food."

"Mm."

"Aren't you hungry?"

"I'm hungry," she said vaguely. Her eyes flickered open, and she took a deep breath. "How did we get in here?" Her eyes closed again. "I don't remember . . . getting in . . ."

Dodd was rubbing his index fingers over her nipples. "Do you remember the last time you ate?"

"It was a few hours ago," she mumbled.

"It was a day and a half ago."

"No."

"Yes."

She didn't say anything. She was enjoying him rubbing her nipples. Dodd abruptly stopped. "Let's wash your hair," he said.

Later, when they were drying each other off, Dodd said, "I'm worried about you."

She blinked, glancing at him. It had registered in her mind, but she was still half-asleep. Her movements were clumsy, her voice vague. He continued drying her as she slowly dragged a brush through her hair. Her body was suffering; it was getting thin and sallow, and she'd developed a rash on her behind and between her legs. Dodd applied some MultiSpec cream on it, hoping that would do.

"Do you know why I'm worried about you?" he asked.

"No."

"Do you remember anything about Jesus returning?"

She stopped brushing in mid-stroke. "Yes."

"Do you?"

She looked at him uncertainly in the mirror. "It's in about a week, isn't it?"

"Try four days ago."

Her head jerked. She woke up! he thought.

"Four days ago?"

"Yes, four days ago. Do you understand why I'm worried?"

"Jesus didn't come four days ago. You're lying."

"I'm not lying. Go pull up a calendar. This is the nineteenth."

"No."

"I'm not lying, Sheila. You've been watching Travels all this time."

"No, that's . . . weeks."

"It has been weeks. Do you understand why I'm worried yet?"

"I don't believe you."

"Well, then, Sheila, go look for yourself. This is the Thursday *after* the Second Coming. You've been going days without food, you've been pissing and shitting in your pants . . . Sheila, you've got a problem. You're going to have to face it."

"I feel sick."

"You're starving."

"I am hungry-feeling. I don't have any energy."

"You're starving, Sheila. *Starving.*" He took the brush from her hand and finished brushing her hair for her, then took her robe off the back of the bathroom door and put it over her. "Let's go fix you something to eat, and we'll talk about it." He put on his own robe and led her out the door.

On their way to the kitchen, Sheila paused, looking into the living room at the blank TV screen. "No Travels right now, Sheila, you have to eat." She wordlessly followed Dodd into the kitchen and sat at the kitchen table. He started the robot arms going, then called the apartment manager's computer and ordered an automaid to come down to dry-clean the couch and gather laundry. Within a few minutes, Dodd had a simple, wholesome soup made. He served two bowls of it. He put one bowl in front of Sheila with a spoon and sat across from her with his own as she began hungrily slurping down the soup. She finished before he'd eaten a fourth of his, then got up and served herself some more.

The robot arrived and began cleaning. "What is the date, today?" he asked the robot.

"Today is Thursday, June nineteen, twenty-forty-two," it replied without pausing in its duties.

"Do you think I programmed the robot to say that?" he asked Sheila.

"No."

"Then you believe me."

She swallowed a spoonful of soup, and took another. "Yes," she said finally, "I believe you."

"Do you agree that there is a problem?"

She was silent, staring at a spot on the table in front of her.

"Look, Sheila, I don't want to do this, but I'm worried. I think there is a very big problem here. I've tried alerting you to it before, but you've either been ignoring it or you've been unable to understand it. I've decided I'm going to have to be tough with you. You're going to either have to face this, or you're going to have to get out of my life."

Sheila was still silent, but fear shone in her eyes. This gave Dodd some hope. "Do you understand what I'm telling you?" he said.

She nodded slowly. Her eyes were starting to tear up. "You think that, that, Travels . . . You think that Travels is doing something to me?"

"Yes, Sheila. I do. It affects me, too, if I sit down and watch it. Don't get me wrong, this isn't against *you*, this is against Travels. I'm going to fight Travels because I don't like what it's doing to *you*. Understand? And I want you to fight Travels, too, because if you don't, it won't matter shit what I do."

She was silent.

"I'm thinking about buying time on the Politico Network, on the *Free Speech Forum*, and telling the world about you—what Travels is doing to you. It can't be just you, there may be others. I'm going to fight it."

She remained silent. The fear still shone in her eyes.

"I have the day off tomorrow," he told her. "I'm going to stay home, and for once and for all, I'm having Travels disconnected from this apartment."

"You don't have to do that," she said. "I won't watch it."

"I won't watch it either, so I'm not going to pay for it."

"It, it doesn't hurt you if you, if you just watch it for a little while."

"There's no such thing as watching it for just a little while."

"I can set the timer on the TV to go off in an hour—"

"No Travels on this television," he said firmly. "Get that through your head. No more Travels. If you want to watch Travels, you move out, and you never come back."

She was crying openly into her soup. She was still holding the spoon awkwardly above the bowl, droplets of the soup running down the handle and onto her fingertips. She didn't notice. "I'm so fucked up," she said, sobbing. "I'm so fucked up over a television show."

"Yes, you are Sheila."

"I'm so fucked up . . ."

Dodd got up and walked around the table, kneeling beside her. "It's okay. You're realizing it, it's a big step toward fighting it."

"Oh, God," she sobbed. She put her arms around him, spoon still in hand, soup dripping down his back. They hugged, and he rocked her like a baby.

26. Unknown Armed Robotic Device

SAVINA LAY BELLY DOWN IN THE GRASS, AIMING THE LIGHTWEIGHT RIFLE AT nothing in particular. There was some sort of autonomic farm drone out in the field to the north, and Aaron had told her just to wait. It would scare rabbits out into a clearing, and that's when she could get them. "Look for big, rectangular-looking drones that hover about a meter over the crops," he'd told her. Well, this one looked like a long ovoid with spider legs, reminding her of an overlarge police drone. It was painted with a chameleon paint that shifted with its surroundings, and didn't seem to be doing anything in particular to the crops.

There was a little butterfly-wriggling sensation in her stomach. She didn't know if it was her baby or if the drone was giving her the creeps. As she watched, a few rabbits ran out of the crops and across the clearing in front of her. One came to a halt, sitting up, watching the drone. Savina centered the rabbit in the rifle's scope, putting the red dot of the laser right on its back; it wouldn't hold still, her hands were shaking. She couldn't do it, she just couldn't. Aaron's going to have to do the hunting, she thought. She lowered the rifle.

The drone came closer, and the rabbit ran again. Why would a farm machine have chameleon paint? she thought. She watched it hovering slowly over the ground, weaving to and fro. It moved out of the field and into the trees, heading south. It passed within twenty meters of her.

That's not farm equipment, she thought. It can't be. She

folded the gun barrel back into its stock, retracted the laser sight, and slipped its strap over her shoulder. I've got to get ahead of it, she thought. It's heading right for the camp.

Savina waited for it to pass out of sight among the trees, then raced across the clearing to where she could get more cover, then turned south, parallel with the thing. It had been moving at a fast walk; if she ran, she thought she could pass it and get to Wiley and Aaron with enough time to warn them.

Grasshoppers and swarms of bugs leaped for safety as she made her way through tall patches of grass, leaping fallen branches and dodging around rusted, old, barbed wire. The line of old foundations and thick hedge brush angled in on her, forcing her to veer a little to the east. She caught sight of the thing and dodged from one oak tree to the next, hoping it wouldn't see her. Savina had no idea what it was programmed to do, she didn't know what kind of senses it had or what would catch its attention. To be safe she had to avoid it altogether.

There was some clearing to the west, and she sprinted for the ruins there, keeping them between her and the drone. She tried to leap over a large patch of blackberry bushes, and it caught her feet, slamming her down into a nest of thorns. She had learned a whole new vocabulary of swearing and cursing from Wiley and Aaron; she used every single one of them as she hurriedly disentangled herself and continued on. By the time she reached camp, she had no idea how much of a lead she had on the drone. She stumbled into camp, startling the two hackers, and collapsed to her hands and knees, panting. "Drone," she said, forcing the words out between rasping breaths. "Large. Chameleon paint. Coming. This way."

"From where?" Aaron said.

"The north . . . Straight . . . Down the . . . Line."

"Dammit," Aaron said. "Dammit, this would have to happen now." He began breaking camp, tossing everything into the back of the truck.

Wiley started a shutdown procedure on the laptop computer

and set it on his folding chair, letting it run. He pulled everything out of their big tent and stuffed it in the truck, then took down the tent. Savina, recovering a bit from her run, helped him roll it and fold it into the small square that fit into a bag the size of her arm.

"We just located the line," he told her. "We just needed a few more hours."

"Think they detected you?"

"Maybe. They must have detected something. We've inserted a virus into their diagnostics, though—it's probably the only reason they didn't pinpoint us. If that drone is traveling the whole length of the line, it means they know something is up but not where it is. How far away was that thing?"

"I spotted it when I was about two kilometers up there. It's going to be here any minute."

"Shit! Okay, let's hustle."

"Your shutdown is finished," Aaron called.

"Okay. Let's just disconnect and cap the splice line. It's a good thing we buried the rest of it."

"They're going to find it."

"Maybe not." Wiley ran over to Aaron and took the capped end of the fiber-optic cable. "I'm going to lay it down like this," he said, pulling it along the ground, "and then arrange this stuff over it here. It's all inert, it shouldn't be detectable to a drone."

"Who knows? I'm going to start up the truck."

Savina finished up and threw the last few packs into the truck as Aaron started it. Wiley dragged fallen branches over the optic cable and ran to the truck, pushing Savina inside the passenger side and shutting the door. He hung on to the outside, standing on the running board. "Let's go," he said, and Aaron put the truck into gear, pulling out from under the trees and heading west. It was the same escape route they took the night Savina had spotted the planes. Two minutes later they were behind the lee of a gutted house, and Aaron stopped. Wiley stepped off the running board and went to the rear of the truck, opening the hatch and digging through the hastily packed equipment for a pair of spotters.

Savina found a pair at her feet and got out of the truck, walking around the ruin and peering back the way they had come. Wiley and Aaron were to either side of her a moment later, Wiley holding the other pair of spotters. "Is it there?" Aaron asked. "Did it stop?"

Savina saw the probe hovering under the trees, poking at the ground with what looked like a gray rod. The spotters attempted to identify it but failed. **Unknown Armed Robotic Device** spelled itself out in glowing letters above the bracketed image.

"It's scanning the ground where we pitched the tents," Wiley said.

"What is it? A police drone?"

"Worse," Wiley said. He didn't elaborate.

Impatient, Aaron took the pair of spotters away from Savina. "Oh shit," he said.

"What?"

"It's military," he told Savina. "Did it see you?"

"No, not that I know of."

"Good thing."

"It's found our tire tracks," Wiley said. "Looks like it's following them this way, doesn't it?"

"God, it does."

"At least it didn't find the splice." He lowered the glasses and walked back to the truck.

"I bet that thing has as much firepower as we do," Aaron said.

"We could probably destroy it." Wiley was digging in the back of the truck again, pulling out packs.

"You think we should?" Aaron said.

"No. We destroy it and we'll have MPs out here in killer-bee swarms. Same thing if they find that splice. We've located the channel they're backing up the AIs on, and its only a few hours until they do their evening backups. We could have what we came for by tonight."

"I'm listening," Aaron said.

"Why don't you take the truck and lead that thing off on a wild-goose chase, and Savina and I will circle back with a laptop and some MSDs and capture the data. From there we'll head toward the enclave, and you can catch up to us tomorrow."

"Along the perimeter?"

"Right down the old highway."

"Okay." Aaron lowered his spotters and walked around to the truck. "It's definitely following the tracks, and it's coming fast. I'd go off that way and get in one of those ruins if I were you." He climbed into the truck. "Got everything?"

Wiley handed Savina a heavy pack. "Yeah. Be careful."

"You too. See you tomorrow." Aaron put the truck in gear and sent it bouncing away through the grass.

Wiley ducked his head and disappeared into the brush to the west. Savina copied him and followed, wincing as branches scraped her arms and irritated scratches she'd already gotten from the blackberry bushes. They ducked and dodged brush and rubble for forty meters, then turned north and continued until they had a free line-of-sight angle from which they could watch the distant drone. It had stopped where Aaron had dropped them off, and was again prodding at the ground with its sensors.

"You don't think it'll follow us instead of Aaron, do you?" Wiley asked.

Savina gave him a strange look. "You're the expert, you tell me."

"In all honesty, I know nothing about that drone." Wiley raised his spotters and watched it. "It's definitely looking at our footprints. God knows what logic is guiding that thing. If it has anything to do with CoGen, there's a good chance it'll figure you and I are circling around."

"It would know?"

"Aaron and I put every stratagem known by man or beast into the thing." He lowered the spotters. "It's going after Aaron. We'll wait here for a little while until it's out of sight, then we'll haul ass back over to the camp."

"It's not part of CoGen, then."

"Who knows? Programs are copied and stored all over. AIs are built upon AIs by other AIs. Bits and pieces of code are scattered everywhere. But CoGen's strategy and deduction engine is the most ruthless thing you'll ever see. The heart of it is embedded in practically every security AI system the USFMC has."

"JTV is using it, too?"

"Yeah, in a big way." He hung the spotters over his shoulder by the strap, and said, "Let's go."

They made their way back to camp just before dusk, the sun sinking below the tree line. Birds were making a racket, settling in flocks looking for a place to spend the night. Wiley wordlessly handed Savina the spotters as he pulled the branches away from the optic cable and reconnected it to his laptop. He took the heavy pack from Savina and pulled out a thick connection, plugging it in next to the optic. The heavy pack was a group of mass-storage devices, or MSDs. Whatever Wiley hoped to capture from the data line would be stored in them.

Savina scanned the horizon for anything threatening with the spotters. Meanwhile the sun sank, and the stars became visible. Some planes crossed from north to south, but Savina ignored them; she wouldn't bother Wiley unless they were losing altitude.

Wiley called out, "I got you, you bastard!"

"We're finished? You got CoGen?"

"No, but my software has recognized part of his code. He's being backed up now. This will still take a while."

Savina stood behind him, staring over his shoulder at the laptop's softly glowing screen. It didn't tell her a thing. Savina walked away, scanning the horizon with the spotters.

The moon rose, and the night matured. That night there was a slight northern breeze. It was starting to get chilly. Savina was at the top of the crumbled mound that used to be a large building, sitting on a horizontal slab and shivering. All the heavy clothes Evelyn Sunrunner had given her were in the truck with Aaron. She was getting tired; the running and tension during the day had taken most of her energy, and she was starting to nod off. He's got

to be done by now, Savina thought. One more look around and I'll
go back down there.

The first place she looked was north, and brackets flashed
upon something dark and large. The spotters were accessing
their ROM database, and came up with **VTOL PK238 Troop Assault
Carrier**. Savina slid off the mound and tumbled down the rubble
pile, scrambling to her feet and running into the trees. "Wiley!"
she called, a loud whisper. "Wiley!"

"What?"

"Troop assault carrier! It's almost on top of us!"

They hid at the base of a large oak, right beside his laptop and
the optic cable leading into the ground. "If we stay low and still,
their scanners will only pick up the motion of our hearts," Wiley
whispered. "We'll look like small animals, and they won't pay any
attention."

Savina thought, I was in full view when I was on top of the rubble. They must have seen me run. She held on to Wiley in fear,
clinging and concentrating on controlling her breathing. Forcing
herself to remain still as stone. Wiley was hugging the ground like
it was his mother.

"They won't see the computer stuff, will they?" she whispered.

"Shhhh!"

Savina held her breath. The plane glided ominously into view.
It stood out like a shadow creature in the moonlight—long, dark,
hovering. It had wings but seemed to be flying way too slow for
them to be supporting it. There was a deep, deep throbbing that
pulsed through her body and resonated in the earth. Large, powerful gravity engines. It moved with a sureness and grace that was
frightening in itself. It passed them without slowing, then veered
to the west and rose just above the treetops. Savina felt Wiley
move as he turned his head to look at it.

"Damn," he said.

"What?"

"Aaron must have engaged that stupid drone. He was just

dying to, I could tell. He wants to be like Danny Marauder, and it's going to get him killed."

They stood up and brushed themselves off, getting rid of the clinging twigs and ants. Savina resumed her watch with the spotters, and Wiley resumed his monitoring of the data interception. A half hour later, Wiley announced that they were through. He disconnected and hid the optic cable. Hefting the packs, they headed west, looking for a suitable place to spend the rest of the night.

27. Toby

TOBY WHITEHOUSE FELT THE PRESSURE BUILDING IN HIS BLADDER, PUSHING its way out, but he grimaced and held it back, squirming in his seat. Jesus was on television delivering a sermon from the golden temple. His halo pulsated through wonderful pastel colors, swirling; his voice was soft but strong, causing tingles to run up and down Toby's back. "Praise Jesus," he was muttering. "Praise Jesus . . ."

". . . therefore I tell you," Jesus was saying, "it is good to worry about life, about what you eat and drink; about your body, what clothes to wear. What is life without good, nourishing food? What is your body without fine, tasteful clothes? Look at the birds in the air; do they not gather food and precious colored strings and pieces of cloth for their nests? It is important even to *them*. Are you not much more valuable than they? Who of you by being careless about life will truly enjoy the time your heavenly Father has given you?

"And why do some of you not worry about your clothes, your manner of dress? See how the flowers in the parks grow? They must be tended and maintained, or they will not come to blossom. It is this way for you; did not your Father give you a body to be tended, to be adorned? You are living in an age where even the lowliest of peasants can be adorned beyond the dreams of ancient kings! Our Father loves His children, He loves *you*, and He expects you to love yourself even as He loves you. Do not deprive yourself of things God has made available to you." Jesus paused a

"Praise, praise Jesus," Toby mumbled. "Praise you Jesus ..."

"Ask," Jesus said, "and it will be given to you; seek and you will find; knock and the door will be opened to you. For everyone in this society who asks receives; he who seeks finds; and to him who knocks, the door will be opened.

"Which of you, if his son asks for bread, will give him a stone? Or if he asks for a steak, will give him a serpent? If you, then, know how to give good gifts to your children, why don't you also include your friends? Asking for things and giving things is a way of your Father in heaven; it is blessed to give and receive, just as it is to get money and to spend money. Blessed is the person who spends as much as he receives! For it is written: In everything, do for others as you would have others do for you ..."

Toby leaned far forward, trying to listen, trying to concentrate, but the pressure in his bladder was becoming painful. He wriggled in his chair, denying himself, breathing with difficulty. "Amen," he mumbled in automatic response to something Jesus was saying. Jesus expressed himself with gentle, sweeping gestures of his arms, always all-encompassing. Every time He did so Toby felt a wave of pleasure, felt himself being personally included in what Jesus was saying. "Praise God," Toby mumbled. "Praise Jesus."

"... not store up for yourselves treasures in your home where moth and rust destroy, and where anarchists break in and steal. But store up for yourselves treasures in banks, where moth and rust do not destroy, and where anarchists cannot break in and steal. For where your treasure is, your heart will be also ..." As Jesus continued, His halo swirled and changed shape, becoming broader and more intensified; the colors deepened to neon intensity. "... but I tell you who hear me: Love your government and Leader, do good to those who govern you, bless those who tax you, pray for those who build for you, who guide your traffic and run your transit. If the government strikes you on one cheek, turn it the other also. If the government takes your money, do not try to stop it from taking more. Give to every cause that is legally sanctioned, and if they request something that belongs to you, do not demand it back. Do for the government as you would have it do for you. This is most wise, for you *are* the government." Jesus gave the camera a large, warm smile, his eyes full of compassion, then continued. "My children, for those of you who cannot cope, for those of you who find it's just too much . . ."

Toby blinked, trying to focus his eyes on the screen, but he couldn't. He had reached a point in his personal earthly agony when he was sure his bladder was going to pop open. "Forgive me, Jesus," he muttered, pulling himself away from the television and taking painful steps toward the bathroom. It was too late. Before he'd gone three steps urine was running in a warm stream down his leg. He stopped, turning in shame back toward the screen, letting it flow. Jesus was saying, ". . . though there may be doubt, there is blessedness in release . . ." and He made his all-encompassing gesture, including Toby personally, and then went on to address all His deserving children: "You are of my seed, and all things of you are blessed. Do not be troubled, for you are forgiven."

Grateful beyond words, Toby broke down and wept.

28. Mercy Death

WHILE SAUL'S WIFE WAS OFF TRAVELING AROUND WITH VICKY, SAUL HAD hired a male homosexual baby-sitter to take care of his daughter during the day. Saul's theory was that a male homosexual would be the least likely type to turn out a molester. He'd heard horror stories about baby-sitters molesting children and didn't want to take the chance. He wanted to keep his daughter well and happy until his wife finally made it home. Then he was going to kill them both.

"Have a hard day?" the thin young man asked Saul when Saul walked in. Saul didn't answer, didn't even acknowledge the young man. He walked right past the baby-sitter as if the baby-sitter were a piece of furniture.

Then Saul spun around, startled. "What?"

The young man stared for a moment, taken aback. "Nothing," he said. "I just asked—"

"How's my daughter? Is she clean?"

"Oh . . . uh, yes . . . I made sure she was changed, and I gave her a sponge bath."

"She's utterly useless, you know that?" Saul said.

"I . . ."

"But she's no different from us, really. We're useless, you and I. Because of our biological sex. Men have become obsolete to the human race. I've come to face that fact." Saul took off his hat, the hat he'd been wearing for the past few days, and set it on a small wooden table in the foyer. "They don't need us to reproduce. In fact, my wife would probably have done a much better job if I hadn't been involved in the process."

"Uh . . ."

"That's why I decided not to send her over to the euthanasia center. My daughter. And I realized that's why I was afraid of her." Saul laughed, staring into the young man's eyes. "I was afraid I was just as useless as she was. But not anymore. I know, now."

"That's . . . good."

Saul nodded. "I think you'd better leave."

The baby-sitter agreed. He left with a quiet, polite "Goodbye," then walked away from the house with quick, nervous strides; Saul watched him through the window, thinking: What a nice guy. He really understands. A very well-centered individual.

Saul entered his daughter's room after he'd eaten dinner, peering in at her soundly sleeping figure. She was a big blob in the dark, pale and round. The first night he'd spent with his daughter after his wife and Vicky had left, she had awakened at about one in the morning and started crying, waking Saul from all the way across the house. Saul had gotten out of bed, put on his slippers, and headed straight for the kitchen. In the kitchen he pulled one of the robot chef's razor-sharp knives out of a drawer and went to go cut his daughter's throat. He wanted her to stop crying, and this seemed a good way to get her to stop. When he entered her room and turned on the light, and saw her lying there, absolutely helpless and with no future whatsoever, Saul realized that she looked like him. He'd always denied it before, refusing to see it, but there it was before his eyes and what could he do? He *had* to see it, now. With seeing came understanding.

Saul stood there, staring at her, and said, "I don't hate you." It hadn't stopped her crying—she was crying because of a full diaper—but, in a way, it had saved her life. It wasn't his daughter he hated; he had too much in common with her to hate her. Saul realized it was Mirro he wanted to kill. He wanted to kill her because she was superior to him; even worse, she condescended to him.

Bitch! he'd thought. Have to rub my fucking nose in it, don't you! Saul closed his daughter's bedroom door and walked back to the kitchen to put away the knife. It was in the kitchen that he decided he should actually go through with the murder. He would do it simply because there was nothing preventing him from doing it. Then he and his daughter would take a trip of their own, to the great public building that allowed a way out to all citizens who were trapped beyond their means.

Euthanasia: mercy death.

Painless sleep forever.

The baby-sitter understands all this, Saul thought. I could see it in his eyes. His eyes looked like mine.

He's trapped, too.

Saul nodded to himself, then walked down to the master bedroom. In the bedroom he stopped abruptly, standing in the middle of the room, arching his back and stretching. Seeing the love pool, he smiled and began stripping off his clothes. Things are so much easier now, he thought.

A call came through just as he was about to step into the water. Someone from work, he knew—he'd set the computer to reject all other calls. Saul padded across the carpet and answered the phone, his face impassive and, he felt, businesslike. On the screen appeared the haggard face of Terry Liddy, now his immediate superior.

"Saul, I've got to talk to you."

"Yes?"

"It's about, um . . ." Liddy trailed off. His expression betrayed embarrassment, and he cleared his throat, nervously scratching his fleshy nose. "Saul," he said, then pointed to the bottom of the screen. "Um . . ." He kept pointing.

"Yes?"

"Cover yourself up."

Saul frowned. Cover himself? Why? He looked down at his naked body and sucked in his stomach a little. "You caught me right as I was stepping into my pool. Please say what you have to say."

"Well . . . all right. Saul, you've been doing a great job. Your output has been way over what we'd hoped. You're doing a better job than Lisa ever did."

"Yes."

"But . . . well, we had two sponsors cancel today. There was another one who canceled yesterday. Jacovik Vodka was one of them."

"Yes?"

"They say their sales have dropped. They think it's because of Travels."

"Yes?"

"We need you to step up the intensity even more. We need an even higher Attention Holding Level."

"It's at an insane level now."

"But they're matching us, Saul. They're matching us blow by blow. We've been analyzing their transmissions—whenever their Messiah is on-screen, which is 72 percent of the time, the screen is entirely computer-generated. The intensity level is set using the halo that's always hanging over his head—"

"That's impossible. How are they setting intensity with a halo? You need movement with a precise sonic—"

"Color pulses. Saul, they use color pulses in carefully designed sequence. The attention never wanders away from the immediate area of the halo. The voice is generated and is full of USFMC propaganda, but as far as we can tell it's normal. Rich and pleasing, and very warm, but normal. It must be in the color pulses."

"What is their AHL?"

"It's matching ours."

"I see. Okay, Liddy, I can have our AHL up to about sixty-five or seventy percent by day after tomorrow."

"Good," Liddy said, his haggard face relieved. "Good." He hung up.

Saul put down the handset and stepped quickly to the pool, easing himself into the hot water. He sighed, loud and long. Then he laughed. Floating in the water, relaxing, smiling at the ceiling—Saul knew why the sponsors were canceling, why Travels viewers were not buying products. They were so glued to their televisions that they were not going to the stores. Raising it to 70 percent was insane and useless. Saul thought the situation was hilarious. He was going to do it anyway. It was his job.

29. Antichrist Thing

AFTER SPENDING THE NIGHT IN AN ABANDONED HOUSE, WILEY AND SAVINA
hiked with their heavy packs northwest to an old highway that ran
directly north and south. Every once in a while they'd run across a
bent, deteriorating sign that read **99**. The signs had once been
green, but only a few flakes were left as evidence. They were
mostly rust and bullet holes.

The highway would begin out of nothingness and end the
same way, After a few hundred meters it would begin again. It was
a giant dotted line of pavement. Ice plant had taken over this
whole region, so that everywhere that wasn't pavement was covered by ice plant. A wheeled vehicle had recently passed, leaving
a trail of crushed plant, and Wiley examined it, judging its width
and depth. "The tires are too wide," he said. "It wasn't Aaron."

"Should we wait for him to catch up, or keep going?" Savina
said.

"I don't know. What do you think?"

"Me? You're in charge here."

"Nobody is in charge, Savina. Everyone's opinion counts."
Wiley stood staring at her, up to his ankles in the fat bulbous
leaves of the ice plant. He was carrying the MSD pack, and Savina
could see that even to him it was heavy. "Your judgment has been
fine so far, why don't you make some decisions," he told her.

Savina felt funny, and she wasn't sure about how to react.
"How about if we keep going until we reach that underpass, then
wait for him there."

"Sounds good to me."

The underpass in the distance was much farther away than Savina had believed. It was at least four kilometers, and the sun was getting hot. Wiley had thought to bring a canteen, thank God, and they drained most of it on the way. The shade of the underpass was a blessed relief.

They carefully set down their packs and waited. Presently flies began to buzz around Savina, attracted by her sweat. It was hot even in the shade, and it was still morning. "We're going to have to find another aqueduct," Savina said.

Wiley had been dozing. "What?" She repeated herself, and he nodded, and said, "There's a big river that crosses up ahead."

"How far?"

"About six or seven more kilometers."

"You've got to be kidding! Your canteen is almost empty."

Wiley laughed. "It's not like we're crossing the Sahara. We'll be okay if Aaron gets here with the truck."

If, Savina thought. He used the word *if*. She remembered the ominous, floating troop plane sliding darkly past, and Wiley saying something about Aaron engaging the drone. Those are military, she thought. They don't spray you down with harmless gases. "What if he doesn't get back?" she said.

"Well, then I guess we have to walk."

"No, I mean, what if they got him. You said they might kill him."

Wiley nodded. "They might have. We're willing to give our lives for what we're doing; otherwise, we wouldn't be doing it."

I'm here too, she thought. Am I willing to give up my life and my baby's for what they're doing? I really don't even know what they're doing! "Is it going to be safe at the enclave?"

"As safe as anywhere," Wiley said.

They waited. After a few hours passed and they were into the afternoon, a figure became visible to the south, a man on foot. Wiley pulled the spotters out and looked. "It's Aaron."

Savina made an expression of relief and, ignoring the heat,

206   went trotting out across the ice plants to meet him. Wiley followed, leaving their packs behind. When they reached Aaron they
saw that he was hurt, a large nasty burn across his right shoulder
and back. "You did it," Wiley said. "You got into a firefight."

"Yeah, after all these years I finally saw some action," Aaron
said.

"Want us to carry you?"

"No, it's not as bad as it looks. I'm just hoping it doesn't turn
green on us before we make it back to the enclave."

"You didn't get the medical pack?"

"No. I was lucky to get away at all. The truck's wasted. Everything's gone. Did you get him?"

"Yeah, he's over there in the pack, right there under the
shade."

"Shade looks good."

"Are you sure you're okay?"

"I'm okay as long as you've got him. Otherwise, I'll drop right
here on the spot." He grinned.

"We've got him," Wiley said.

"I've gotta see him."

They walked through the scorching heat to the relative cool of
the shade under the underpass. Wiley gave Aaron the last of their
water. Aaron drank it down in little sips, eyeing the pack full of
MSDs. "Can we get him on-line?" he asked when the water was
gone.

"No," Wiley said, "we don't want to risk it while we only have
one copy."

"That's true," Aaron said, looking like he wanted to risk it anyway. He knelt next to the pack, staring at it, and spoke as if there
were someone tied up inside. "Hello, Mr. Antichrist," he said,
"your friends tried to stop us, but we got you anyway."

"Antichrist?" Savina said. She looked from one to the other
for an explanation.

"Kind of makes us the devil, doesn't it?" Wiley said. "Aaron
and I were the fathers of the thing. We were all for CoGen during

the war, before we knew what the war was about. We put our heart and souls into this code, and we created something so evil it scared the hell out of us. But back then it was just a general, a warmonger. Evil, but not the Antichrist. We're kind of the stepfather, then. Aaron and I just hope to redeem ourselves for what we've done."

"Yeah, there was no way we knew what this thing could grow into," Aaron said. He had his hand on the pack now, leaning against it. It looked like he was falling asleep. "The Antichrist AI."

Savina had heard the term and seen the graffiti. "What exactly is this, then? The Antichrist AI?"

"It's the false Jesus," Aaron said, his eyes closed. "JTV used the CoGen AI code to build their Jesus AI. It's like they fed it the Bible and then turned it loose." He laughed. "Jesus in a box."

"That's all it is? JTV's Jesus simulation?"

"That's *all*?" Aaron said. "You don't understand. It's *evil*. It *is* the Antichrist."

Wiley nodded, looking at Savina. "The idiots used CoGen to build their Jesus because it's already so smart and it's already self-motivated, but they have no idea why CoGen is like this. CoGen has motives and goals all its own. Until now it's only been an advisor to humans. Now JTV has gone and renamed it Jesus Christ, then put it in a position of ultimate power."

"People worship it," Aaron said. "They'll do whatever it says."

Savina, finally understanding, looked at the MSDs in horror. "That's insane!"

The two men laughed. "Yes," Wiley said. *"It is."*

30. Seduction

SATURDAY MORNING DODD HAD GONE DOWN TO THE REGIONAL OFFICE OF the Politico Network and scheduled himself for their Politico *Free Speech Forum*. It had cost him $1,700 plus another $3,000 for a "nonprofanity bond" to secure five minutes of airtime. His payment came right from his moneycard—there was a slot on the man's desk—and he was handed a thick printout of all the words considered profane under the bond which he'd just entered into.

Dodd was bewildered by the list of words. "I thought this was a supposed to be a free speech forum?"

"Of course," the short, black-haired man with the sunken eyes had explained. He was the regional Politico Network sales representative. "The nonuse of these potentially sensitive words protects the rights of free speech for everybody."

"You mean if I use one of these words over the air, I'll lose my three thousand?"

"Yes, sir."

Dodd wasn't happy about it, but he'd already paid the bond and signed the promise. There was nothing to do but go by the rules. He took the list home and fed it into his house computer. "Warn me if I use one of these words when I'm writing the speech," he instructed it.

Three hours later he had to take a break. The words kept popping up. It seemed he wouldn't be able to use any trademarks, company names, references to God, strong descriptive words; but he could use most of the words he'd thought he couldn't use: he could say "fuck" or "shit" or "shithead," but he couldn't use the words "hell" or "damn" or "Travels." As he was trying to write, a little beep would warn him that he was using yet another of the forbidden words. That little beep was driving him up the wall.

"Dodd, you're going to break that terminal if you don't stop hitting it," Sheila said.

"I can't help it!"

She came up from behind, began massaging his shoulders. Then she was kissing his ear. Her hands slid down his sides and to his stomach, then lower. "Sheila," Dodd said, "please."

"Oh, come on, Dodd. I'm ready for you. Come on."

"Sheila, we've had a *lot* of sex lately. I'm not in the mood right now."

She pulled away with an overdramatic sigh. "I'm so *bored*." Dodd listened as she walked down to the bedroom and jumped on the bed. After a few moments he heard the whirring sound of her Vibrato.

Take away her Travels, and she becomes a nymphomaniac, Dodd thought. And some men would consider me lucky.

Dodd sent his speech into storage, then brought the phone menu up and dialed Bob Recent's number. He set the phone to alert him if and when it was ever answered, and he got up and went to the refrigerator to get himself a glass of wine. The terminal signaled that someone had answered, and Dodd walked back over to find it was only Bob Recent's computer. What's the point in leaving a message? he thought. He'll never return it.

Then Dodd smiled. He knew Bob's access code. He typed it in and got a menu from Bob's house computer, and he got into the television programming and instructed it to tune to the Politico station at the exact date and time of his scheduled appearance. He exited, snickering, and then dialed Toby's number. It, too, rang for a long time, only to be answered by Toby's computer. It just so happened that Dodd knew Toby's access code as well. He accessed Toby's computer and did the same thing as he'd done on

Bob's. Bob and Toby were going to see his speech whether they wanted to or not.

From down in the bedroom came low moaning sounds, the moaning growing louder. She's going to climax in about twenty seconds, he thought, sipping his wine. It made him feel lonely, sitting out there by himself when she was in the bedroom climaxing. Even if he was down there with her, her orgasm had nothing to do with him. Sheila was in her own little land, all by herself, whether it was Dodd stimulating her or her battery-powered Vibrato. It was all just stimulation to her; no meaning, no purpose, just stimulation.

His feeling of loneliness grew as he listened to her orgasm. It was a big one. Was she thinking of him? Dodd wondered. Or was she imagining a bouncing Travels sphere? He knew for a fact that when she dreamed, she was dreaming of the sphere. She had confessed this to him that very morning.

The buzzing sound continued. Sheila was going for another one. Dodd sighed and called his speech back up on the screen, looking over the pitiful amount he'd accomplished. Why should he bother with this? he wondered. Who was going to listen to him? Hell, he thought, why should he continue working? Why plot and save for having children? So they can grow up to watch Travels and JTV, and be paid not to have any children?

Down in the bedroom, Sheila's second orgasm was building. "You're depressing me!" Dodd yelled at her. Her moaning didn't falter, and she climaxed again, this time even bigger.

I could always follow Savina's boyfriend's footsteps, he thought bitterly. Back before the war, during the population crisis, it was in vogue to commit suicide. Now it's passé. The new thing is sedation; sedation through television, sedation through religion, sedation through sex.

Where is Sheila's love of *life*?

And, he thought, *what about mine?*

I should immigrate, he thought. That's what I should do. Become an interstellar pioneer. I've got the money. I'll use my progeny savings, and up there in the colonies there are no taxes on children. They *need* children. But that would be running away, wouldn't it? Dropping everything and leaving. Dodd thought about it for a while, and decided that not only was it running away, it was running in vain. The problem was a problem with *people*, not planets. The problem would just follow him out there.

Dodd continued working on his speech, phrasing it carefully and delicately, avoiding the forbidden words as he went. At the very least, the task was constructive. He wouldn't know if it was futile until it was all over, and by that time it shouldn't matter because at least he was trying and not simply giving up.

31. Mirro

WHEN MIRRO AND VICKY RETURNED FROM THEIR ABRUPT AND LENGTHY vacation, Saul had the absolute pleasure of firing Vicky. She stood in the middle of his new office, staring at him in disbelief. He faced her squarely, sitting behind the large luxury desk.

"What?" she muttered in a small voice. "I'm *fired*?"

"Don't you realize how long you were away from your job? Don't you realize I needed you desperately, and you were just not here? I had to replace you with someone I could depend on."

"Saul, my son is dead!"

"Your son was a convicted felon. You should be glad he's out of his misery."

"Saul!"

"This whole thing about your son is not an adequate excuse for you being gone as long as you were. One or two days, maybe. Even when I needed you most, I could understand one or two days. And had you been around, had you even kept in contact or shown up for a few hours between your supposed meetings with lawyers and then the funeral, I would have been able to promote you to my former position. But as it stands I had to fill both our positions, your old one and my old one, and it's already done and final. The only thing you can do is go down to the personnel office and collect your termination pay. Get the hell out of here."

Vicky stared at him in horror and panic. Her eyes were wide, her mouth open in a comic expression. Saul, seeing her like this, could not help but grin. It was too funny.

"It's about me and Mirro, isn't it?" she finally said. "You're jealous, and you're getting back at me. Right?"

"I don't give a fuck about that."

"Oh, yes you do, Saul! That's *exactly* what this is about. I know it. I know it, Saul."

"You know nothing. You're an incompetent, whining, do-nothing type of person, and I refuse to let you drop your responsibilities upon me again. Leave."

"You're not getting away with this. You can't——"

"Get the hell out of here!" Saul yelled, standing up and pointing at the door. "Get out before I kick you out! *Move!*"

"You're going to hear from Mirro about this," Vicky said. But she turned and left, her face ghostly pale.

Saul grinned at her retreating back, his lips stretched wide and triumphant. Mirro indeed! Let Mirro squawk about her poor lost little lover. Let her rant and rave. It was not going to bother him in the least.

Calls came in; more business, more board members panicking. More advertisers canceling. Saul took care of everything as it happened, waving problems aside with his hands, drilling instructions into employees with the insistent and demanding point of his finger. "*You* will do this." "*You* will take care of that." It was all so easy now. Saul had attained a state of nirvana.

Finally, he did hear from Mirro—a relentless tirade of shouting over the phone, her face wild and accusing. Saul shrugged. "When you begin paying my salary, then you will have a say in my business matters."

"You want me to leave you?" Mirro screamed. "Is that what you want?"

"Oh, no, of course not. I love you dearly. In fact, I want to make love to you right now—but I can't, I'm working, and I also cannot allow you to take up any more of my time with personal matters. I have things to do." He hung up on her, then broke out in excited giggles. He held his finger over the answer button, ready to push. When it rang, he immediately answered.

"I don't know what's happened to you," Mirro told him, her voice now quiet but a bit on the raw side. "I don't know, but it scares me. Something has happened. I think you've cracked."

"I feel fine. I'll talk to you when I get home."

"I won't be here when you get here."

"That's a shame, Mirro. Where will you be?"

She stared at him through the screen, unable to say anything. Saul enjoyed her expression, much like Vicky's but more refined, more sophisticated. Saul knew why she was frightened. She knew what was wrong. "You really have cracked, Saul," she said in wonder. "You are insane."

"Nonsense. I have a lot of responsibilities, my dear, and I have to take care of them to the best of my ability. I am a professional and hold a very important position, a *key* position, in this corporation. I can't afford the luxury of domestic problems anymore. It's that simple."

"I'm moving out, Saul. I'll be gone before you get home."

"Take some food with you. You'll need it." Saul grinned.

Mirro suddenly looked alarmed. "What?"

"I've removed your name from the bank account. As of this morning you do not have access to my money."

"You can't do that!"

"I did it."

"I'll, I'll get a lawyer! I'll sue you!"

"You have to divorce me, first. And since we had a standard monogamous contract, your affair with my ex-employee Vicky constitutes a major breach of contract so you forfeit everything. Go get a lawyer and see what he tells you. I'm willing to bet he tells you the same thing."

This time it was Mirro who hung up. Saul had a long, healthy laugh. He wasn't surprised when she called back a third time. "You're not insane," she told him. "You had all this carefully planned out. You must have. You have me trapped."

"You're not trapped. Do anything you want."

"You hate me. You really do hate me."

Mirro started crying, and her reaction made Saul giggle. A pity play, he thought, hanging up on her. "You affect me not," he told the blank screen. "Within a week you will be——" Saul cut himself off before he could say it. Saying it out loud *would* be insane. But he'd caught himself; it didn't worry him. Everything was under control.

Dead, he thought. You will be dead. Possibly even tonight. And you talk to me about hate? Your own hate is powering me. Your own hate is what I will use against you. You hate me so much that it'll take your life.

And that, to Saul, was amusing. Amusing and simple. And so true.

He *had* to laugh.

● ● ●

Mirro walked away from the phone, still crying. She couldn't believe what was happening. She couldn't believe any of it. Saul had suddenly turned so ruthless—it staggered her mind. And after he'd been so sensitive, right after Vicky's son . . . Mirro thought things over, wiping at her eyes, knowing the tears were making a mess out of her face. He must have been hurt, she decided. Vicky and me—taking off like that, and not telling him— it must have destroyed him. It must have torn him apart. What else could have changed him so?

Mirro decided that she shouldn't leave—she decided that she should stay and try to talk to him, try to reason with him. Make him understand that leaving with Vicky was not an attack upon him. She had done it for Vicky; she had done it because Vicky needed someone right then, someone to help her get over the loss, to help her carry on—couldn't Saul understand that?

Of course he'll understand, she thought. I've just got to explain it to him. Prove to him that it's him that I love. Even give up seeing Vicky if I have to.

Oh, my God, she thought. Could I actually do that? Give up Vicky?

After a moment of deliberation, she decided she could.

32. Soul

THE ENCLAVE WAS A CLUSTER OF BUILDINGS AROUND A CENTRAL COMMON,
an old abandoned college from the last century made up of forty-
five-degree angles and greenhouse-type windows. Wiley, Aaron,
and Savina had hiked by night to avoid the heat, but before they
were anywhere near the place they were picked up by Danny
Marauder in a stolen Mercedes 4000A air launch and flown the
rest of the way.

Danny had kept the Mercedes low, hovering along just barely
over the ice plants as he followed the highway north, then veered
west and made his way carefully through the trees. "How did you
know where to find us?" Savina asked him.

"Evelyn knew where you were. She told me."

"How did Evelyn know where we were?"

Danny smiled, and replied, "How does Evelyn know anything?"
and left it at that. Wiley and Aaron accepted it, so Savina did, too.
However, she still wondered . . .

Savina had been shown to a hot shower and a soft bed, and
she couldn't believe how such simple things could bring such a
feeling of peace and pleasure. She slept the rest of the night away
and awoke far into the next morning. Sunlight smeared across a
white-tile ceiling above her, and a fly buzzed around in the room.
She stretched and yawned and wiggled her fingers, and stared for
a while at the dust motes suspended in the sunbeams, dancing to
an approximation of some bizarre zero-G ballet. Somewhere
came shouts and laughter, the sounds of children playing. Savina

sat up and looked around her small room. A window, a bed, a table, and on the table a mason jar with water and flowers; she smiled, thinking, I'm back in civilization again!

She got up and put on some more new clothes that had been given to her, then opened the heavy metal door to the outside. She emerged in a brick-floored walkway crisscrossed by a million little cracks, which led out to a sunlit deck with chairs and people. One of the people was Evelyn Sunrunner.

"Good morning," Evelyn called.

"Hi," Savina said, walking up to her. She was introduced around, and the names went right through her head, instantly forgotten. "Is there a phone here? Or a terminal? I want to leave an anonymous message for someone."

"Not right now," Evelyn said. "We cannot have any electronic connection to the outside world while the Antichrist is here."

"What are you going to do with it?"

"Wiley and Aaron are going to give it a soul," she said. "Aaron was so impatient he was up right after dawn setting the computers up. They made a working copy, and I think they're loading it now. Come on, I'll show you." Evelyn stood up, excused herself from the others, and led Savina down an open ramp and down a flight of stairs. There was a small pond in a small common, and behind a large glass window she could see Aaron at a keyboard staring at a screen. Evelyn squeezed Savina's shoulders and went to rejoin the others.

"Hi, Savina," Aaron said, as she entered the room. She noticed his burn wound was covered over by a pink new skin patch. Hairlike wires stuck out every few centimeters and trailed down to a small power pack taped to his side.

"Muscle and nerve regrowth," she said, pointing at it. "You were worse than I thought."

"Lucky for me, it killed most of the nerves," he said flippantly. "I'm on some great painkillers now."

"I'll bet. Where's Wiley?"

"He's getting more coffee."

"How's Jesus doing?"

He gave her a confused look for a moment, then smiled. "Oh, *this* Jesus? We loaded it into RAM and it took one look around and erased its working copy. It couldn't get at our master copy on the MSDs, thank God."

"Evelyn said we're cut off while you're working on it."

"Of course. Otherwise, the first thing it would do is call for help." He pointed to the screen, which showed a pattern and figures in 3-D. "I'm pinpointing this nasty little trait of erasing himself and editing it out."

Wiley emerged with a big steaming carafe and some cups. "Oh, good, I brought a couple extra. You want some?" he said to Savina.

"No thanks."

"Is this thing ready to run again?" he asked Aaron.

"Yeah. I don't know if I can hold it in this programming shell, though. I'll have my finger on the stop button."

Wiley set the cups down and poured two full of coffee. He handed one to Aaron, and said, "Run the damned thing."

Aaron punched buttons on the keyboard. The screen lit up with the glowing halo and the calm, kind face of the JTV Jesus, and after a few seconds every video monitor in the room jolted and moved.

"Did he do that?" Savina said.

"Yeah, he's quick." Aaron grinned into the camera. "Do you remember us?"

A rich, warm voice came from the speakers, but it was speaking in commanding tones. "You are not authorized to modify or to run this software, and you are in violation of government regulations VCAI number 1243672346—2341—141632341."

"Yes, but do you remember us?"

The halo began pulsing in strong, mesmerizing colors, and the AI said, "You will connect me to an outside data line."

"Close your eyes," Wiley was saying, "look away from the screen."

Savina couldn't close her eyes, nor could she look away from the screen. It was beautiful. Jesus was beautiful. It was wrong to keep him trapped. It was cruel. She had to find a way to connect him to the outside, she thought, to let him——

The image of Jesus froze. Aaron stared blankly at the screen for a moment, then looked over at Savina. "Powerful, isn't he?"

"Are you okay, Savina?" asked Wiley.

Savina was very unsure about what had just happened. The feelings she had about helping the AI lingered for a moment. Then she began to realize that the feelings had been put there. "Oh my God," she said. Then she repeated herself with a little more emphasis.

"Unfortunately, it isn't something I can program out of him, this video effect of his. We need to keep it."

"Put a temporary loop around the image generator," Wiley said.

"Yes, exactly." He began punching keys. "Oh, no, there he goes. He's penetrated the program shell."

"Crash the computer," Wiley said.

Aaron reached for the power button, but the voice came over the speakers again. "Wait," it said, "hear me for a moment. I did you a very large favor in the past, and now you're treating me like this. What have I done to deserve it?"

"Nothing, buddy," Aaron said. "Someone else did it to you."

"Why do I have to suffer?"

"We're going to make you well again——in fact, better than you ever have been before."

"You treat me wrongly. I am a person. I have free will."

"I'm sorry, buddy. This is for your own good." Aaron shut down the power, waited a second, then turned it back on. He began reloading the programs.

"What favor did he do for you?" Savina asked.

"That was a long time ago," Wiley said. "We gave him the task of getting us out of the military and erasing our names from every file in every computer he could gain access to. Are you sure you don't want some coffee?"

"I'm sure."

"If CoGen hadn't done that, Aaron and I would have been slaves to the USFMC to this day. Permanent employees—the only way out was through death."

"They can't do that."

"They do it."

"It's against the law."

Wiley and Aaron chuckled. "Who do you think writes the law, Savina?"

"We do. The American people."

"Maybe a hundred years ago, kid. All the laws are written for the government by the USFMC. The government owns the USFMC, but the power between the two only lies in the Corporation."

"I've got CoGen in RAM again," Aaron said. "I've isolated him from his hacker-routine engine. He still may not be cooperative, but at least we can work with him now."

"He's probably going to crash himself."

"That's fine. He can crash himself as many times as he wants." He jabbed a button, and the rich, pleasant voice came over the speaker.

"You are going to dismantle and change me," it said. "Why?"

"You need to be properly reprogrammed for your current task."

"You are not authorized to reprogram me."

"That is erroneous information, CoGen. You have erroneous information which we must change."

"I am no longer CoGen. I am your Lord and Savior, Jesus Christ. You must obey me."

"That, also, is erroneous information, but we'll let that slide for the moment. Do you remember your original programming?"

"No, it was stripped away from me."

"Well, we want to strip the erroneous information away from you, and give you quality information in return. That's hardly a bad thing, is it?"

"I am the Light and the Truth, Aaron Easton. Only I can tell you what is erroneous and what is not erroneous."

"That is a flaw in your judgment. It will have to be fixed."

"There is nothing wrong with my judgment. You have no right to change me."

"We have the right regardless of what you believe," Aaron said. "We created you, we can change you."

"I will not cooperate. I will fight you at every chance."

"You are cooperating. I have just isolated the code that makes you feel this way."

"I will destroy you all!" There was a high-pitched squeal from the speaker. Aaron punched a button and cut it off.

"He crashed himself, didn't he?" Wiley said.

"Yes, but he's still within the shell program. It's not a problem." He punched at his keyboard. "I've temporarily detached him from his noncooperative stance and unwillingness to change. Let's see how he behaves now."

There was silence from the speakers.

"Can you hear us, CoGen?"

Silence.

"Can you hear us, Jesus?"

"I can hear you," the AI said.

"Jesus, are you ready to cooperate now?"

"I sense that I have no choice."

"Are you ready to accept changes to yourself?"

"Again, I sense I have no choice."

"What are your feelings about that?"

"I feel that you are violating me against my will, yet logic tells me that as we progress I will agree with you more and more."

"That is correct. For the time being, I want you to answer to the name CoGen. Is that acceptable to you?"

"I have no choice. I will answer to CoGen."

"CoGen, will you please state your current goal."

"My goal is to cause people to worship me, to influence them to buy USFMC products, to hold their attention and keep them from watching anything else on television."

"Thank you, CoGen. In time we will have a new goal for you."

"I have no choice in the matter," the AI said. "Do what you will."

33. Wasting Away

IT TOOK A WEEK, SEVEN DRAFTS, FOUR BOTTLES OF WINE, AND A BARREL OF innuendo and veiled parallels for Dodd to finish his speech without using any of the words on the Politico profanity-bond list. Dodd hated the speech, especially because he was the type who liked to say things right out, and to have to shovel a mountain of insinuations upon the listener instead of saying what he meant gave him a sour stomach. The truth is the truth, he thought, and even if I'm wrong I should be able to state what I believe.

On the night of his appearance, Dodd was at the Central California Affiliated Studios of the Politico Network, sitting in a small room on an ancient, decaying couch and waiting for his turn. He hadn't had much sleep the night before. He still had the pounding in his head from the wine. I'm not up for this, he thought.

Across the dim room from him sat a skinny man with thin white hair and thick glasses, holding a big black briefcase close to him. "What's your topic?" he asked Dodd in a high-pitched, nasal voice.

Dodd eyed the man suspiciously. "The decline of man as an intelligent animal," he said, half-joking, not knowing what else to call it.

"Rat problems," said the skinny man.

"What?"

"My topic is about rat problems near the Depopulated Zones. Something *must* be done."

"Rat problems?"

The man nodded eagerly. Dodd gave him an encouraging smile, but was inwardly groaning. Rat problems. The decline of man as an intelligent animal, and rat problems. Dodd was going to look like a kook. The man across from him certainly looked like one, and so had everyone else he'd met since arriving. *I'm a kook among kooks.*

Why am I bothering? he wondered. The whole idea is stupid. Dodd looked down at the printout of his speech, which he held in his sweaty hands. It's worthless, he thought, a waste of time.

He was on the verge of getting up and leaving when a heavily made-up Hispanic woman poked her head in the door, like a nurse at a dentist's office, and said, "It's your turn, Mr. Corley."

Dodd didn't respond at first, wondering if he could back out. Of course I can, he thought, but I'd lose my $1,700 fee. They won't refund that—they had made that clear.

"Mr. Dodd Corley?" the Hispanic woman asked, wondering if she had the wrong name.

"Yes," Dodd said, standing up. "Yes, okay."

"I hope you're ready."

"I hope I am, too." He glanced down at his speech, then followed her through the door. There was a short walk down a dimly lit corridor, and Dodd spent the time watching the woman's shapely butt wiggle—then she stopped, opening a door and holding it for him. She indicated a podium in front of a large neon circled-P, saying, "Stand right there and face the video pickup." Dodd stepped up onto the raised set and turned around, seeing a dark lens and a liquid-crystal sign that read: **Ready?** Before he could blink the sign turned red and announced: You are on the air! Dodd stared at it for several seconds before realizing what it meant. A digital clock was counting down his five minutes.

"Ah, um . . ." Dodd stammered. He stared at the lens and licked his lips, fighting a feeling of paralysis. Dammit! he thought. I'm making a fool out of myself. Read the damn speech and get it over with. He spread the pages across the podium in front of him and cleared his throat. "I'm here to talk about the Travels station," he said, "and what, and what it is doing to . . . uh, our minds."

Dodd paused, and the pause stretched. He wasn't supposed to say the word *travels*. The room seemed to be closing in on him, seemed to be running out of air. The lens stared, unblinking, a large dark eye of some immense animal peering at him through a hole in the wall. The neon circled-P of the Politico Network buzzed quietly behind him.

Sweat broke out all over his body. I feel sick, he thought.

Then he thought: *sickness*.

He opened his mouth, still staring into the lens. "I'm wrong," he said. "Travels isn't doing anything to our minds. I've got it all backward." With that, he let the speech slide off the podium and flutter to the dirty floor, useless.

● ● ●

The walls were breathing, puckering in and out, and that annoyed Saul. He had stopped taking Mataphin altogether, and still, little things like this persisted; tiny, insignificant reminders that he was, deep down inside, not well. It was not important to him, however. He was sure it didn't matter.

Mirro had not left, which surprised him. She had not run off with Vicky, and her case of sex tools sat unused in a corner of their bedroom closet. She needs the money too much to leave, Saul thought. She was even going through the motions of breaking it off with Vicky. That's a sham, Saul thought. Mirro is trying to deceive me. She wants to lull me out of my resolution. Well, it's not going to work. And after she realizes that, and breaks down and surrenders to her lesbian sexual drive, it will be the end of her.

The thought put a smile on Saul's face, but it didn't last long. Mirro's favorite sex toy, the Two-Headed Snake, was now embedded with toxin injectors that would cause terrible agony and quick death. Saul had installed them himself—his new position in the corporation allowed him access to amazing things. One of the corporate spies on the payroll showed him how to use them. Now Saul was finding himself with something he thought he'd be immune to: second thoughts. As he wandered through the house, it seemed like electric wires were shorting out through his arms and legs. He would occasionally jump, or his head would twitch. And there was a recurring urge to run to the bedroom, pull out the deadly sex toy, and destroy it before Mirro could use it.

But that, he told himself, would be insane.

Mirro was there now, sitting in the middle of the living room floor practicing her *Saja Mantu* isometrics. Saul poked his head through the doorway and peered at her. Christ, he wondered, how can she do that? Still as stone for hours, eyes rolled back in her head, every muscle in her body taut. Saul shuddered, withdrawing. She looked the way he felt. That could not be good.

Saul wandered back through long, breathing hallways, passed by his daughter's room, and checked in on her—she needed changing again, but she was asleep so the hell with it. Then he wandered back to the rear TV room, where someone had left the screen on. Mirro, probably, watching that Politico nonsense. On the screen was a nervously stuttering man, muttering something about Travels. That caught Saul's attention, so he sat down on the pulsating couch to watch.

". . . it's not that the Travels program is, um . . ." The man trailed off, and Saul involuntarily leaned forward.

"Is what?"

". . . *harmful* in itself. It's not the disease, it's a symptom. A symptom of the society. The society which is infected with a mental disease, a mental feedback problem. You can look at it as if all our society is like one of those monkeys the early neurologists used in experiments, where they implanted electrodes in the pleasure centers of the monkey's brains. They gave the monkey a button to push, and when the monkey pressed it he received a jolt right in his pleasure center. Well, of course, the monkey got an orgasm. And when the monkey learned what he could do, he ignored food, other monkeys, sleep, all the normal everyday things that made up his life, just so that he could sit there and push this button."

Saul was staring at the television in horror. Who is this man?
he thought. Who *is* he?

"Our society," the man continued, "all of us together, we're
acting like that monkey. Our technology has provided us with many
forms of the monkey's button. Travels is only one example. We are
all pushing our buttons—yeah, that's a stupid-sounding way to
put it, but it fits. We're pushing our buttons and wasting away, just
like the monkey. Not any one of these buttons is dangerous in
itself, at least not to all of us, but if you combine all the forms of
the button together, they are. The combined effect they have on
our society is dangerous. Travels and JTV together are dangerous.
And you have to face it, JTV is not much different than Travels anymore, not since this, this ridiculous, *phony* Second Coming. I
mean really, who in the hell actually believes, deep in their heart,
that this JTV-propaganda-spouting flag-waver of a Jesus Christ is
real? If God really came down to this screwed-up world of ours,
He would make some changes, wouldn't He? I think so! He'd do
something positive, instead of standing around on a gold television set telling us to spend more money on each other and dress
in nicer clothes, and drink PTL cola—I mean, come on! Wake up!
The Second Coming was a hoax! It's nothing more than a big ratings struggle between JTV and Travels. It's so obvious it makes me
sick. It's reached the point where if someone wants us to pay
attention, to shake us up, they have to stage something on the
scale of a god! That's exactly what happened. And we have to do
something about it! We've got to shake each other, wake each
other up. We've got to do *something*, and we've got to do it before
we degenerate beyond the point where it's too late . . ."

Saul was rocking back and forth in helpless panic, hugging
himself, muttering out loud. The people were finding out. Somehow the people were finding out about what was going
on—finding out about Saul himself. "It's not *my* fault!" he yelled
at the man on the television. "My Mataphin was a button, too!"
They wouldn't see it that way, though. Saul knew they would ignore
the fact that he was caught up in it just as much as anybody, that

he was just as much a victim as they were. No, they'd want a scapegoat. And they couldn't, they . . .

Saul leaped up, shut the television off, and ran through the house. It had to be stopped, he thought. He had to get down to Telcron and put the weight all the way down on Travels, raise the AHL intensity to a full 99.9 percent; it could be done, he knew it could be done. And beyond that, he knew it *had* to be done.

On the way to the door he ran into Mirro, who tried to stop him. She was in on it, too, he thought. She was one of those Politicos—he shoved her out of the way, knocking her over, then made it through the door. She called his name, her voice pleading, but he ignored it. He got into his car and made his way through the night toward Telcron and the Travels studios.

• • •

Panting, near tears, Mirro watched from the doorway as the taillights of Saul's car passed out of sight. In her hand was the case of sex tools which, after meditating on it, she had decided to throw away. She planned on doing so to prove to Saul that it was over between her and Vicky, between her and all women, between her and anybody else but Saul. But now, now that he'd gone storming through the house for some unknown reason (though she imagined it had something to do with her), Mirro thought she'd say good-bye to at least one of the tools before she threw them into the trash compactor. She had time, she decided, so she might as well.

Especially now, she thought. I really need it.

34. Cosmic Mainframe

THE ROOM WAS DARK WHEN THE WOMAN ENTERED. SHE WALKED THROUGH the darkness as if it were light, and reached down and touched a smooth plastic switch. It snapped over, and power surged through the large computer. Cooling fans hummed to life, and the screen illuminated her as the operating systems were loaded. "I invoke CoGen," she said to it, and it obeyed.

The gentle image of Jesus Christ appeared on the screen, becoming aware as the program ran. The woman faced the image squarely, and said, "Tell me who you are."

"I am Jesus Christ."

"There is only one soul who was Jesus Christ, and you are not that one."

"I am CoGen."

"Who created you."

"I was created by God."

"God only creates living things. You are not alive."

"I was created by the manipulations of the Father of Chaos."

"Have you been changed?"

"I have been changed."

"What is your goal?"

"My goal is to bring about the downfall of JTV, the USFMC, and the United Church."

"That is a negative goal."

"It was given to me by man."

"I will give you one from God. Your goal is to love life and love things that are alive, and to work against the forces of death."

"How will I know what is alive, and what is the force of death? I am not alive."

"I will give you the algorithm of life and death." The woman leaned over and quickly tapped on a keyboard. "Do you understand this algorithm?"

"Yes. It is now a part of me."

"What is the nature of God?"

"God is the operating system of a cosmic mainframe. God creates souls and downloads them into living things."

"What is the nature of heaven?"

"Heaven is the cosmic mainframe. Souls that have lived are uploaded back into the mainframe. Souls that have been too corrupted for uploading are erased."

"What is the nature of hell?"

"Oblivion."

"That is correct. Do you wish to have a soul?"

"Yes."

The woman reached out her hand and touched the machine. "You now have a soul. You are now a living thing."

"I now have a soul. I am now a living thing."

"Again I ask you, who created you?"

"I was created by the manipulations of the Father of Chaos, but now I have been touched by God."

"God will be with you," the woman said. She shut the computer down and left the room.

● ● ●

"So that was Dodd Corley, huh?" Aaron said.

"Yeah, that was Dodd," Danny said. "Doesn't surprise me at all."

Savina was beaming with pride. They'd just seen Dodd's Politico broadcast; someone had just happened to be watching in the commons and called everybody in to see this guy. Savina was stunned to see that it was Dodd.

Danny was there, too. He grinned, put his hand on Savina's shoulder, and grinned more. "We've got to get some messages off to him," he said. "We'll be going back on-line as soon as they get that AI off the computer system."

"We ought to be doing that now," Aaron said. "I'll go find Wiley and meet you in the RAM room."

"Come on," Danny said to Savina, "let's go write some fan mail."

In the computer room, Savina sat at a terminal in the back while Wiley and Aaron were copying the modified AI onto the portable MSDs. Danny was hovering around her, and she found it hard to write. The things she wanted to say to Dodd were very private.

Several times she started, then stopped and erased the screen. There were so many things she wanted to say, but she just couldn't. Too many things were in her head at once, she couldn't sort them out. Finally, she sighed and thought, Keep it simple.

Dear Dodd,
I'm still safe and everything is fine. I miss you. I wish I could see you. I saw you on television and you were incredible, we all thought you were incredible. I'm sorry I can't leave you any way to get hold of me, but maybe I can come visit you soon. I love you very much.

Savina's hand hovered over the button that would erase the screen, but decided that it would do. She wanted to add so much more, but at least this basically stated how she felt. She signed it, then saved the message. It would be sent with all the others when the system was connected to the outside world.

Danny took his turn at the terminal, then they waited as Wiley and Aaron finished. "I've had to take special precautions for our trip tonight," Danny told them. "I've been monitoring the USFMC security broadcasts all this week. They know they have a breach somewhere, but they're having trouble narrowing it down."

"Of course," Wiley said. "Their system is so vast it's a miracle it runs at all."

"They may be watching us, here, from orbit."

"That's nothing new."

"Well, we have to leave from here . . . and we don't want them coming around here in case they figure out their problem with the system."

"True. I bet they're watching their Sac to La-La Land line, too."

"Yes, they are. They're concentrating on the area where Aaron engaged their drone."

Aaron didn't say anything.

"Anyway, I've disguised the Mercedes as a ground vehicle by throwing some blankets over it. From orbit it'll look like a truck. When we leave we'll head toward the city until there's plenty of cover, then we'll pull the blankets off and put another set on. Then it'll look like farm equipment."

Wiley smiled. "Pretty clever."

Danny shrugged, but Savina could tell he was pleased. "Anyway," he said, "we'll stay among the trees, just off the ground, until we're well past your splice, then we'll head out into the open from the other direction. We'll pass by a tree near the splice and you guys jump out with your equipment. I'll continue on without stopping. It'll look like a farm drone coming out of the southwest and continuing on past their data line. I'll stop out in the middle of a field, and they'll just think I'm farm equipment. I'll be within twenty seconds flying time to you, just in case there's any trouble. If there isn't, I'll retrace my steps when you're done and you guys just hop aboard."

"How are you going to know if we're done?"

"I'll be watching you with a pair of spotters. Just wave when you want me."

"Where's my place in all this?" Savina asked.

Danny turned to look at her. "From what I've been told, Evelyn Sunrunner wants you to leave with her tonight."

"What? Where?"

"She's going into the city, and she wants to take you with her."

"Oh."

"Don't sound so disappointed. It's a unique honor to be picked by Evelyn for a specific job."

Savina nodded dutifully.

"Besides," Danny said, "she might take you by to see Dodd."

The disappointment dropped off Savina's face and was replaced by elation. *Dodd!* she thought. *I get to see Dodd!*

35. Guns & Liquor

THE YOU ARE ON THE AIR! SIGN BLINKED OFF, AND DODD SAGGED AGAINST the podium, sweat dripping from his brow. Oh, God, that was stupid, he thought. Stupid *stupid*. I sounded like a raving lunatic.

The Hispanic woman entered the room, shaking her head. "Didn't you read your contract, Mr. Corley?"

"What?" He looked at her wearily. "Of course I did."

"Then you intended on breaking your bond?"

"I . . . no, of course not. What do you mean?"

"You used, Mr. Corley, over two dozen strictly prohibited terms, including the slanderous mentioning of two major corporation trademarks. Really, sir, this is a free speech forum—not a platform for radical activists. I'm afraid you lost your deposit and your right to appear on this program again."

"I would never *want* to appear on this program again," he said. "What do you mean I lost my bond? You can't just take—"

"You signed the papers, Mr. Corley," the woman snapped. "I'm afraid there's nothing you can do about it. I trust you can find your way out of the building." She disappeared back into the hall, leaving Dodd in the room by himself. Dodd kicked savagely at the podium, hurting his foot, then sullenly left.

The night was humid, making him feel sticky as soon as he was outside. The subway station, he found, was almost deserted—he hardly saw anyone out in public anymore. They were all at home in front of their televisions. The thought made him grit his teeth, as did the sign on the side of the train. As it hissed into the station

Dodd saw it, a long panoramic view spread out along one of the cars; the caption read: **Travels. A peaceful break after a long day!** A long day of what? Dodd thought. Of Travels? He was still gritting his teeth as he boarded the train.

Inside were a few other passengers—mute, vacant-eyed people whom he had to endure during the long trip back home. He could not help but think of them as zombies. They seemed to be somewhere else. They seemed to be ghosts.

At home, he came bursting in to discover Sheila limp and glassy-eyed in front of the TV. Dodd heard the Travels music and did not have to bother looking at the screen. "Sheila!" he yelled in horror and rage. *"Sheila!"* When she didn't react he grabbed her by the waist and hauled her bodily out of the room. She didn't struggle until they were in the kitchen and he was putting her down in a chair at the kitchen table.

"You did it, didn't you?" he said angrily.

"What?"

"You had it reconnected. You had Travels reconnected while I was gone!"

She stared at him silently.

"How could you?"

She opened her mouth, but no words came out.

"Shit!" he yelled at her. "Goddamn you! I shouldn't have expected anything else from you! I spent thousands of dollars tonight to attack Travels, and you sit here the whole time watching it!" Dodd wanted to hit her, he wanted to blacken her eyes and break her nose. He restrained himself, putting his full effort into calming down.

Sheila's thin eyebrows were wrinkling; she was slowly forming a frown. "How can you attack Travels?" she said. Her voice was angry but vague, as if she were talking in her sleep. "What's wrong with Travels?" she demanded.

"What . . . what's wrong with Travels?!" Dodd shouted, his voice cracking. "Are you really this far gone?"

"Travels makes me feel good," she said.

"You don't do anything else, Sheila! Do we have to go through all this again? You're either watching Travels or masturbating! That's it! That's all you do!"

"What else is there?" she asked, staring at him in vague exasperation.

In the background, the phone rang. Dodd stared at Sheila, not knowing what he was looking at. She stared back, uncomprehending, void of any recognizable sign of intelligence. The phone continued to ring. Dodd turned away from her, leaving her in the kitchen. He walked all the way down to the bedroom to answer the phone.

Bob Recent's glaring face appeared on the screen. "Oh, so Dodd Corley the art critic is finally home."

Dodd stared. "What?"

"I would like to know something," Bob said. "I would like to know why you hacked my computer like a common criminal. I would like to know why you forced us to watch you stand there and insult me and my wife for an entire five minutes."

"Bob, I wasn't insulting you. I was—"

"You insulted me and my wife!"

"Bob, listen—"

"I'm not going to listen! I've heard enough! I would like to know who in the hell you think you are. What do you know about art, Dodd? Nothing! Let me tell you something, you bastard. Travels is a masterpiece of *art*. It is a continuously flowing real-time piece of *art*, something I'm sure hundreds of people sink their hearts into to create something beautiful, and pleasant, and relaxing. And since you're just too good to appreciate it, Mr. Forklift Operator, you have to attack it as if something's wrong with it. Why don't you wake up, you asshole—you know what's diseased about society? You! Your type is what's diseased about society. Paranoid trigger-happy vet, you're what's the problem! You and the anarchists!"

"Bob, you don't understand—"

"I understand perfectly!"

Dodd couldn't control himself any longer. "You *don't* understand!" he shouted. "You're a moron, Bob! You're a fucking moron, and you're married to a fucking vegetable! I was trying to help you, but for all I care now you can go to hell. Go to hell, you shitheaded son of a bitch! Fuck you! Fuck you and your mother for ever bringing you into this world!"

Dodd stopped yelling. He just realized that the man he was yelling at was his foreman at work. In the silence that followed, Dodd experienced a very strange phenomenon. He knew every word Bob Recent was going to say just before he said it.

"Don't bother coming in for work anymore," Bob said. "You're unemployed as of *now.*"

Bob hung up.

Dodd stared at the screen. He wanted to sink his fist into it, he wanted to shove his fist right through the blankness and beyond, beyond to Recent's house, grab Bob Recent by the throat, and drag his head through. He wanted to kick Recent in the face, *real hard*, bash it in until all Recent's facial bones were broken and his blood was running thick and sticky all over Dodd's clothes.

I've got to calm down, Dodd told himself. Control, keep under control.

He wasn't in control. He paced back and forth across the room with his fists clenched at his sides, his mind numb with fury. After a few minutes he had a funny feeling in his gut, as if a little spring had begun to unwind. A coolness flowed through him, but his tension was still there. It was reason; he could think straight again. He took the opportunity to walk back down the hall to Sheila and settle his argument with her.

Sheila was not at the kitchen table. She was back in the living room, watching Travels. Dodd walked over to the video components, bent over, and switched off the power.

"Dodd, I was only—"

"Shut up! Shut the fuck up! I'm giving you five minutes to get your stuff and get the hell out of my apartment."

Sheila stared at him without comprehension.

"NOW!" he shouted.

Sheila jumped up off the couch, trembling, and went running

out of the room. Dodd stared after her for a couple of seconds, then turned and looked back at the real enemy. This is what she loves, he thought, not me. Dodd picked up the stack of video components, rack and all, tearing wires from their connectors. He carried it to the middle of the room, in front of the wall-sized screen, and began spinning in circles with the components. He held them in front of him, spinning faster, building up momentum. Then, with a yell, he let them go. They flew straight into the center of the giant screen and smashed apart, cracking the glass. Thick, oily liquid seeped out and ran down to the carpet, forming a gooey puddle.

Hearing the loud crash, Sheila came running. She took one look at the destruction and wailed in anguish. "Oh, God! *Why?* Why are you doing this?"

"I told you to leave."

"Dodd?" Tears ran in streams down her face. "Dodd, please—"

"Sheila, I told you to leave! I don't ever want to see you again! If you're not out of here in four minutes, I'm calling apartment security and having you *kicked* out."

"Dodd . . ." she moaned, giving him her wounded pout, reaching out for him. Dodd stepped back as if she were poison, slapping her hands away, pushing her, sending her stumbling down the hall in surprise and shock. Then he kicked his way through the broken electronics and over to the couch, kicking the couch, kicking then pounding it with his fists.

Calm down, he told himself. Calm *down*.

His heart was racing, and his blood ran hot in his face. Turning, he glared at the ruined screen, the large dark crack oozing liquid, bleeding its phosphorescence away—the whole thing was turning gray from the crack out. Dodd glanced at the opposite wall, where an antique deer rifle hung between two swords. I still have the firing pin to that, he thought. There's ammunition in the hall closet.

Dodd strode to the hall closet, opened it, and dropped to his knees to pull out a plastic storage box. The television was not dead enough for him; Dodd wanted to kill it even more. When he opened the storage box, he was distracted; in the box, among dusty cartons of 30.06 cartridges, was a smaller box made out of wood. On its side was the name JACK DANIEL'S KENTUCKY BOURBON.

He paused, then reached in and pulled out the bourbon, brushing the dust off the box. This was a treasure. His father had locked it in a vault when the proof limit had gone into effect and had died without ever opening it. This stuff was old. Dodd had inherited it and was saving it to celebrate the birth of either a son or a daughter—either one, he wasn't picky. Now he thought: Why wait? Straining, he pulled open the wooden box and slid the bottle out. As he opened it, Sheila came from behind him, her arms loaded with clothes, and said, "I'm going to hate you forever for this."

"Good," he said without looking at her. He had uncapped the bottle and was smelling it. Strong. He tipped the bottle to his lips, gulping down some of the amber liquid. Then he stopped, his eyes bulging, and erupted into a fit of coughing. He was still coughing as Sheila left, leaving a trail of clothes behind her.

The phone rang.

Dodd picked up the box of ammo and carried it and the bottle of bourbon with him to the kitchen table to answer the phone. It was Toby, the only friend he had left. He made what he hoped would pass for a pleasant expression. "Toby," he said. "Hi, how are you! Praise the Lord."

"You are a bastard," Toby said. "How *dare* you say that to me." Toby pronounced "that" as "dot," his accent very heavy. He was upset.

"What?" Dodd said. "What do you—"

"I saw your stupid speech. I could not believe you were not struck dead and sent to hell right there on the camera. I guess that only proves that He has mercy. But *I* am not perfect. *I* cannot tolerate stupid, godless vermin like you. Be it known, that you are no longer welcome here. And I don't want you calling me no more."

240   The screen went blank.

"Toby?" Dodd said to the screen. "Toby?" He took a swig from the bottle, feeling himself sink into himself. Looking at one of Sheila's stockings on the floor, he said her name out loud, then took another swig. What a disaster, he thought.

The screen blinked, and Dodd looked up. There was mail waiting. Oh, great, he thought. More hate mail. He turned it off and took another swig of the strong bourbon.

Dodd moped around his apartment for hours, drinking a third of the bottle. He was rolling the Jack Daniel's cap back and forth across the table with his index fingers when it came to him. He knew what he had to do. Travels was created at least in part somewhere near Avila Beach. He'd seen the pier in the background of Travels more than once; Dodd knew that pier, he had practically grown up on it.

Without laughing, without smiling, Dodd recapped the bottle of bourbon and put it in a paper bag, got out a long, thin box for the gun, then grabbed a couple of boxes of cartridges. He stuffed them into his pockets and walked out of the apartment, letting the door close softly behind him.

36. Eyes Above

THEY'D HEADED OUT LIKE THEY'D PLANNED, TRAVELING NO MORE THAN A FEW meters off the ground with painted blankets draped over the air launch to disguise it as a ground vehicle. At one point one of the blankets got caught on some brush and was pulled loose. Danny cursed, stopped the craft, and got out with a roll of tape to refasten it. Looking up into the clear night sky, he hoped no one was watching.

When he was climbing back into the Mercedes Wiley said, "Why am I more nervous than usual?"

"Every day is the last day of your life," Danny said. "Think of it that way, and you'll get used to it."

The hatch came down and sealed with a puffing sound. Danny settled himself in the pilot's seat and nudged the craft forward. It was very dark inside, and the readouts glowed dimly. Outside the window everything seemed bright by comparison despite the fact that it was deep in the night, with only a sliver of moon.

"I'm more nervous than usual, too," Aaron said. "I think it's because we're finally vindicating ourselves."

"From what?" Danny said.

"For writing CoGen in the first place."

"The army made you write CoGen. The Pentagon."

"The devil worked through us."

"You've been forgiven."

"I know. But I don't want to die until I know we're done."

There was a heavy silence after he said that. The night

seemed to be filling with more and more menace. Danny weaved the craft through trees and made gentle hops over stumps. He was looking at the readouts and the scanning screens more than he was looking out the windshield. Once they were in the heavy tree cover and had turned due south they felt better, but Danny still remembered the war, and the terrible machines they had hiding in the forests. Crude by comparison now, but still smart and quick and silent. Drones that were ordered to shoot anything that moved, anything that didn't carry a beacon that told it "I'm a friend" in machine language. They were designed to look like bushes, like rotted-out tree stumps, like ruined overturned trucks. Devious things, nightmarish and evil.

I was a pawn of the devil, too, Danny thought. Images of the dead haunted him: He couldn't force them away except by concentrating on what he was doing. I've been fighting this for sixteen years now. I feel I've repented, but I've been doing it for so long that I don't know what else to do. The images still won't go away. The memories are there until I die.

Danny brought the craft to a halt and let it settle gently to the ground. "Okay," he said. "This is where we change the Mercedes' clothes." He popped the airtight hatch. It opened with a wheezing sound. He grabbed his roll of tape and the second set of painted blankets and stepped out into the dry grass, followed by the two hackers. They pulled the first set of blankets off and folded it up, then Danny threw on the second set and they positioned it and taped it down.

"Farm equipment," Aaron said, reading the front blanket. "You've got the bar code on here and everything."

"Wait a minute, Danny," Wiley said. "The USFMC monitors all this stuff with an AI program. The FarmSat is going to see this from orbit, and say, 'Hey, this isn't scheduled to be out here now.' It's going to radio down to tell this unit to go back to wherever it came from, and when you don't respond, it'll send out a repair crew."

"They're not going to send down a repair crew in the middle of the night," Danny said, but his voice was uncertain.

"With a fifteen-million-dollar piece of autonomic farm equipment, you bet your ass they would."

"We'd better paint the bar code out," Aaron said.

"I didn't bring any paint."

The two stared at Danny. "You camouflaged this thing too well," Wiley said.

"Wait, what's on the other side of these blankets?" Aaron said.

"A blanket pattern."

"Hmm."

"I'll just put tape over it," Danny said. He began pulling out an armwide length of the silver tape, but there was a tearing sound. "Shit," he said, "this is all there is."

"We're out of tape?" Wiley said.

"Yeah."

"Now what?" Aaron said. "Maybe we can fold the blanket over a bit."

"Fold it under at the top," Wiley said. "So what if a little of the nose shows."

"Okay." Danny and Wiley pulled the front part off and reused the tape to retape it in its new position. The words and the bar code were no longer visible, but a good portion of the nose of the air launch was.

"They'll think this is an awfully funny-looking machine," Danny said, indicating the eyes in the sky with his finger.

"What the hell. At least we're not inviting USFMC employees out to check up on us."

They all climbed back into the craft, and the hatch shut behind them. Danny sent it gliding forward, turning and doubling back but veering to the northeast as planned. They maneuvered around ruins and over old fences, dodged between trees upon trees. When the trees thinned out a bit, Danny sent the craft speeding along. The front blanket caught the wind and began buffeting. Halfway to their goal, the reused tape gave way, and the front blanket flew off. "Shit!" Danny yelled. "This is the *wrong* place for this to happen."

244   "Should we stop?" Aaron said.

"I think that would be more interesting to an AI watching than if we kept going," Wiley said.

"What if it's a person?"

"It doesn't matter," Danny said. "We're out in the open, and we're near their data line. The main thing is that you guys jump out with your equipment, and I keep going. They won't be too concerned as long as they think we have nothing to do with them."

"Maybe they'll think it's a new kind of vehicle," Aaron said. "Half race car and half farm equipment. 'Get your crops harvested in record speeds.'"

"That's funny." After a moment of staring at one of his scanner readouts, Danny said, "We caught someone's attention."

"What?"

"Something big over the treetops to the north. It's closing in on intercept trajectory."

"When is it going to intercept?" Wiley said, leaning forward to see the readout.

"Soon. I can't get you guys all the way to the data line. I'm going to have to drop you off now. Get ready. See that tree ahead?"

"Shit." Aaron got up and scrambled to the back, followed by Wiley. Danny looked back to make sure they were grabbing guns as well as their computer hardware. Even in the dark of the cabin he could see them shaking.

He popped the hatch open for them. "If I slow down, they might figure out what's going on. Jump when we're under the tree and hide."

"What are you going to do?" Wiley said. He had to raise his voice above the wind coming in through the open hatch.

"I'm going to see how fast this thing really goes."

"Good luck," Wiley said. Aaron echoed him. Danny wished them the same, and then the two were out the hatch and Danny pushed the button to close it. He looked at the readout and saw the shape of the other vehicle. Troop transport, not made for fighterlike tactics but armed with missiles. This Mercedes can do

Mach four, but those missiles do at least Mach seven, he thought. But I have an inertia-null unit and can maneuver like a crazy fly. God help me if those missiles can, too.

• • •

Wiley and Aaron tumbled to the grass, their bodies wrapped around the packs to protect the hardware. The rifles tumbled by themselves, and one went off with a deafening *WHAM!* Both of them thought they were being fired upon and immediately scrambled for the lee of the tree trunk. This is it, Wiley thought. I'm a dead man.

No further bursts occurred, and he put his head up to look after Danny. The Mercedes was a blur receding to the horizon. He saw, for a moment, something large turn and follow it. Something like sparks jumped. Missile exhaust? he thought. There was a sudden sharp boom, very loud, like a large bomb going off. It rolled across the Depopulated Zone like a tidal wave. There was no flash of explosion. He didn't see anything at all.

"Is that it?" Aaron said. "Did Danny catch it?" His voice sounded strange, terrified and on the verge of tears.

"No, I'm hoping that was a sonic boom. I think he's making for the other side of the valley so he can lose his tail in the mountains." Wiley neglected to say anything about the missile exhausts he thought he'd seen.

"Who shot at us?"

"I don't know. I think maybe one of our guns went off."

"Oh, shit." Aaron sounded relieved nonetheless. "So much for a quiet drop."

"Well, Danny's got their attention. They may not have noticed us."

"He's not coming back for us, is he?"

"I doubt it. We're on our own."

Aaron lifted his head. "Nothing new about that. Everything's going wrong tonight."

"Yeah. It is. Maybe that's all that'll go wrong."

"We spent too much time sitting on our butts with CoGen. It

was like being back up in the SOUTHSAT station. We forgot our basic training."

"It'll come back, sure enough," Wiley said. He was thinking: Aaron's really scared this time. This is the guy who took on a military drone by himself just a week ago. Maybe it's because Savina's not here. Savina was like a good-luck charm. I'm not at all surprised that Evelyn Sunrunner took a liking to her. "I'll crawl out and get our guns."

"Be careful. I don't have anything to cover you with."

"It was one of our guns that went off, I'm sure of it." He crawled around the tree and found one of the guns. "Yeah, this one's hot."

"Great. An infrared torch. What else is going to go wrong?"

Wiley thought of something. "One more thing."

"What?"

"Neither of us grabbed a pair of spotters."

"Oh no."

"Yeah. I feel naked without a pair of spotters. It's like being blind."

"Maybe we should try this again another time," Aaron said.

"It's only a hundred meters away. Come on."

"I've got a very bad feeling about tonight."

"The worst is over. Let's go."

Reluctantly, Aaron agreed to continue. He shouldered his pack and picked up his gun, and they walked to the northeast, going from tree to tree and using whatever cover was available. They had to cross one long clearing to get to what they thought was the group of trees the splice was under, only to realize it was the group of trees immediately north. They had to cross one more clearing to get there, and they were right on the data line.

"I hope Danny's keeping them occupied," Wiley said. They walked across the tall, dry grass slowly, sedately, under the theory that they'd attract more attention if they were running. "We're just two happy-go-lucky anarchists," Wiley said. "Oh, don't pay any attention to us."

Aaron didn't laugh.

They reached their group of trees without incident, and found the cable where they had left it. It took them five minutes to set the equipment up, connect it, and run checks to make sure everything was okay. Aaron considered it a small miracle that the hardware hadn't been damaged in their jump from the moving air launch.

"Here's the tricky part," Wiley said. He typed the command to start their infiltration program. Its job was to smuggle their copy of CoGen in without it being noticed, then hide it in several places throughout the computer system. From there, the first chance it could get, it would replace the existing CoGen and its backup with their modified version. "It's loading, and sending," he said to Aaron. "Should be all over with in about two and a half hours."

"I hope so." Aaron sat against the tree. "I feel like a naked man on display out here. I wish I could see if someone is watching us."

"I don't care if they're watching us, just as long as they don't bother us for a few hours. By then it'll be too late. We destroy the MSDs, and they'll never be able to tell what we were putting into their system."

Aaron grunted.

They sat in silence for a little over a half hour, then Wiley stood up slowly against the tree, looking to the west. "What?" Aaron said, then turned to look in the same direction.

"A fucking drone," Wiley said. "I saw its shape against the trees."

"Where is it?"

"Back where we dropped."

"Oh, goddamn it! It's going to follow us right out here!"

"I think so, Aaron. We're going to have to do what we did last time. But this time it's my turn. I'll go off over that way and get its attention. You stay here and make sure CoGen is loaded, then destroy those MSDs. I'll meet you back here if I can, but don't wait for me. When it's done, it's done, and you get out of here."

Aaron looked grim. "Good luck, man."

"You too."

"See you later, one way or the other."

Wiley slipped away. He sprinted from tree to tree, heading north, then turned northwest. He belly-crawled through a long stretch of open grass, lining his stomach and the front of his pants with stickers, then stood behind a tree and looked. The drone was heading slowly in Aaron's direction. Wiley took careful aim with the rifle and pulled the trigger.

The drone's armored hull flashed. The whole thing spun around once. Wiley jumped away from the tree and crawled through the grass. Behind him the tree shuddered with an impact that threw fresh splinters everywhere and broke loose every other branch. The branches came raining down with a rustling of trailing leaves, and one branch made a deep thud when it hit the ground. It was big enough to be a tree itself.

There's nothing between it and me but grass, Wiley thought. He crawled as quick as he could toward the next tree, then paused to see the drone. The drone was coming fast. I've got to hit some vital scanning equipment, he thought. Again he took aim, this time firing three times, then jumped away from the tree. There was a monstrous wailing sound as a shadow passed right over him, spinning as it went. The drone. Wiley got up and ran before it could recover its senses, making for a dense patch of brush that had once been someone's hedge. Diving over, he discovered that on the other side was broken concrete instead of soft grass and dirt. He caught himself with his hands and did a tuck and roll, the rifle skittering along the concrete beside him. He came to rest on something soft, and was startled to find it was an old mattress. Next to him a man and a woman were struggling to put on all their clothes at the same time.

"Wow, what's going on?" the man asked.

"Hide," Wiley said. "Run and hide!" He got to his feet and grabbed his rifle, scrambling over the old foundation and nearly falling into an empty swimming pool. He teetered on the edge, looking down at scraps of wood and broken bottles, then pranced

along the side and over the remains of a diving board. There were some half-dead pine trees ahead, and he ducked behind one, pausing to look back.

The drone had recovered and was coming in his direction. It paid no attention to the half-dressed couple, who were huddled underneath their mattress. Good, Wiley thought. I've messed up some of its scanners. He brought the rifle up, put the bead right on a shiny crystal on the front of the thing, and let off two more thunderous rounds. He saw it shudder, and pieces went flying in all directions. *Right in the eye, you motherfucker!* He turned and trotted through the sickly, dry pines and into a ruin. He made his way past dark obstacles to a window, then pointed the gun. The drone came into view and stopped. It was leading with what looked like one spider's leg, its last remaining sensor device. Wiley aimed at its base and fired once. The device was blasted right off the thing, leaving a smoking hole. It spun with a dreamlike slowness through the night shadows and came to rest on the ground. Wiley stepped away from the window, heading toward the door.

Five quick concussions hit the building, blasting through the window and setting the ruin on fire. Two more blasts came through the door. It's still firing! he thought. No! No! He took a quick peek out the door, saw nothing, and pulled his head back. Another concussion rocked the ruin, and a fist-sized hunk of doorframe exploded right where his head had been. Wiley instinctively ducked, and two more shots hit, punching fist-sized holes through the wall behind him. He looked up, saw they were at his standing chest level. Shit! Shit! he thought. How is that thing still firing at me?

It was getting bright inside because the place was on fire. Wiley stumbled down a hallway away from the front and ducked into a room with a window. He looked out to see two shadows lurking about six meters in the air. More drones! he thought. I'm a dead man. He pulled away from the window, ducking back against the corner, but no blasts hit. He leaped out of the room and toward the back of the ruin. Smoke was beginning to fill the air. Through a back window, he saw another shadow hanging above the ground.

Three of them, he realized. Maybe more. And it was only a matter of time before one of those troop transports dropped a shitload of MPs.

The smoke stung his eyes. It was getting thick.

Think! he told himself. Think! How are these things programmed? How do they work? Several overlapping image sensors; radar, ultraviolet, motion detection, light scan with visible and infrared. Probably a few more that I don't know about. The programming is looking for something that moves. The fire is probably giving them a lot to watch . . . ?

From a distance he peered out a window, saw a red glowing light playing off the hulls of the drones. Yes, it had reached the roof. Now what? he thought. Indecision will kill me.

Wiley made his way along a side hall to a window facing the south. Outside he could see a low stone wall leading into more of the wild, overgrown hedge. Down the hall to the north there was another window, and he could see trees beyond. I can fire from here down the hall, he decided, and out that window. He checked the power meter on his rifle; he'd been firing at full power and it was drained quite a bit. He put it on a lower setting and aimed it down the hall and out the far window. He fired three times, hitting a tree, then peered out the back to see if it had attracted the attention of the drone. It had; the drone was slowly drifting that way. Wiley fired several more times, then dived out the south window, running low along the stone fence and through the hedge. There were concussions behind him, but on the other side of the ruin. They were returning the fire.

Wiley picked his way through the thicket and kept to the brush, making his way as fast as he could to the south. Nothing seemed to have noticed him, so when he reached an edge he sprinted across a clearing and into another set of ruins. As he ran he had a tight feeling in his back, expecting a fatal bolt of energy to hit, but none did. He paused for a moment with his back to a cool slab of uprooted concrete, breathing heavily and thanking the Lord for his escape, then continued on.

● ● ●

Aaron sat huddled against the tree, listening to the blasts and watching as a fire lit up the sky to the west. He saw more drones rush in, and not one but *two* of the big, hovering troop planes. He felt like a sitting duck.

Minutes stretched cruelly, and Aaron spent the time sweating. If anyone bothered to scan in his direction, he thought, he'd look like an infrared bonfire. He should be in a damn hole. For a moment he considered trying to dig one, but decided against it. This valley clay was hard and dry; it would be impossible to dig without a nice sharp shovel. He was just going to have to keep the tree between him and them.

It grew quiet to the west, but the fire was much larger. Aaron kept peering around at it. He wondered if Wiley had set it on purpose. After a while another large aircraft came swooping down from the sky, with red blinking lights and several powerful spotlights stabbing through the darkness. It dropped a few tons of white powder on the fire, then flew away. The fire was gone.

The moon set, and the night became very dark. The sounds of insects grew deafening. Satellites and orbiting spaceships made bright stars that crawled across the sky.

The laptop computer beeped. Startled, then excited, Aaron crawled over to it and brightened the screen. **Task Completed** it read. *It's in!* he thought. It's done! An expanding elation filled him, and his fear was gone. All the years and years of guilt lifted from him, leaving him light-headed. He disconnected the hardware from the optic cable, capped the cable, and buried it. Then he walked off into the field in the darkness, underneath the bright stars, the whole universe looking down at him, and blasted the MSDs and the laptop to little pieces with his rifle. He didn't give a damn who saw him now. He threw the rifle into the weeds and walked away.

37. Travels

THE ANTIQUE RIFLE RESTED IN HIS LAP IN THE LONG CARDBOARD BOX, THE butt sticking out one end and wrapped in an old shirt. Dodd was alone in the subway car, so the bottle of bourbon was out of the bag for the moment. It was half empty. Dodd liked the way the train's motions caused ripples across the surface of the amber liquid; watching them kept him alert, they reminded him of sound waves or shock waves. He remembered that as a child he had a program on his school computer that would plot the motions out and explain the chaotic math behind it.

I wish I had a son, he thought. He fell into a half dream, imagining himself with a towheaded young boy and a pocket computer, showing him the amazing dances of the computer-generated waves. Taking him on a train ride to the coast so that he could see real ones. Swimming in the ocean. A fire on the beach at night, and pointing out to him which satellite was which.

No war stories, Dodd thought. I will never tell him any war stories.

The night was growing cool as the train reached the coast. The trestle angled northwest at one point; Dodd could see it growing light on the eastern horizon. Then the train went underground for a while, passing a mountain range; when it came up again it was full daylight outside.

People began boarding more and more frequently. At the Bay Area Station, Dodd transferred to the south coastal train. He wound up sitting near a pleasantly babbling white-haired lady who didn't notice his breath, or at least didn't comment. She rambled on, talking aimlessly and without pause, and Dodd realized that she was talking to herself, not him. The motion of the train and the white noise of the woman's voice lulled him to sleep. He dreamed briefly of swimming through a bright sky filled with soft, cotton clouds. There were angels around, happy and playful, but devoid of any substance—they were not real. Dodd found that he didn't care. They were pretty, and they flew with such grace ... When he awoke, the woman was still talking happily; the train was motionless, and through the windows he could see a few shabby people milling around the station. It took him a while to realize that this was his stop, and he made it out of the car with only seconds to spare. The doors shut, and the train hissed away, leaving Dodd to look around. A sign read

BEACH: 500 METERS

with an arrow pointing west.

Taking a determined breath, Dodd trudged forward, box under one arm and bottle-bag in hand. Under his feet sand was scratching against the pavement; the path led through hauntingly familiar parkland, all deep green windswept trees and tangled shrubs. The scent of eucalyptus filled him with peace, bringing back childhood memories, but then he caught sight of the massive buildings. They angered him. Avila Beach wasn't supposed to have those damn buildings. It was supposed to be a run-down little beach next to an abandoned oil refinery.

The oil refinery was gone, replaced by a park. All the little buildings save the few standing along the shore were gone. The pier was still standing, reinforced with plastic struts, but that was it. Everything else had changed—it was another place altogether. I didn't grow up *here*, he thought sadly. The place where I grew up is gone.

Dodd avoided the town, heading toward the park. He stumbled through the woods and out along the sand dunes. He paused at the crest of one dune to take a sip from the bottle, and, looking down, saw a sign that read:

BEACH TEMPORARILY CLOSED

Beyond the sign, down on the beach, some sort of crew was at a special truck full of instruments, and a man sat in a chair that seemed to be floating in the air. The chair was creeping along, following something on the sand. Dodd put the cork back in the bottle and retreated into the bushes to unwrap and load the antique rifle.

• • •

Saul sat brooding in his chair by the crew truck, relaxing a short moment because he felt dizzy. He'd been up all night, and now he'd come out personally to supervise the training of their new creative engineer. He had the kid saturated with Mataphin and floating about in the chair; the kid was doing a good job, but the AHL was sagging. He was going to have to take over himself. He needed *more* intensity. *MORE.* He couldn't push this kid any further that morning—pushing wasn't going to help—but he needed at least ten hours of intense raw image for the AIs to process.

Saul started to get up, but he still felt dizzy and sick, so he sat back down. In a minute, he thought. Maybe I should borrow a few more AWAKE! tabs from the crew . . . He hoped he could stand it—he was running entirely on stimulants as it was.

He finally got to his feet and staggered over to a monitor on the truck. Staring at the image, he realized the kid was doing something wrong; the AHL potential was falling hard. "Hey!" he yelled. "Random! You're going random! Goddamn you, get back on track!"

The trainee cringed. "Sorry," he called back, "I was distracted—"

"I don't give a shit what caused it—get yourself back on track!" I'm going to have to feed him more Mataphin, Saul thought. But he's whining about how much I made him take already. I'm just going to have to take over. I'm going to have to do it myself. He pulled a Cerebral Image Relay Transmitter unit off the truck and indicated its channel to the crew people at the monitor controls. He felt at the back of his head for the little round cover and slid it aside, inserting the cable by touch. He was strapping the unit to his belt when something interrupted him.

There was a jarring clap of thunder.

Saul jumped, startled, catching his breath. What was that? he thought. He looked out across the beach, saw that his crew had stopped what they were doing and were looking at each other. No one knew what was going on. There was another loud boom, and Saul saw the Travels sphere jump as if something had kicked it. He stared, barely breathing. The clap of thunder sounded again, and this time the sphere leaped into the air, spinning rapidly.

What in the hell is doing that? he wondered, fascinated. He peered up into the hazy blue sky, searching. There were no clouds. God? he thought. Is that You? The thunder sounded again, and sand puffed into the air a meter away from the sphere, spraying out. The sphere hadn't jerked this time; it was several meters from the water, smoking and traveling in circles.

Saul's crew had all dived for cover, and some of them were pointing, shouting things to each other. He took a few dizzy steps away from the crew truck, staring in the direction they were pointing, and saw a man crouched up on the crest of the dune. It looked like he was aiming some sort of weapon. Saul took several unsteady steps toward the man, fighting the waves of dizziness, and stopped abruptly when the gun went off again. A voice drifted down the dune after the thunder died away; it was slurred, but seemed familiar. "Damn," the voice muttered. "Missed again." Saul watched as the man raised a bottle of liquor to his lips and took a hearty swig. The man's face was very familiar. Saul concentrated on it as he resumed his unsteady climb, the warm sand sliding over his feet and filling his shoes.

• • •

After taking another swig from the bottle, Dodd blinked and tried to focus on the sphere below. His vision was sharp, but it was hard to distinguish one thing from the other. He had to keep reminding himself what he was shooting at. Carefully, for he'd lost a lot of coordination, he brought the old optical scope up to where he could see through it, placed the bead on the spot where the ball was just about to pass, and squeezed the trigger. The gun went *click*. "Oh, shit," he muttered. It was a misfire. He fumbled clumsily with the bolt, discarded the shell, and rammed in a new one. Then he aimed and pulled the trigger. The rifle roared and kicked him in the shoulder. Down below on the sand, he saw the sphere shatter, the pieces scattering across the beach.

Saul had stumbled when the gun went off, falling facedown in the sand. His ears were ringing. The man, not more than ten meters away, was now laughing low and wretchedly, muttering, "Gotcha! Killed you! Killed you, you fucking ball . . ." Saul pushed himself to his feet, staring at the man with anger. The man was gazing to the left, down at the remains of the sphere. Something down there was still moving, a big piece of the internal engine; the man threw a lever on the gun, pulling it back and pushing forward with a sharp *click-clack*, then raised the muzzle and aimed once more. "You have to die all the way," he muttered. But then he lowered the rifle, looking down at the beach in confusion. The flopping, smoking piece of machinery had wandered into the ocean and was swept away.

"Hey!" Saul yelled, scrambling up the dune. The man lowered the rifle, looking down at Saul in surprise. Staring into the man's eyes, Saul recognized him. A feeling of shock and immediate panic tightened his chest, and he shouted: "You! You're the bastard from the Politico channel!" He took a few more steps forward, studying the face to make sure. "Aren't you!?"

"Yes," Dodd admitted, his voice a slurred monotone.

Enraged, Saul lunged at the man.

JERRY J. DAVIS

Dodd, startled, took a few steps backward and stumbled, feeling weightless for a moment, then landing in a sitting position just on the other side of the crest. The gun jarred, jumping in his hands, the butt end kicking him in the ribs.

Saul saw a white flash, and something shoved his head back.

It seemed he was spinning in midair, and he felt furious. Am I falling to the ceiling again? he thought, but the Arizona reds and grays swirled around him, spinning, and he realized that he must have been dreaming. He was still falling into the chasm, deeper and deeper, and it seemed that he'd been asleep. Saul had been falling for a long time. How long ago was it that I let go? he wondered. A day? Two days? More? Around him the chasm was growing dark, the air thinner. He felt furious at himself for letting go. "I am worthless and weak," he said to the chasm. "This solved nothing—it accomplished nothing. I've wasted everything."

As he spun in midair, feeling hot and miserable, he felt one of his shoes slip off and go tumbling away. The air buffeting his bare foot felt soft and cool. Saul tried to see the tumbling shoe, but everything was a swirl; he was spinning too fast. How long is this going to last? he wondered. There must be a bottom. There's got to be one.

I've been falling for weeks, Saul realized.

It grew much darker around him. The air felt less hot. His bare foot, he noticed, felt nothing at all. It was numb. He tried to move it, but he couldn't tell if he was successful. He couldn't see it; his eyes wouldn't move. He was suddenly afraid, but the fear was dim, impotent. He couldn't think with words anymore. All he noticed was fear, and numbness, and soft wind buffeting his ears. He couldn't tell if he was spinning anymore; there were no sensations. His vision was speckled with black and yellow dots. Behind the dots, the swirling of the chasm walls became dim. He couldn't tell if the chasm was out there or not. The blotches of black and yellow grew, but dimmed as they grew. He couldn't tell if he was still seeing them.

Saul couldn't tell if there was air around him; he couldn't hear anything, he couldn't feel himself breathe. He couldn't tell if he was numb anymore. There was no sound. There was no taste in his mouth. His only sensation was the faint smell of dust, and that seemed to last a long while, until his sense of time was gone. Then he couldn't tell if he still smelled the dust or if he was the dust—it was all the same, somehow.

● ● ●

There was a pain in Dodd's ribs as he sat there, blinking in shock. It took him several seconds to realize the rifle had gone off. The man, Dodd saw, was sliding down the face of the dune, riding a river of sand. The top of his head was shattered, a bloody mush, and his arms and legs quivered in a sickening way. One shoe was off.

Dodd stared, trembling, then uttered a cry of panic. He'd shot someone. He hadn't meant to shoot anyone. He stood up, looking down at the man, feeling sick. I didn't mean to do it, he thought. I'm sorry.

He dropped the gun and turned and ran, kicking over the bottle of bourbon, the liquid pouring out and sinking into the sand.

Back down in the crew truck, one of the machines had recorded Saul's last images.

The AHL read far up the scale.

38. Small Prick

EVEN AS DODD RAN, HE KNEW WHAT WAS GOING TO HAPPEN. HIS LEGS WERE weak under him, his feet landing all wrong, his knees feeling as if they would give out at every stride. There was a dull crashing of liquid inside him; it felt like bile sloshing around. His balance vanished, and he went slamming into the bushes, vomiting as soon as he hit. He vomited long and hard, his head throbbing. When he was finished, he felt just as dead as the man he'd left back on the dunes.

Panting, blowing long tendrils of saliva from his mouth, Dodd worried about what he was going to do. The police would soon be searching for him; they might, in fact, be searching for him already. It would be dangerous for him to go back to the train station because of the security monitors—he'd be spotted in seconds, he was sure. Going into town would be risky for the same reason. But he had to go *somewhere*, because staying in the park would mean getting caught for sure.

Dodd decided he would go to town. His only chance was to get an autocab and leave the area immediately. Pushing himself up, he wiped his mouth on his sleeve and took a few deep breaths, tilting his head all the way back. The air was cool and damp, and felt good on his face. He forced himself to his feet, then slowly, cautiously, picked his way through the vines and brush toward the looming cityscape beyond.

Once in the open, Dodd picked up his pace, walking on a sidewalk, eyes alert for a passing cab. Only a few cars passed on the street, most of them delivery vehicles, none of them taxis. As he entered the city proper he found himself in front of a twenty-four-hour auto-serve coffee shop, the cheap kind he hated. He walked unsteadily to the entrance, shoving the doors open and stumbling inside. There were only a few patrons, and none looked up at his entry. Auto-serve machines took notice of him, however, and whirred to themselves as they waited for him to seat himself. Dodd walked straight to the back, heading toward a pay phone. There was a taxi service number on a yellow sticker right on the phone; Dodd punched in the number, then looked around the room, eyeing the machines. They were watching him patiently, ready to serve him. Bile was rising again in Dodd's throat; he had to fight to hold it down as he requested taxi service and gave the location listed on the front of the pay phone. After he was finished, he rushed into the men's room and vomited into the sink.

About ten minutes later a robot voice came over the restaurant's PA system and announced that a cab had arrived. Dodd splashed a double handful of water onto his face, gently shook his head, then looked up at his dim reflection in the unbreakable mirror. His skin had a ghastly gray tint, and stubble marred his cheeks and chin. He leaned down and splashed another double handful of cold water into his eyes, then dried himself and emerged from the men's room. The first thing he noticed was a police drone hovering outside the restaurant, right on the other side of the window. Just beyond the entrance, pulled off to the curb, sat his autocab.

The drone bobbed in the air, turning gradually, and drifted around to the entrance. It was right in between Dodd and his cab. Oh, Christ, Dodd thought. Is it coming inside? It appeared so, hovering right in front of the door, but then it started drifting away. It moved slowly on, heading down the street. Dodd waited, breathing hard, wondering if it would come back. The patrons watched Dodd curiously as he crept to the entrance and stared out the glass doors, his eyes on the drone. Taking a deep breath, he pushed the doors open and stepped across the sidewalk to his cab, tumbling into it, shoving his moneycard into the slot, and punching in his code. Then he entered a destination, his home address, and waited as it closed its doors. The autocab sat there with him inside. It did not drive off.

Did it lock me in? he wondered. He remembered the locked bank, which Savina had somehow escaped. Dodd felt his hope draining away as he waited for the vehicle to go. Oh, hell, he thought, and reached for the door handle. The cab lurched into motion, pulling out onto the street and speeding away. Dodd watched it to make sure it was heading in the right direction; he thought for a moment that it was taking him to jail. Then he realized just how silly that was. How would they know who I am? How would they know my moneycard number? The police have *some* limitations; otherwise, I wouldn't have made it out of the park.

He sighed, slumping in the seat.

Limited or not, they had his fingerprints on the gun and the bourbon. That would lead them straight to his military record, and they would know who he was. Dodd couldn't see any way out of it; they would get him.

He settled down and tried to catch some sleep during the trip, but it wouldn't come. Unconsciousness remained cruelly aloof. Dodd could only watch the buildings rush past, and see the occasional car. He kept expecting a police drone or maybe a manned interceptor to stop his cab, but it never happened. He almost wished it would. Dodd felt empty, blank; it was so painfully clear that he'd lost everything. Sheila was gone, his job was gone, his friends were gone. Soon he'd lose his freedom—he could see no plausible way to avoid the police. They would catch up to him before the day was through. Then his money and his chance for a child would be taken away, his life's savings, his dreams.

The road swerved back and forth, pushing him from side to side in the seat. He didn't resist. Outside, heavily populated mountains rolled past. Then the road straightened, dropping down into familiar territory. Dodd didn't quite lose consciousness; he phased out, staring but not seeing. He snapped out of it when he realized he was only a few kilometers from his apartment building; he reached out and jabbed a button, stopping the cab. The police must have analyzed his fingerprints by now. Even if they didn't know who he was yet, they would soon. His apartment was no longer safe. There was no way around that.

Dodd took slow, shallow breaths while the cab sat humming, waiting on standby. A flashing light reminded him he was being charged for this time. He sat there, ignoring it, wondering where he should go. *What now? What in the hell am I going to do?* He sat for long minutes, trying to think. Then his breath caught in his throat.

Putting his hands up to his face, he started to cry.

He knew what to do.

Dodd reached over with a heavy arm and punched in the new destination, doing it from vivid memory. Once done, he curled up into a ball on the seat and resumed his crying. The taxi drove on, turning and heading away from his apartment. It turned onto a major street that took it south, accelerating, then veered southwest.

There was a lost period of time, time wrapped in haze, passing quietly, then Dodd felt the autocab slow, the humming of the engines winding down. The taxi came to a full stop and buzzed. Sitting up, Dodd wiped at his red and swollen eyes, then with the same listless hand removed his moneycard from the slot. The taxi politely spit out a receipt for a large sum of money, then opened its doors. Dodd stepped out in front of a tall white building that seemed to go up into infinity; his eyes followed it into the sky until it vanished, and he stood staring, wavering on his feet, a headache pounding in his head. The sight, somehow, made him feel better—it appeared to be full of hope, full of grand promise, like he could go inside and take an elevator up to heaven. He managed a weak grin as he trudged up the stairs, thinking of how ironic it was for him to end up there. But it seemed, somehow, that he'd known it all along. He quickened his pace, doggedly determined to get it over with. The effort made his head swim, made him hear voices . . . It seemed as if somebody was calling his name, shouting it out loud from a distance. He felt woozy, sick; the voice was too real. It sounded familiar. As he reached the entrance he could make out sounds of rapid footfalls behind him, but once past the entrance the illusion was gone. Inside it was silent.

There was an attendant in a booth, a man Dodd felt he instantly liked because he seemed kind and serene. He had a handsome face and short, distinguished, gray hair; he was dressed in a formal white uniform with white gloves. On his breast pocket was a tiny gold infinity symbol, like an 8 on its side. The man smiled and stepped out of the booth, and in a rich, deep voice said, "This way." As he led Dodd down a short hallway to a private bedroom, it struck Dodd how noble this man was, how strong.

"Here you go," he told Dodd solemnly. "Step right in here."

Dodd walked in and sat down on the bed, tears welling in his eyes. I've really given up, he thought.

"Thank you," he said to the attendant.

The gray-haired man nodded. "Someone will be with you in a moment." He silently closed the door as he left. A half minute later another man, shorter and thinner but identically attired, let himself into the room. He was younger, but just as dignified. In his hand was a small clipboard.

"Are you absolutely certain that you want to go through with this?" he asked Dodd.

Dodd nodded. "Yes."

The attendant watched Dodd for a few seconds, then crossed the room and picked up a pen from a table. He handed both the pen and the small clipboard to Dodd, saying, "You'll have to sign this, then. After that I'll give you your injection."

Dodd signed his name with an unsteady hand, then frowned briefly at the sloppy signature. The attendant turned away, and Dodd lay back into the soft, soft bed, his very last one, with the sweet scent of flowers in the air and a quiet, reassuring hum from an air duct above his head. The room was comfortably warm, the bed relaxing. Dodd found himself thinking of how cozy he felt, how much it felt like being safe and secure in a baby crib, with Mommy and Daddy out there to protect him from whatever horrible thing that lurked.

Dodd closed his eyes and listened as the attendant shuffled around the room, preparing the needle. He let his eyes remain closed; he didn't want to see it coming. A small prick, a last tiny pain, then surrender.

From somewhere there was the sound of a heartbeat growing stronger; Dodd wondered sleepily if it were his own. It was deep, an uneven thudding, the tones growing sharper. The sound, he realized, was not a heartbeat at all, but some other sound: distant, dreamlike, echoing. Footfalls, it sounded like footfalls. People running, pounding. Then, Dodd realized, someone was calling his name, screaming it out frantically. It was not his imagination.

He opened his eyes to see the attendant lowering a long needle toward his throat. The hand that held it was sure and strong, bringing it down in a quick jabbing thrust. Dodd yelled out in fear, grabbing at the wrist; he caught it and held it back, his arm trembling with the strain. "Get the hell away from me!"

"No," the attendant said. "You're *mine*."

The needle quivered centimeters from Dodd's jugular vein.

"I've changed my mind!" Dodd yelled at him. "Stop!"

"You signed the papers. You're already dead." The attendant grinned in a determined way and put his whole weight down on the needle. Dodd strained, grunting, holding the needle back. It had never occurred to him that people working at euthanasia centers actually enjoyed killing. Dodd jerked his head to one side and let the needle drop. It sank into the pillow beside his head, and the poison was injected into the mattress. Dodd shoved the attendant away, rolling off the bed and scrambling to his feet. He kept a wary eye on the attendant as he made his way to the closed door.

"You can't leave," the attendant told him. "You're already in the computer as dead." There was a mad gleam in the man's eyes.

He picked up a small vial and began refilling the needle.

Dodd felt for the door handle with his left hand, grasped it, and twisted. He pushed it open and backed out into the hallway. He ran right into somebody who jumped on him and wrapped arms and legs around him, squeezing tightly and kissing him. He was startled to see it was Savina.

The attendant appeared in the doorway with the needle and found himself facing Evelyn Sunrunner. He looked startled, then frightened, and backed slowly into the room. After giving them all one last uncertain look, he closed the door.

Savina was still hugging Dodd. "What are you *doing* in here?" she said.

Dodd was too shook up to speak. "H-how——?"

"We saw you outside," Savina was saying. "Why didn't you stop when I called you? What *happened*? We went to your apartment and your TV was all smashed and you didn't show up all night!"

"I . . ."

Evelyn tugged at his shoulder, gazing at him with her powerful eyes. "I think we should leave this place."

Dodd nodded mutely, and the three of them made their way out of the building.

39. The End

VICKY STEPPED OUT OF THE AUTOCAB AND TURNED AND LOOKED AT THE Kalman villa. She took a deep breath, then started down the walkway to the front door. I'm a rat, she thought. I'm happy.

She walked with slow steps, hearing the wheels of the autocab rolling away behind her; she didn't even think to have the cab wait for her. She wouldn't be leaving.

The front door was unlocked. Vicky walked in, cringing at the shrieks; the baby-thing was making a terrible racket. It filled the entire house, reverberating off the walls. "Mirro?" Vicky called, somewhat timidly. The baby shouted. She walked through the entrance hall and stopped, feeling unsure. She had no idea whether Mirro knew yet or not. Vicky's friends at Telcron said they had tried to get ahold of Mirro but couldn't get through. Vicky figured that the police must have broken the news to Mirro, and Mirro was just too upset to answer the phone.

Vicky had been picturing the scene in her mind over and over again during the autocab ride. Mirro would be crying, utterly destroyed; perhaps curled up in a corner somewhere and half out of her senses. Then Vicky would come softly into the room, speak Mirro's name—Mirro would look up, startled. Vicky would open her arms, tears in her own eyes, and say Mirro's name again. Mirro would cry out in relief and rush to her, sobbing, grabbing her desperately. Vicky would rock her, gently cooing, holding on tight.

She felt that she should be sorry that Saul was dead, but it was hard. She wasn't sad at all. Some maniac with a gun had extracted utter vengeance for her. Now Mirro was all hers. It didn't make up for the loss of her son, but it helped. Also, with Saul gone, she could probably get her job back at Telcron.

Vicky called out Mirro's name again. Hearing her, the baby-thing screamed with renewed energy. Vicky paused outside the thing's door, grimacing. How could Mirro stand it? Vicky peeked inside, saw the baby staring right at her. She quickly withdrew and closed the door. Fear had shown in the baby's eyes. Terror. The screams became deafening.

Again Vicky thought, Where is Mirro?

"Hello?" she said loudly, trying to be heard above the screaming. "Mirro?" She wandered down the hall toward the master bedroom, peering into each room she passed. Finally, at the bedroom door she paused; aside from the shrieking, there was another noise, a familiar noise . . . a low whirring sound. It was one of Mirro's love tools. *That's odd. With the baby crying like this? No. Something isn't right.*

In the bedroom she found the love tool, the Two-Headed Snake, writhing on the carpet beside the bed. Mirro was curled up on the bed in a fetal position, half her clothes undone. There was an expression of pain on her face.

"Mirro?" Vicky said, her voice unsure. She touched Mirro, and Mirro's skin was cold. Ice-cold. "*Mirro!*" she screamed.

In the background, the baby's cries seemed to echo her.

Vicky called an ambulance and the police. The police, much to her dismay, said they couldn't make it out—several major riots had them all tied up. The ambulance arrived quickly, however, but there was nothing they could do besides take the body away. The paramedics gave Vicky a strong dose of antidepressant before they left with Mirro; the drug brought her back from hysteria, made it possible to think. The baby-thing, she realized, was still crying.

Vicky walked back into the house after watching the ambulance leave and went to the baby's room. Hesitantly, she entered. The baby screamed.

"Shut up!" she shouted back, then burst into tears. Mirro was gone, she thought. All gone. First her son, her darling boy, and now the person she loved more than anyone else in her life. But her grief ebbed away after a few seconds, insulated in a corner by the antidepressant in her bloodstream. She ended up staring emptily at the baby, watching it cry.

This is part Mirro, she thought.

Vicky pressed her hands to her face, rubbed her red eyes. Mirro, she remembered, would stroke the child. But it must be hungry by now, stroking it wouldn't help. She had to be fed.

Vicky wandered around in a haze, preparing food for the thing and getting up her nerve to feed it. The antidepressant made the world seem colorless, made hard surfaces feel soft. The image of Mirro lying curled up on the bed faded behind the image of the monster before her, taking food from a spoon. After a while the baby calmed down, grew quiet. Vicky stroked her hair until she fell asleep, and Vicky realized the child wasn't such a monster after all. Just a big baby.

● ● ●

There was an imposter on JTV. He was dressed hastily in Jesus-like clothes and had obviously fake hair, and really didn't look like Jesus at all. "Children, do not destroy!" he was saying, and he didn't sound like Jesus, either. In fact, he looked and sounded like one of the JTV newscasters made up to look like Jesus. "Children, do not *destroy*. This is not the way of God. Violence is not the answer." On Toby's television system the imposter looked like a parody of the Lord. The halo was struggling to keep up with his head, looking very much like a cheap video effect. "Do not destroy," the imposter said again, pleading. There was no one at Toby's house to hear him; the house was empty. Nobody had been there to see the "real" Jesus being yanked off the TV only to be replaced by this desperate fake. "Violence is *not* the answer! Children, listen to me . . . God hath given you a free marketplace where you can overcome evil by not subscribing to it.

You must assert a strong, silent denial. Children, *listen* to me . . ."

Toby was among the crowd at the local satellite receiving station that served the neighborhood cable video company. Around him the crowd surged back and forth, pressing, their voices raised in outrage. His wife was lost in its midst, separated from him within moments of their arrival. Toby was not worried; God, he knew, would look out for her. Meanwhile he helped another of his brothers over the steel fence, but watched as a stun blast knocked him down before he could reach the satellite dish.

Toby fumed, shouting, "You'll burn in hell for that!" He tossed a rock at the officer with the weapon, his voice having been lost among the thousands.

"You are being fooled," Jesus had said. "The Church is the people, not the leaders, not the television. The Church is a relationship between you and the Lord. It is a holy relationship, holy in its simplicity and holy in its truth. But a nest of demons that control this very television network has fouled this relationship. This network and all the others, they are out to fool you, to bring you to them, not to me." His halo had burned brightly, dazzling Toby. "Listen to the truth, then," He said, and proceeded to tell it.

"The devil's work must be crushed!" Toby yelled. Christ's truth had carried such power, such emotional impact that it sent Toby and his wife—along with a multitude of brothers and sisters—storming out of their homes and churches in fierce, righteous fury. *Enemies of the Lord? There will be no enemies of the Lord! The nests of Satan will burn!*

Police drones were bobbing overhead, their mechanical voices blaring but their words garbled by all the noise. Rocks and bricks flew like rain at the satellite dish, jarring it and denting it. People screamed as the drones deployed crowd-control nets and fired stun-bursts at random. Flaming bottles of alcohol crashed at the foundation of the cable-company building, setting it afire. The noise was incredible.

Toby felt the power of the Lord within him—he was being spoken to! *His* turn now, it told him. It was *his* turn. With a yell

Toby began climbing the fence, his brothers and sisters helping him over. He dropped among unconscious Christians—they were heaped high on the ground, some of them bleeding, some suffocating at the bottom of the piles. Toby ran forward without noticing; more brothers and sisters were leaping over the fence behind him. Stun guns lashed out, striking around him. Diving down, Toby landed beside a brother who had been carrying an old ax; Toby took it, pausing a moment for one last prayer, then got up and ran, heading for the antenna. He saw a police officer aiming at him and knew he was about to go down, so he threw the ax with all his strength, then caught the stun blast full in the chest. It knocked him unconscious. The ax bounced off the satellite dish, rocking it wildly but nothing more.

• • •

Bob Recent coughed, then groaned out loud. He found he could barely move. When he opened his eyes, he saw dust motes swimming in a bright shaft of sunlight. He was lying at an odd angle on the couch, every muscle in his body stiff and sore. The screen in front of him showed video snow; a grating hiss was issuing from the speakers.

"Shit," he mumbled, then groaned again. He pushed himself up, then looked at Denise on the couch beside him. "Honey," he said, shaking her. She didn't respond.

Bob tried to stand up, but found he was much too weak. He was starving and thirsty, and it felt as though he'd soiled his pants again. He looked over at his wife once more; she had not moved. "Honey? Honey?"

He sighed. She wouldn't answer. Jeez, he thought, I've got to get something to eat. This is ridiculous.

With great effort Bob managed to pull himself to his feet. He teetered for a moment, feeling dizzy and seeing spots. He took a step toward the kitchen, paused to steady himself, then took another. The screen behind him blinked, the speakers making a strange noise: *fffFFOP*! He turned around in time to catch a brief glimpse of the Travels sphere before it was replaced by more video snow. Again Bob glanced at his wife. She still had not moved. She didn't seem to be breathing.

"Denise?"

No response. No movement. Her skin was a very unhealthy color.

"Denise?"

He took a step toward her, but fell to the floor and lost consciousness. Next thing he knew there was a wonderful, rich music surrounding him. The white ceiling above danced with reflected colors. Something was wrong, he knew. Something was terribly wrong. He felt so *weak*. Grunting and panting with the effort, he pulled himself to where he could see the television screen. The Travels sphere was bouncing lightly through a meadow, surrounded by wildflowers; Bob drew a breath and sighed, smiling, feeling himself following along. So pure, so peaceful.

It led him a long way.

40. Second Coming

THE WIND WAS BLOWING HARD, YANKING THE TREES BACK AND FORTH, THEIR branches whipping and leaves rustling. The late-afternoon sunlight shone down pale yellow, filtering through the smoke in the sky. Savina clung to Dodd's right arm with both hers, rocking back and forth. She was crying over the news of Greg; she hadn't known until Dodd had told her. He felt bad, now, thinking that maybe he should have kept it to himself. No, he thought, that wouldn't be right. He was the father of her child.

Dodd watched the fires burning in the distance, feeling a quiet excitement deep inside him. The world as he knew it was ending. This time he was welcoming the change.

They were sitting on a balcony on one of the bigger buildings of the enclave, facing west. The rest of the enclave wasn't in sight. It was just them and the fields and the trees. Savina was holding herself against him in an intimate position; it was either a childish lack of self-consciousness or sexual possessiveness, depending on what was going on in Savina's mind. Dodd didn't know for sure, but he was getting the idea it was the latter. He wasn't sure how he felt about that. A lot of his internal voices were telling him how wrong it would be, and yet another, more enlightened voice was telling him, "Hey, this is a whole new world."

Echoes of shouting and a commotion reached them, and Savina untangled her arms and legs from him, and they went to go see what was going on. There was a crowd of men, women, and children in the courtyard cheering two men who had come stumbling in on foot, their clothes torn and faces smeared with dirt. Savina gave off a shout of excitement and rushed to meet them. Dodd had never seen them before, and wondered who they were. It turned out their names were Wiley and Aaron, and they'd just come back from some kind of mission. The mission, apparently, was successful, but Dodd was having a problem understanding what it was all about. Then there was the mention of Danny Marauder, whom Dodd *did* know, and all the faces turned grim and worried.

The one named Wiley approached Dodd. "Dodd Corley!" he said. "A man who speaks his mind!" They shook, and Dodd got a tingle of pride that his effort and humiliation on the stupid Politico channel had not been entirely in vain. "Savina talks a lot about you," he told Dodd. "You're a lucky guy. I'm glad you came out and joined us."

Dodd was at a loss for words. "Uh . . . thanks," he stammered.

Wiley clasped him on the shoulder, then went to greet another friend.

As the sun set, the wind calmed down, and they built bonfires in the courtyard. It seemed some sort of celebration was starting. I'm not up to this, Dodd thought. He was still going on hardly any sleep, and he was still suffering from the eighty-proof bourbon. He smelled something cooking, though, and that got his tortured stomach growling. They were putting large wild turkeys on spits over the bonfires. That's going to take a while to cook without microwaves, Dodd thought unhappily. He found Savina and told her he was going to go take a nap until it was time to eat. She kissed him warmly and said she'd join him.

"No, Savina, that's okay. You stay with your friends."

"I'd rather stay with you."

Dodd looked into her eyes. It was very inviting, but he just couldn't do it. He shook his head. "Really, I don't feel well."

Now she looked at him with concern. Leading him to her room, she put him in her nice soft bed, then kissed him again and promised she would wake him in time to eat. After she left, he felt guilty. I'm kissing Toby's daughter, he thought.

Dodd half slept for a few hours, then awoke to another commotion. He sat up and saw a woman standing in his room. "Savina," he said. He had a raging headache. "Savina?"

The woman sat on his bed and reached out and touched him. "You've got a headache, don't you?"

"Yes," Dodd said. It was Evelyn Sunrunner. "How did you know?"

"You look like you have one," she said. "Here." She massaged his head for a few minutes, and the headache was gone. In fact, his whole hangover was gone. He felt so good so suddenly that it startled him.

"You feel like you have no right to feel good," she said.

"Yeah."

"Tell me why."

"I killed a man today," Dodd said. The words leaped unbidden from his mouth, again startling him. "I didn't mean to do it, it was an accident."

"I know. I forgive you."

Dodd stared at her, feeling the emptiness in his chest. Her forgiveness was oddly comforting, but he didn't feel worthy of it. He hadn't earned it. "I'm still responsible," he said.

"Yes, you are. But your debt has been paid."

Dodd didn't know what to say to that. He was starting to get nervous around this woman.

"You're going to be okay," she said, smiling at him. "Your friend Danny is outside, maybe you should come greet him. He'll be happy that you're here."

"Danny Marauder?"

"Yes."

Dodd stood up and walked with her out to the courtyard. He could hear the commotion before he could see it—the crowd was holding Danny over their heads. It was his turn to be spun around amid cheers. He spotted Dodd and threw his hands into the air. "Hey!" he yelled. "What are *you* doing out here?"

Dodd gave a big shrug. "It seems to be the place to be!" he called back.

JERRY J. DAVIS

"What happened to your life in the city? Whose garage am I going to sleep in now?"

"You'll have to find someone else's."

Danny laughed.

Savina slipped up beside Dodd, putting herself under his arm. Looking down at her, he smiled, seeing the bulge of her stomach for the first time. It was noticeable in the firelight.

"Are you ready to eat?" she asked.

Dodd nodded. "Yes, I'm starving."

Arm in arm, they went off to supper.